# Peaks of Madness

## A Collection of Utah Horror

Copyright © 2019 All rights reserved

Forty-Two Books, LLC. 42 Books

Salt Lake City, UT.

www.fortytwobooks.com

Cover art by Carter Reid, www.thezombienation.com

Printed in USA on acid free paper. Times New Roman, 12 pt font.

ISBN-13: 978-0-578-45143-5

Library of Congress Control Number:  2019904529

## About the Utah Horror Writers

Utah Horror Writers is a nonprofit organization of writers and publishing professionals.

Find out more: www.utahhorror.org

## Editors

Daniel Cureton, MA

www.danielcureton.com

Johnny Worthen, MA

wwww.johnnyworthen.com

# Peaks of Madness

## A Collection of Utah Horror

An anthology of original Utah horror by the
Utah Horror Writers

April 2019

Edited by Daniel Cureton and Johnny Worthen

**42**
Books

Salt Lake City

Other books by the Utah
Horror Writers

---

*Old Scratch and Owl Hoots: A Collection of Utah Horror*, 2015, Griffin
Publishers, ISBN 978-1505517347
*It Came from the Great Salt Lake: A Collection of Utah Horror*, 2016,
Griffin Publishers ISBN 978-0997197099
*Apocalypse Utah: A Collection of Utah Horror*, 2017, Griffin Publishers
ISBN 978-0997197051
*The Hunger: A Collection of Utah Horror*, 2018, Twisted Tree Press
ISBN 978-0999020029


All titles are available on Amazon Createspace

# Letter from the Editors

In this 5th installment of the anthology you will find original content by authors across the state of Utah. Each has taken the time to submit, be judged under blind peer-review, and work with editors to polish their craft up to standard for publication.

Enjoy the scares,

Daniel Cureton and Johnny Worthen,

January 12, 2019

Salt Lake City, UT, USA

## Acknowledgments

The Chapter, Editors, and Publisher would like to thank all those who took the time to submit, edit, and help produce this publication.

# THE MADNESS WITHIN

## MANIA

Part .V-Introduction

## DELIRIUM

Part .III/V[th] -Biographies

## HYSTERIA

Part I-Flash Fiction

# LUNACY

## Part II-Poetry

# PYSCHOSIS

## Part III-Short Stories

# MANIA

## Part .V

*Introduction from the Publisher*

At the August 2018 chapter meeting, I volunteered to be the publisher for the 2019 anthology. Having previously published several volumes in an ongoing peer-reviewed literary journal, I was familiar with the process and felt that moving forward into the fiction realm would be an exciting and great adventure, allowing me to work with different authors than I had previously.

Forty-Two Books was started in the fall of 2018 to prepare for the release of the 5th installment of the Chapter's anthology collection. The history of the anthologies can be found in the previously collections, but in case you are a new reader, here it is from the introduction of *Apocalypse Utah*, the 2017 anthology:

"A little over three years ago, author and friend C.R. (Cody) Langille introduced me to the HWA organization and the fledgling local chapter of the Utah Horror Writers. One of my first meetings with them, they introduced me to their idea of a local anthology of Utah Horror. As they discussed publishing options my ears perked up because I had started a publishing company the year before. I tentatively interrupted the conversation with a little, 'Um, I started a company last year. I'll do it.' From there we had a Utah-based publishing company, an artist for the cover from Utah—Carter Reid—and local writers working on Utah horror stories.

The first anthology, *Old Scratch and Owl Hoots* [2015], was a learning experience for us in the Utah Chapter of HWA as well as for me as a young publisher. I guess I did a decent job producing the anthology because they asked me do the second, *It Came from the Great Salt Lake* [2016]. Of course it could have just been I was the easiest option having done one volume already.

*It Came From the Great Salt* Lake rose from a Facebook banner image Cody used for his profile once of a monster rising from a lake. Someone commented with what became the title and the idea of our second anthology was born.

As Cody and I talked about plans for more anthologies, we both loved the idea of exploring the end of the world in Utah-themed stories. I requested the stipulation that we avoid dystopian government stories, but rather, how could the end of the world happen if you were in Utah. When spreading the idea for *Apocalypse Utah* [2017] at writing conferences and conventions, I heard many great concepts from mythical to military and everything in between. My response was always the same, 'Make it scary'" (Godard).

*The Hunger* was published by Caryn Larrinaga at Twisted Tree Press in 2018.

The Chapter is creating a great legacy of content and writing in the state of Utah. The act of producing and pushing content to the public eye shows the vibrant and diverse culture that exists in Deseret. A healthy society embraces and encourages its hidden components (as horror often is). Regardless of its historical origins and political affiliations, a culture that expresses itself in the many ways in which peoples exist and live is a culture that flexes with change and re-invests in itself for the future. Horror is often one of the elements of culture that is suppressed and banned by the dominate structures in a society (governments, officials, churches) because of the inherent nature of what it contains: upsetting, disturbing, moral defying, and challenging ideas which can transform an individual.

I define horror as my graduate English science fiction teacher did, Dr. Eric Swedin, from Weber State University, "In speculative fiction, horror is anything you don't want to happen." From the things that go bump in the night, to gore, repulsion, fright, terror, and what makes us uncomfortable, horror at its core is not about shock value or exposition. Though exposition, grindhouse, and body horror have their place, the use of horror in human culture dates back to ancient times with folk myths and fairy tales—scaring children into behaving—warning of danger, and exciting the minds to the possibilities of adventure.

Horror can act as a medium to express imagination, ethical lessons, and to understand what it means to be human by reflecting on a situation which isn't real, but very well could be. The genre and the creativity within invites discus-

sion, confronts assumptions, and makes us turn inward to answer the questions about how we feel and how we will live
our lives after encountering the most terrifying and horrific
monsters of all: ourselves.

Each story is a piece of art, put together in a collection
that is a public exhibition. Creative writing, as a fine art, allows us to tame the inner demons and befriend the outer monsters of the world. As in the words of Karl Paulnack, director
of the music division at the Boston Conservatory, "Art is part
of survival; art is part of the human spirit, an unquenchable
expression of who we are. Art is one of the ways in which we
say, 'I am alive, and my life has meaning.'" Horror thus gives
life meaning.

It is my aim as a publisher to produce fine craft and
writing that is of high caliber—showing talent—old and new.
In this installment, Forty-Two Books is pleased to present the
best and most original horror of Utah:

## Peaks of Madness

In Screams,

Daniel Cureton, MA

Forty-Two Books, LLC.

Salt Lake City, UT

January 23, 2019

**Works Cited**

Godard, Daniel. "Introduction." Worthen, Johnny and Stoker, Callie. (Eds.) *Apocalypse Utah: A Collection of Utah Horror*. Griffin Publishers: Salt Lake City, 2017.

Paulnack, Karl. "We Need Music to Survive." *The Christian Science Monitor*, 4 June, 2009, https://www.csmonitor.com/Commentary/Opinion/2009/0604/p09s02-coop.html. Accessed 24 Jan., 2019.

Swedin, Eric. Personal Interview. 25 July, 2016.

# DELIRIUM

## Part .III/V

*Author Biographies*

**Anna Marasco** A perfect 50/40 split between Gryffindor and Slytherin, Anna Marasco likes to embrace both her light and dark sides. She is an award-winning author and international award-winning poet who is presently working on a second Master's degree, this one in creative writing. When she isn't writing, she can be found in her codependent relationship with the only man she will ever tattoo on her body: her horse, Henry.

**Betti Avari** lives nestled within the peaks of Northern Utah, spending her sleepless nights tucked under a fuzzy blanket, typing out her latest nightmare. Writing is her coping mechanism. She would be nowhere without Stephanie Gittins, the genius that coaxed her writing out of hiding; The Clandestine Writerhood Guild; and most of all, her family's tireless support of her passion. She has been previous published in the Utah Chapter of the Horror Writers Association 2018 anthology *The Hunger*.

**Brenda Bowen Wright** has always been a writer, but only recently has begun to put her stories on paper. After a career teaching middle school, nothing much scares her any more. Brenda has spent her entire life in the State of Utah living and working in many cities, now calling downtown Salt Lake City her home.

**Brian Mealing** loves to write poetry, often inspired by fairy tales and horror. He also loves comics, sci-fi, and other fandoms and is a member of the Horror Writers Association. Brian lives in the scenic Rocky Mountains, where he curses each snowfall awaiting the warm summer.

**C.H. Lindsay** is a writer, poet, housewife, and mother, but not necessarily in that order. She spent thirty years as an event planner, organizing, and running science fiction, fantasy, and horror conventions while spending a decade acting in musicals. Now she prefers to stay at home with her family and write novels, short stories, and poetry. This is her seventh anthology. She's a member of SFWA, HWA, SFPA, and LUW. Mostly blind, she lives in Utah with her "seeing-eye husband," son, and a cat who thinks she's another child.

**C.R. Langille** spent many a Saturday afternoon watching monster movies with his mother. It wasn't long before he started crafting nightmares to share with his readers. An avid hunter and amateur survivalist, C.R. Langille incorporates the Utah outdoors in many of his tales. He is an affiliate member of the Horror Writer's Association, a member of the League of Utah Writers, and received his MFA: Writing Popular Fiction from Seton Hill University.

**Charles R. Bernard** is a writer who lives in Salt Lake City, Utah. His work has been featured in *Thuggish Itch* and will appear in the forthcoming anthology *American Cult*. He is a contributor at Madness Heart Press, where he blogs about horror culture. He resides next to Salt Lake City Cemetery; a sprawling necropolis whose tombs and markers stretch out over a square kilometer of grounds. You can read more at saltcitysinner.blogspot.com.

**Daniel Cureton** grew up in South Carolina, moving to Salt Lake City, Utah in 2008 to pursue university studies. He has an MA in English from Weber State University. Daniel is an Avant-Garde writer. His poetry exposes the deeper meanings of experiential living and his speculative stories are idea platforms. He has previously been published in *Peculiar: A Queer Literary Journal*, *The Rocky Mountain Review*, *A*

*Shanghai Poetry Zine*, and *Enheduanna: A Pagan Literary Journal* for which he is the editor. Read more at www.danielcureton.com.

**Daniel Yocom** does geeky things by night because his day job won't let him. This dates back to the 1960s through games, books, movies, and stranger things better shared in small groups. He's written hundreds of articles about these topics for his own blog, other websites, and magazines after extensive research along with short stories. His research includes attending conventions, sharing on panels and presentations, and road-tripping with his wife.

**Elliott Dobler** has days when he has feelings too strong not to write about. A few of those feelings wind up as stories or poems on elliottdobler.com. Elliott lives in Utah and rides motorcycles when it's warm. He has an on-going battle with depression and poor writing. Rodney Mullen, Kurt Cobain, John Hughes, Jairus, Wes Anderson, Elliott Smith, Jimi Hendrix, and Edgar Allen Poe are a few of Elliott's heroes. Oh, and certainly his dad, who lives in Florida.

**Edward Matthews** lives in Salt Lake City with his wife, two children, and an incessantly howling hound dog. By day he slogs away as a government cog, but when night falls, he retreats to his loft to scratch the itch of the dark things that inhabit his brain. This is his second offering to the Utah horror collection series.

**Glenn Hammer** digs up trilobites because real dragons are too hard to find. He is a rabid science fiction fan who loves alternate history, archeology, and miniature war-gaming. He's worked in night security, motion-capture for x-box video games, and solves technology problems. He is fascinated by the War of 1812, but prefers it with airships, lightning guns, and dinosaurs. Dig him up on Facebook and Goodreads.

**Jeff W. Kramer** is a graduate of Indiana University and Stanford Law School, and a top-rated former Los Angeles trial lawyer. He was the Mayor of Malibu, where twenty-seven miles of coastline and endless vistas of the sea helped keep him sane. He now makes his home in Salt Lake City, enjoying the Wasatch Mountains and southern Utah red rock as his new playgrounds. It is often said the law is a jealous mistress. Jeff's solution was to dump her for writing, always his true love—fiction writing, that is.

**Johnny Worthen** is an award-winning, best-selling multi-genre author, voyager, and damn fine human being! He is the tie-dye wearing writer of the nationally acclaimed, *Eleanor: The Unseen*. Among his other titles are the adult occult thriller *Beatrysel*, mystery *The Brand Demand*, and the new horror thriller, *What Immortal Hand*, a dark journey through American wastelands on a quest for memories, faith, and meaning. Johnny teaches writing at the University of Utah while writing and editing professionally.

**Joni B. Haws** loves a good, scary tale, but can only watch horror movies with the sound turned off. She lives in South Jordan, Utah with her husband and three children. One any day you might find her belting power ballads behind the blur of a crochet hook, devouring a plate of nachos, or restocking books in her Little Free Library. Find more from Joni at www.jonibhaws.wordpress.com

**Joshua P. Sorensen** is from Orem, Utah. He graduated with a Masters of Military History from Norwich University. His extensive travels inspire him to write poetry and short fiction. Drawn to horror writing, he particularly enjoys writing monster fiction. His other loves include history, nature, and all things geek. Joshua's current life goal is to bring delightful chills to all ages, particularly the young. He can be found on Facebook: #SorensenVagabondWriter and Amazon: amazon.com/author/joshuapsorensen

**K. Scott Forman** has published several short stories and poems and was an editor and contributor at Fast Forward Press. He received an MFA degree from the Jack Kerouac School of Disembodied Poetics at Naropa University and was the recipient of the Robert Creeley Scholarship. Scott teaches English at Weber State University. He is a member of the Horror Writers Association and the League of Utah Writers. He enjoys long walks, sunsets with blood in them, and Metallica at volumes determined unsafe by the Surgeon General. Scott currently lives in the Rocky Mountains with a collection of guitars.

**Keri Montgomery** writes mainly speculative fiction. She's a contributing author to the Amazon bestseller *Rise Above Depression* by main author and inspirational speaker Jodi Orgill Brown. Keri's short fiction can be found in the 2018 League of Utah Writers anthology *At First Glance* and also in the upcoming 2019 anthology. When not writing, she enjoys firefighting with her local department, convincing her kids that museums are cool, and wishing for superhuman skills.

**Kevin Blankinship** is a professor of Arabic at Brigham Young University. He teaches Arabic language and literature, Islam, and the Qur'an. His research focuses on classical Arabic literature with a special focus on poetry. Currently he is writing a book about the blind author al-Ma`arri and the poetics of death. His work has benefited from grants by the Fulbright-Hays Program, the American Institute for Maghrib Studies, Southern Denmark University, and the University of Utah. In addition to scholarship and teaching, he reviews books for general audiences, write original English language poetry, and works as a freelance translator. You can read his work at *The Atlantic*, the *Los Angeles Review of Books*, *Jadaliyya, and Bridges*.

**Laurie Heath** has been a belly dancer, burlesque dancer, and knitter. She loves asking the question, "what if?" and discovering where it might lead, knitting a story out of the tangled webs of dreams and questions. She loves inspiring women to be fierce and live with passion whether it's through dance, writing, or some other form of expression. When she isn't writing short stories or poetry, she is cooking up delectable dinners (especially pasta), crafting, traveling with her partner, Craig Kingsman, or hanging out with their cats, Mystery and Mayhem. You can follow her adventures on Facebook https://www.facebook.com/pg/writinglaurie.

**Levi Robinson** has been deeply passionate about storytelling ever since he was a young boy. From screenplays and comics to song lyrics and short stories, he spent his life dreaming up fiction. He is only happy when he is creating. Levi has lived in Utah most of his life, where he has sought out like-minded individuals to share and collaborate with. He is constantly compelled to use his imagination to tell stories as a way of expressing himself and to share his voice with those around him.

**Maegan Langer** has a Bachelor's degree in biology from Brigham Young University. When she was seven years old, her mom let her stay up late to watch *Alien* on TV and thus began her lifelong love affair with sci-fi/horror. Her essay, "Alternative Goddess" appeared in the March/April 2008 issue of *Cicada* magazine. These days, her main focus is screenwriting. She enjoys a quiet life with her pets in the beautiful foothills of Alpine, Utah, having never discovered any dead bodies under her house.

**Marilyn Felkner** is a native of Utah, although she lived briefly in Denver during the late 1980s. She graduated from Westminster College where she majored in Math, and minored in English and Biology. In 2001 she went back to school and graduated with a diploma in Graphic Design. Marilyn has been filling writer's notebooks with short stories since the 80s and focuses primarily on emotions, the grandeur of nature, and the whimsy to be found in everyday life. This is her first foray in the Horror genre.

**Michael Darling** is a No. 1 Amazon bestselling author. He has worked as a butcher, a librarian, and a magician. Not all at the same time. He nests in the exquisitely beautiful Rocky Mountains with his equally breathtaking wife, their normal-if-you-don't-look-too-close children, and a disturbingly large St. Bernese dog that looks like he stepped out of *Peter Pan* and is probably a furry-faced attempt to extend the Darling brand. Michael's award-winning fantasy and science-fiction stories are frequently featured in anthologies. He continues to work on his bestselling *Behind Beyond* series and has three fantasy and science fictions novels scheduled for release in the next year.

**Michael Glassford** works with clients to protect their families and businesses from potential court and conflict, and gives them the confidence to live well and preserve their story. Michael's exciting debut Y.A. adventure, *Fog of Fortune*, was published in 2014 and it won best Young Adult Manuscript with the League of Utah Writers, 2014. He recently published a legal non-fiction book titled, *You Failed At Marriage, Don't Fail At Divorce*. Michael is also a freelance editor, hobby farmer, and an undercover pirate. You can find his books on Amazon, www.michaelsglassford.com, and www.legallifeplan.com

**Mike Nelson** grew up on a small farm in northern Utah where he entertained himself with daydreams. A corn field could become an impenetrable jungle, a hideaway, or an enchanted forest. The hayloft in an old barn could become a pirate ship, a castle, or a frontier fort daydreams are the stuff of writing. "Noveling." He is father of three works: *Thorns of Avarice, Treehouse in the Hood,* and *Clairvoyant.* Find him on Amazon.

**Miranda Renaé** is a lover of both horror and romance—especially when the two collide. She spends her days as a title clerk and as a foster mother to a very pampered litter of orphaned kittens. At night Miranda braves the rabbit hole and writes her way through nightmare.

**P.A. Sterling** Grew up in Utah. She has always wanted to be a super hero but somehow ended up writing software for computer games. To fill the void she got involved in full contact martial arts, skydiving, and now works full time in public safety. Aside from writing, she enjoys studying foreign languages, imagining fantastic worlds, racing 140.6 mile triathlons, and hanging out with her retired running buddy, a 13 year old lab-mix named Bella.

**Sariah Horowitz** explores the world on digs, in books, and in her writing. She has a degree in archaeology but she thinks of herself as Archie Oogly's Ex (Archaeologist) because no one will pay her to play in the dirt. While on her digs, she imagines fantastical situations that could happen with a little magic in the mundane world. She is a member of the League of Utah Writers. Dig up more of her writing at sariahhorowitzwriter.wordpress.com

**Steven F. Craner** has lived in Utah his whole life. Married for 43 years, he has 5 children, 4 grandsons, and no pets at the present. Steven enjoys gardening, blues and root music, outside bonsai, reading, writing poetry, and spending time traveling in Utah, Idaho, and Montana with his wife. He wrote his first short story after encouragement from his creative writing instructor and has been working on his first novel for several years.

# HYSTERIA

## Part I

Flash Fiction

# THE OLD MILL

## P.A. Sterling

Near the edge of the city, a narrow road branched off from the town's main thoroughfare, made a sharp turn, and dropped into darkness. The tires of my cruiser made little noise as I steered the vehicle along the winding road that followed the bends of a dried up creek. There were houses on this little street, but they were set way back and accessed through gated drives. If you didn't know they were there, you'd never see them behind the trees and hills. The whole area looked deserted until, turning a bend in the road, the cruiser's headlights swept across the bone-white stones of a three story building. The crumbling building was surrounded by chain link fence with several poorly mended gaps and holes.

As I drove past, I shined my cruiser's spotlight on the old building. Since there were no cars pulled off to the side of the road, I didn't expect to see anything unusual. Most of the building's windows were boarded over, but a few on the third floor gaped black. I focused my spotlight on these, but the beam didn't penetrate. The roof on the south wing of the building had collapsed ages ago leaving the walls intact to the middle of the second floor. The remaining jagged half-windows looked like the crenellations of a medieval castle.

I inched past the building then turned off the spot. Damn, this shift was talking forever and I still had an hour to go. Further down the road, I backed my cruiser into a gated side street. It was late enough that there would be no traffic coming and going and if somebody did need to drive out, I'd see their headlights in my mirror.

I had one report to write and this was as good a place as any to finish it. The radio was playing the same song I'd heard at least a dozen times this shift so I reached over and turned the damn thing off then opened the car window to let in the crisp October air.

Two days before Halloween. It used to be my favorite time of year. Still was, though I rarely had time to celebrate it now. I usually worked and let the younger officers have time with their families.

I loved the smell. It reminded me of home and easier times when I didn't have so many adult worries weighing heavy on my mind. The air smelled of dead leaves and fire-place smoke—a nearly imperceptible breeze blew a smatter-ing of dried leaves down the road in front of my car—the soft scraping sound they made against the asphalt sounded loud in the deserted darkness.

It took a moment to pull up the case and open the syn-opsis screen on my computer. It was a simple vehicle burgla-ry report—something I could practically write in my sleep—but as I started to type, I got a strange feeling somebody was watching me.

I looked up and an old lady stood at the widow of my car. I silently chided myself for letting her walk up on me. I was usually much more alert to things like that. "Situational awareness," they called it. Officers in bigger cities had been ambushed while sitting in their cruisers before. It happened.

I smiled at her. "Evening."

"You need to stop them."

I was taken aback by her blunt, almost accusatory tone. "Stop who?"

"They are lighting fires."

I turned to get a better look at her. She was an older lady, mid-fifties with short, gray hair and a wrinkled face.

"Where? In the field?" Across the street from my car was a small park. The city left it in a natural state, overgrown and wooded. We'd had several reports of homeless people setting up camps over the summer. I'd found a few, but they'd been deserted and I didn't remember seeing fire pits in any of them.

"You need to stop them." She repeated.

This conversation was going nowhere fast. "I'm sorry ma'am. I want to help you, but I don't understand what you are saying. Who is lighting fires? Where? Can you start at the beginning and tell me what is going on?"

My computer chirped as a call came in. I turned to see what it was, only for a second, but when I looked back, the woman was gone. I glanced up and down the small street. There was no sign of her at all. And the gate behind me was still closed. Weird, but stranger things had happened.

I turned my attention back to the call screen. It was not a police call, just information about the local fire department running to a medical.

I sat there for a minute, thinking of the half-finished report, but the things the woman had said tugged at my thoughts until I pulled open Google and typed in the name of the abandoned building. The top response had "haunted" in the title.

I hesitated a second before clicking it. The webpage talked of a man and woman who died in a fire in the old mill. I glanced over my shoulder at the condemned building. Something moved in one of the top-floor windows like a curtain pushed by a breeze. Just a shadow shifting in the night. There were no curtains in the building.

A shiver ran down my spine, and I rolled up my window. I could finish the report somewhere else. Suddenly this place didn't seem so inviting anymore.

As I pulled forward the beams of my car's headlights arced across the road to illuminate the pale form of the old woman. I stood on the brakes and jerked the wheel sideways, but I knew it wasn't going to be enough. I tensed, but the thud never came. As the woman passed through the car, I noticed she was pointing back toward the old mill.

"Oh, hell no." I muttered as I stomped on the gas.

# NORAD

Joshua Sorensen

*We hate you. Worst leader ever.*

"Mr. President"

The President rubbed his temples. The voices had become louder and more numerous. When he first started hearing them, he had consulted doctors and psychiatrists. They all gave him a clean bill of health. "Chock it up to stress," they told him.

He had reason to be stressed. The crisis with Russia worsened every day. The World sat closer to total nuclear war than at any other time—closer even than during the Cuban Missile Crisis. The President and his family had been evacuated to NORAD. Most of Congress had been dispersed to prevent a total loss of government in the event of an attack on Washington.

*Schwein. Ibn al-Kelb. Cabron.*

Multilingual voices poured in as well.

His wife's psychic gave him a different answer. "A massive psychic event," Madam Serena explained. "You hear the inner voice of people around you. Maybe the entire World."

"Mr. President"

He looked up. One of the interns stood in front of his desk, holding a file folder.

"Yes, Debbie. What can I do for you?"

"It's Sheila. General Smith needs your signature on these documents."

*What an asshole.*

That came from Sheila. Why would she hate him? Was she one of the interns that he had slept with?

It was one thing hearing disembodied insults; but receiving them from somebody right next to him was new. Stress didn't do this. Was Madam Serena right? Was he really receiving the thoughts of other people? There had to be a way to silence this reception.

The President stood up and walked around the desk. He stopped behind her. Reaching around her, he grabbed the file. Sheila flinched.

*Don't you touch me, you pig.*

"Paraphrase it for me," he said, opening the folder.

"Supply requisitions."

"Hand me a pen."

Laying the document on the desk, he used her pen to sign the tagged lines. As he turned each page, a plan began to form. He carefully envisioned his next few steps. A giggle at his own brilliance escaped his lips. He closed the file and handed it back to Sheila.

"Don't forget your pen."

As she reached for it, the President attacked. His hands shot upwards and closed around her neck. Sheila let out a scream, but it was smothered as he closed his grip around her throat.

*Aaah.*

Her mind continued the panicked scream that her body couldn't. She flailed about, vainly attempting to break free from his hold. His fingers closed python like around her neck, constricting tighter and tighter.

*I don't want to die.*

Her mewing self-pity just angered the President. Sheila's body went limp, but he crushed until he heard the sickening crack of her larynx collapsing beneath his grip.

Then, silence.

He couldn't hear her anymore. He shook Sheila's body, but still not a sound. No internal voices. The President had silenced her. His plan worked wonderfully.

The office lay in chaos. Papers fluttered in the air to land haphazard about the floor. The struggle had swept the desk clean. And of course, there was the dead intern. How do you make a body disappear, a mile underground, in the mountain fastness of NORAD?

*Murderer. Monster. Villain.*

Sheila may be silent, but the other voices barraged him in a cacophony of hate. Could he silence them the same way?

Picking up a letter opener from the floor, he stabbed himself in the left shoulder. He pulled Sheila up and placed her right hand around the handle extending from his flesh. Then he slammed her corpse against the wooden desk.

"Guards! Guards!"

Secret Service agents ran into the room. Seeing the

altercation, they rushed to the aid of their President.

"She tried to kill me, in the name of Mother Russia."

Ushering him away from his assailant, the agents shielded him. "We need to get you to the doctor."

"There's no time. Get me to the Command Center."

Pain shot through his arm like jolts of electricity and the voices yelled ever louder in his head as the agents half-carried the President into the Command Center.

General Smith rushed towards him in concern, but the President waved him off.

"The Russians just tried to assassinate me!"

"All of their strategic air assets have started taking off. We've been monitoring the situation, but they've scrambled like this several times in the past week."

"They are going to attack. We need to strike them before it's too late."

The blood drained from the general's face. "Are you sure, Mr. President?"

"Yes. We mustn't delay. Bring me the football!"

In the end, it was surprisingly simple to launch the nuclear arsenal of the World's last superpower. He gave the order, General Smith confirmed, and done.

The task completed, he consented to be taken to the medical facility. As he lay on a gurney, doctors caring to his wound, the voices echoed in his skull. Despite the migraine and the pain from the stab wound, the President smiled. Soon, silence would reign. The voices would blow away like dust in the wind.

As the doctors finished the last of the sutures, the first

missiles impacted across the planet. The Russian counter-strike hit shortly thereafter. Cheyenne Mountain shook under the force of multiple nuclear explosions.

The bunker complex would survive. It contained enough supplies for years and equipment to dig an escape route when the time came.

But none of that mattered. The nuclear blasts covered the World and chunk by chunk, the voices stopped.

Beautiful silence.

The President broke into a giggle.

Suddenly, like a tidal wave, the voices rushed back into his head. It was just like Madam Serena had said, "A massive psychic event." The death of billions of people. An event so massive that it transcended the normal boundaries of time.

The President screamed in anguish, locked in his mountain fastness with the death screams of his victims flooding.his conscious. A pained giggle died in his throat.

# THE RIVER

Elliott Dobler

The raindrops rap heavily on the tent forming watery black stars above me. Each pauses in its virgin form before breaking and spilling in thin dark veins down the red nylon ceiling. Dear God, the night is bleeding, I think. I lie very still. It's what I've learned to do.

I listen for the river. Henry says the river is essential to our kind of camping. He likes how loud it is. He says it covers up night noises that nobody should hear. I like the sound of the river too, but for a different reason. I strain to hear it now, but the rain hushes its comforting roar. I don't know what to do.

I continue watching the raindrops. They beat constantly on the tent like tiny wet fists wanting inside, to reach me, save me. They are black stars from heaven, I tell myself.

My eyes grow wide to focus. I force myself not to blink. I try to not see anything but my black stars. I try to not hear anything else. I wish I could reach for them, to feel something else, but my arms are pinned, as if nailed to the ground.

I try and count the black stars. But they come too quickly. And this is too much. God, this is too much. But I keep trying, watching. They come faster and louder.

Faster and louder, the pounding, the bleeding. It's hot inside the tent. Oh God, it's so hot. My sleeping bag is open wide yet I am burning. My eyes bulge and swell, stinging with tears and foul sweat. The sound is a deafening crash of static in my ears. My mouth twists in a silent scream.

One day not long after Henry married mom he smiled and said it's time I become a man. The outdoors—camping, hunting, fishing. It's what men do, Henry told mom. Like father like son, he told me.

The raindrops aren't enough, I realize. I panic and try again to listen for the river. I need it to focus, to float away. We always camp near a river. Henry loves it. I rely upon it. We drink from it, eat from it, we sometimes bathe in it. The river sustains life, Henry says. Maybe it takes it too.

Henry teaches me stuff. Like, how to make fire, tie knots, how to survive. He once taught me how to clean a fish. Use only a fillet knife, he said. No other knife will do. He showed me his favorite knife and told me it was special and how the bone handle was from a magnificent elk his grandfather killed. Henry then pinned a twisting fish on its back and slid the knife into its soft belly. Afterwards, he washed the knife and placed it gently back in his tackle box. I asked him about the leftover bloody mess. He scooped it up and tossed it into the river. He grinned down at me. The river takes it all away, he said.

The black stars come harder. Faster and louder. The tent moves in a horrible rhythm under the rain. It's so hot in here yet I'm burning from the inside out. The burn, the blood, the sweat. The stink. Oh dear God, take this from me.

A black star hits the exact center of the tent and splits in two. Split and bleeding from the middle, pooling below the pain. The unspeakable pain. Oh God, why have you—

Henry's shouts come in angry urgent bursts, and I am frightened. I can't help it and I scream. I hate myself for it, for screaming. But nobody can hear. And nobody listens. Nobody ever listens.

The river takes it all away he had said.

The tent is motionless. That part is over. But still I can't move. The crushing weight of shame covers me like boiled clay. It rises and falls, rises and falls. It is deathly heavy.

I'm crying now. Henry hates it when I cry. He says it makes him feel sad and that he doesn't like to feel sad, because it reminds him of when he cried as a boy. Once when we were camping, he cried for a long time after he looked at my face and saw me counting the rain.

Like father like son, he said.

I can finally shut my eyes. Tears spill, mixing with sweat and saliva. I don't see the stars anymore. Through closed eyes I can see it— see the river. I think now I hear it over the rain. It whispers to me. I see the fish… its soft belly.

Without a sound, the fingers of my left hand creep into a fold within my sleeping bag. I find it, the elk bone, undisturbed in its hiding place. It is cool in my hand. I grip it tight, tighter, tighter.

The river takes it all away, he said.

Something is swelling within me. I feel it unfolding and snapping—deep, raw, alive. A blackness beating, bleeding, and boiling thick in my chest. It feels ready to explode. My fist is locked like iron around the knife. My eyes open. Henry, he—

- - -

I stand naked in the falling rain and stretch my arms up to the black night, which is thick with storm and guilt. I finally feel my stars. They cover me, wash me. More tears come, helping the rain rinse away slime and sin. Eventually, I sit on the bank of the river and bow my head, gathering strength for what is next. I look at the knife in my hand for a long moment, turning it over and over. I turn towards the twisted and broken tent. I think of what is still inside.

Henry taught me so much. He really did. I had once asked him what to do with the blood and the mess. The river takes it all away he said.

## WHAT'S THE BUZZ?

Marilyn Felkner

The buzzing in his head sounded like sand paper on a rough-hewn board. His friend, Hank, had told him, "Tom, you must have some of those cicadas in your yard. Back East those things hum all day like static from a radio station." Then Hank had laughed. If the buzzing hadn't been so bad, Tom might have laughed too. He worked as an exterminator. In the last ten years he'd probably done more than his share to bring about a dramatic decline in the insect population. Of course, no one really cared if an insect species was endangered, and studies that showed pesticides might be too effective were scarce.

Tom had inherited his house and the lot it stood on from his dad who'd passed away a year before. Both of Tom's older brothers had died in a automobile accident when they were in their 20s. His mom died of cancer shortly after that, but his dad thought that her death had more to do with a broken heart than cancer. Now Tom had a lot of time to think about death and the meaning of life. He didn't have many friends.

The house and lot backed up to the Wasatch-Cache National Forest. Tom had grown up hiking the trails located just a quarter mile from his back door. The closest trail led to a hidden waterfall and, in the opposite direction, connected with a trio of lakes. When he was young, he and his brothers would hike along the ridgeline or cross over down into Bailey's Canyon. Those had been happy times, when Tom felt like he was in harmony with nature, not working to eliminate it.

Tom was having trouble sleeping, and when he did finally doze off, he would dream about flying insects swarming him. It was so real, he would wake up swatting ineffectively at the air. Even when he was awake, he would see insects flying at him—insects that weren't really there.

After work Tom put on his hiking boots, crossed his backyard, and parted the evergreen curtain that marked the beginning of the Forest Service land. Did he hope to reconnect with the love of nature he'd once known? Ordinarily, a hike brought Tom peace and helped him clear his head, but today the buzzing was worse and Tom felt like sludge was gathering behind his eyes.

An hour in he stopped to rest on a log and closed his eyes for a moment. Soon he felt bugs crawling over his limbs. He scratched absent-mindedly, then jumped to his feet when he realized there were no bugs, just claw marks made with his own fingernails.

The next day at work he mixed the chemicals wrong. The solution was three times as strong as it should have been. After the mixup, Tom's boss gave him a day off to "get your head together." The buzzing in his mind was like being in a sawmill. He had trouble collecting his thoughts. Completing simple tasks like tying his shoes or brushing his teeth felt like calculating the number of light years between galaxies. He wandered aimlessly about the house, then decided a hike in the woods might help. It was a postcard-perfect day, with a deep blue sky, just a few fluffy clouds, and a bright sun that warmed the air but didn't have the intense heat of July.

He placed his steps with care, trying to outwit the confusion he felt from the buzzing in his head.

When he reached the meadows a swarm of angry bugs flew straight for him.

Tom ducked and rolled and writhed on the ground before he realized he had to be hallucinating.

He stood up and looked around. An empty meadow.

As he hiked back, the buzzing never let up but intensified to the point of pain. He was unable to form coherent thoughts. The buzzing seemed to guide his steps. He left the trail. A part of his brain knew he wasn't headed the right way, but he couldn't coordinate his thoughts and actions any more.

He went deeper into the forest until he stumbled over a half-buried log. A massive yellow jacket burrow was on the far side. They bounced off his skin like children on a trampoline as he regained his feet. He swatted at them. That was a mistake. Yellow jackets signal the others when attacked. They responded like a single undulating creature, each of them attaching itself and then stinging repeatedly.

Tom felt like a hundred drills were piercing his skin. The yellow jackets crawled into his hair, up his pants legs, and inside his t-shirt. Some part of his brain screamed, "Run!" but the muscles in his legs and feet were slow to respond. In the midst of the pain he was only capable of fragmented thoughts. "Menaces to society...eradicate...am I the problem?"

Tom lowered his foot, but instead of landing on solid ground, it punched through the burrow, raising another wave of the yellow and black warriors.

He fell. The yellow jackets were in his ears and his

eyes. They covered his hands and arms. His body reacted to the venom with a surge of histamine. The swelling in his airways blocked the oxygen he desperately needed.

"Tom" had ceased to be.

In the days that followed, bloated and covered with stings, the flesh rejoined the elements that had made it. By natural pattern and endless tradition the physical being was broken down and returned to the earth by insect and pest.

## ALPINE SLIDE

Maegan Langer

It's almost midnight in Alpine and Dale Ross is limping through the bare, twisted trees. The old injury in his leg is acting up ever since the weather turned colder. He feels the heavier step in his left side squelch the wet leaves underfoot. The black foothills loom up behind him like sleeping gods. He grips his heavy flashlight tighter.

It was a good idea at the time—moving here to this mountain town. Spectacular views, charming little Main Street and one-hundred year old City Hall building; a few acres of untouched scrub oak and sagebrush where the kids could grow up. But that was before.

Dale stops at the lip of the dark gulf bordering his back yard.

There's an empty animal control truck parked in front of Dale's house. It's been there since this afternoon. Dale knows this because he just checked. Now he's doing the very thing he's told his kids not to do: he's climbing over the fence that blocks the gulley. He's sliding down the muddy slope— why couldn't there be a moon out tonight?—cursing to himself as his leg throbs. He's approaching the gaping hole in the side of the hill. He's shining his flashlight inside. Decades of ruin have punched their way through the rubbled concrete that lines the tunnel. Roots and rocks, mud and regrets.

Don't do this, Ben, Maggie, little Emma. Don't be like your dad.

The clock tower chimes in town, echoing throughout the valley. Dale steps inside.

A steady drip, drip, drip of water from the recent storm leaks through the cracks. Dale wipes moisture off his brow – or is it just cold sweat? He has to rest for a moment, bracing himself with one hand against the side of the tunnel, letting his palm sink into the soft winter moss growing there.

What if it's happening again? His brain, scrambled by that car accident coming around the Point, playing tricks? He couldn't take it, the way the kids looked at him every time he lost a word or tripped over his own thoughts. The way Jessica looked at him on the days he couldn't get out of bed. The Relief Society dropping by with their salty casseroles and dry brownies. The Bishop repeatedly asking, "Is there anything we can do for you, Brother Ross?" Not even trying to disguise the pity in his voice.

Dale prays there really is something down here, beyond the raccoons who steal the cat food his wife leaves out for the strays. There has to be. What about the dead deer that keep turning up out back, the severed rat head in the baby's crib? Jessica blames Dale for that one. She took the kids to her sister's in Pleasant Grove for a few nights after that. He was the one who said Maggie could have a pet rat. But he had to – it was the only thing she wanted for Christmas.

And the thing inside the house—the scratching, scuttling behind the walls. He hears it whenever he's in his office trying to work. Never mind that he's always home alone when it happens. Now the family's dog is missing.

It's all in his head or it isn't, but he has to know.

Dale continues on, feeling his way along the wall of the tunnel with one hand, holding the flashlight out like a weapon with the other. There's something putrid down here. The sourness tickles his nostrils, brings tears to his eyes.

A human face appears out of the dark.

Dale throws himself against the opposite wall. He crouches, trying to recover the air in his lungs, to calm his hammering heart. He stands, slowly, points the flashlight at the man in the tunnel: propped upright against the wall in the moss and mud. His eyes are closed. He could be sleeping.

"Brigham?" Dale says. Brigham, the friendly neighborhood animal control officer, whose heart may be bigger than his brain. That's why he offered to search these tunnels for whatever may be hiding down here because Dale is not imagining things.

Dale steps closer. The flashlight flickers. He shakes it to steady the beam. "Brigham? Buddy, you okay?"

Brigham doesn't say anything. The gray skin of his face begins to twitch. His jaw drops open. Something is moving around inside. Despite himself, Dale angles the beam for a better look.

A cockroach crawls out of Brigham's mouth. Then another, followed by a flood of black insects. Brigham topples forward onto Dale, collapsing like a cheap suit. There's nothing left inside to support the man's skin.

At first, Dale is too scared to move, even to scream. But then a new thought occurs to him. He crawls out from under what's left of Brigham. The poor bastard is little more than an empty burlap sack now.

He struggles to his feet—damn leg—and feels around

in the pocket of his baggy sweatpants for his new smartphone, the one Jessica got him for his birthday. A way to keep in touch with the kids, write notes to himself so he wouldn't forget things. She'd already loaded his doctors' appointments for the next three months into the calendar, with reminders. She thought the phone would make things easier for him.

She was right.

He holds the phone up, checking that the flash is on. The camera captures the soft, deflated remains spread over the ground like a river of skin, the concave lids – the eyeballs were long gone. Something dark and foamy oozes from the nose and mouth. A lone cockroach flails in the tiny black pool. Was that there before? But it doesn't really matter. Dale has what he needs: proof.

# FRESH

### Keri Montgomery

Fred hesitated before he entered the kitchen, listening to his wife Martha hum a sweet lullaby from her childhood. Her aged voice hit the pitches and rhythms just as it did in her twenties—when he first noticed Martha on stage and longed to spend every day in her presence. Forever. After fifty-six years of marriage, he still loved to eavesdrop on her light-hearted cooking, even though his own aged body ached with wear and could never be as jovial.

He glanced down at the car keys in his hand, the subtle smile fading from his lips as a familiar weight entrenched inside his stomach. Then came the ache. His deep and smitten longing for his wife wasn't enough. She deserved better than him.

"You forgot the gallon of milk," Martha said as he entered the room. "I can't make a cream sauce now."

Fred set his keys on the counter next to her open recipe book. I couldn't stop, dear. Too tired. The market's busy after work, even this late at night. Everyone's in such a hurry. I'm too old for it. Please, forgive me."

"Oh, honey." She wiped her hands on a floral dish-cloth—the only soiled item in the entire kitchen. "I know things are hard, but cheer up. I'm making something special for dinner."

Fred clutched Martha's outstretched hands in his own and rubbed his thumbs along her soft winkled skin. "What would I do without you?"

She smiled. "Eat at one of those nasty fast food places every night. Miss out on home cooking. I'm saving your health and your sanity."

He chuckled. "So, how was your evening without me?"

"Productive," Martha said, her eyes brightening. "Come, help me in the garage."

Fred shuffled after her, hands in his pockets, mind wandering. Somehow, he needed to make retirement stick. No more evening part-time jobs that wore him out, but real retirement so he and Martha could enjoy the rest of their golden years together before death stole them away. If he could give Martha his full attention, maybe things would be different.

"Should only take a minute," Martha said.

He stopped on the cement step and reached for the light switch, but his hand recoiled at the last second. The shadows hid what he didn't want to face—mounds of abandoned projects that called to him with guilt—a broken lawn mower, unpainted fence posts, a bike he'd bought for Martha but never got around to repairing the flat tire. The dark hid his shortcomings. If only he had his wife's energy.

"Honey?" Martha called. "Ready?" She opened the SUV's back hatch.

Fred joined her at the tailgate, eyeing a dark mass heaped atop their checkered picnic blanket. The bundle filled the space from end to end, its girth mostly in its middle, and hooked green bungee cord encircled its black tarp wrappings.

"I think you'll need the wheel barrow," she said.

Fred couldn't take his eyes off the mass. In his chest, an irregular heartbeat lumped hard against his breath and forced him to lose a moment of air. One of these days, her projects were going to give him a heart attack. "I thought we agreed to go smaller, not bigger. This one will fill the entire downstairs tub. And break my back getting it there."

She pointed into the dark. "Use the wheel barrow. Were you listening? I managed to drag and lift it earlier. You'll do fine with the barrow. Fred, honey, are you okay? You seem stressed tonight."

"I'm...fine." He retrieved the rusted wheel barrow from a junk pile and placed it at the tailgate. His grip, now clammy, caught rough along the plastic. But he knew she was watching. And waiting. He hated to see disappointment on her sweet, innocent face. Fred managed to half-lift, half-roll the heap toward the SUV's edge until gravity took the mass . It landed with a heavy *thump* into the barrow, nearly knocking it over. A cringe stiffened in Fred's face, but he forced it away before turning to his wife.

"Perfect," Martha said. She began humming the childhood lullaby again while fiddling with the ropes, her song echoing off the rigid garage walls. As she adjusted the wrappings, a man's arm flopped loose from between the tarp edges.

Fred stiffened.

Martha ran her fingers on the man's plaid sleeve, shaking her head. "This one was homeless and living in the park. Died of natural causes with no one to take care of him. Happened just after I got there tonight. So sad."

Fred stared at the darkness above him, unable to glance down. Not yet. He couldn't. Not until she asked and he had to do...

"I don't want the body to go to waste," she said. "Fred, we need to honor him. Just like the others."

He looked at her, at her silver hair and deep wrinkles that were gained after years of being faithfully by his side. She deserved so much more than his shortcomings.

"Will you help me prepare dinner again, honey? We need to hurry while he's fresh." She smiled wide.

Fred's mouth went dry. "Of course, my love. You're such a good cook."

# <u>LUNACY</u>

## Part II

Poetry

## DEMONS DREAMS

C.H. Lindsay

Nightmare vortex

spins its darkness

through tepid sleep.

Injects terror

into arteries of awareness.

Sucks light, snuffs life.

# LESS TRAVELED BY

Joshua Sorensen

A Forest road
Amber light drifts down
Lighting the way
Warming the flesh
I took the one less traveled by
Grass overgrown
It tapers to a barely visible trail

The ground slowly ascends
Golden leaves intermix with warm
Orange hues
Rough road
Strewn with rocks

Not a sound
Quiet loneliness
Only rustling leaves
I stumble on interspersed stones
I reach out
Catch myself
A yelp of pain
A twisted ankle

The trail continues ever upwards
Trees more crowded
The leaves' warm glow replaced
Ruddier hues
Like crimson blood
Paint the landscape
Warm
Visceral

Conifers like piles of rot
Decaying mounds
Sanguine life replaced by death
Aspen bones reach skyward
From decomposing flesh

Dark tentacles encroach the slope
Purple ink
Night obfuscates the end
I took the one less traveled by
And thus the difference

# BEHIND THE WALL
### Kevin Blankinship

*After Poe's "The Cask of Amontillado,"*
*as told by Fortunato*

A merry night indeed! In carnival
when bells tinkle, the demons and the ghouls
come forth to raid the quiet hearths of lives
that march and march along in quiet dread,
before the shadows fuse into a heap.

Restraint cast off us like a mooring line,
we pass around the full and bursting bowls
and dishes, goblets brimmed with ruby red.
Wine! Oh yes, the vine's most gentle daughter
all casked and barreled and decanted there,

And none so regal as my darkest lover
Amontillado, sherry Spanish-born
upon the sylvan frontiers of Jeréz,
aged in oak and locked away in vaults
by you, dear sir, with puncheons and with kegs.

It's why I'm here tonight, my dearest friend,
you'll kindly hark beyond my jester's bells:
Sherry! Amontillado! Bring around
a bottle and we'll drink it to the night
released from politesse or shame. Aha!

But wait, where do we go? You see, the crowd
awaits us in palazzo up above
not here in tunnels low—Oh! Now I see,
niched in dark recess you've got your drink!
Vintage nestled, Médoc, Blanc, De Grave,

and bones? The bones that line the ample crypt?
But so damp in these hypogeal cells!
The niter fills the air with white webwork—
ugh ugh ugh! But my cough it grows the worse
with damp and musty breath—Wait, why do you

stare? What's that, spade
and mortar? Why
do you clap me
in fetters? How can you

just stare? And where
have you got that
Amontillado? No! No
stop, stop, lay no

more bricks! No
more air, I cannot
breathe, the guests
will think, what will

they think? Please
no I beg, no
more air, damp and
must. Must be, be

quiet, quiet now
when bells tinkle they
bring the demons, ghouls
and darkest lover

drown out my vision
with quiet dread, the
shadows that all
fuse into a heap.

# BRAINSTORM

C. H. Lindsay

Kaleidoscopic thoughts
swarm
like butterflies:
in a delirious dance
to eternal
dissonance.

## NECROPHILE LOVE

Daniel Cureton

Fiend of the night
you came to Deseret
for the deeds
with saccharin charm

The University too easy,
the Saints let you in their doors-
Elders and girls so trusting
blind to bludgeoning psychosis.

As you hit so hard.
The cracking,
deep,
in the skull
The glorious ideas.
The succulent sounds.
The warm feelings-
that coursed inside.

The ease of strangle.
The rush of the beat.
The thrill of the feel-
as the feet kept still.

oh Ted-

The push of your thrust,
into the hard body
throbbing against my walls
balls shrinking deep,

as you came inside
within my stiffened space
fulfilling the corpse desires
screaming ecstasy of compulsion

loving me to death
the art of murder-sex
I never knew love
before you corded me
Ted

Exhibition for one
The truest love
like the kind you gave
in my filth laden grave

PEAKS OF MADNESS
I'm yours
Forever in the cell
your memories electrified
never forget the high
as you stiffen, bulge, and die

# GOURMAND

Joshua Sorensen

Ladies and Gentlemen of the Jury,

I cannot express how imperative it is that you set me free. The law may relay in doldrum tones the grievousness of my supposed crimes. But what knows the law of a man's desires? What knows the law of the real world?

They say that justice is blind. I offer up to you that not only is justice blind, but also lacking in other senses. She is deaf. Her sense of touch dulls like moribund meat. And her smell and taste buds are equally stymied by lack of so much capability as to be worthless.

Ergo, how can justice truly bring penalty on a man for seeking the most delicious of fruits. The most sweet of meats. The most aromatic of delights. Is it a crime to enjoy life-giving nourishment?

For those that have never tasted the flesh of man can never properly judge those of us that have. How can one say whether our actions be right or wrong to enjoy the wonderful gourmet that is spread before us, if one does not also partake?

Therefore, I would say to you that you must set me free.

Sincerely,

The falsely accused gourmand before you.

## MAJNUUN, OR TO HAVE
Kevin Blankinship

Why am I so afraid
of spirit possession?

In Arabic, the word crazy
is *majnuun*
"jinn-possessed"
the feeling that
something
else
has come to be inside you.

Another word, haunted,
is *maskuun*,
"lived-in,"
inhabited,
occupied
but not by you.
Why am I so afraid
of being possessed?

Long ago, a prince fell
in love, but he couldn't
have her
and it drove him mad.

He lived in the
woods, talked to
animals, ate bark and leaves.
The Arabs call him
Majnuun.

Why am I so afraid?

When I occupy, I
possess. When I possess, I
have, and when I
have, I am. But if I

don't occupy, possess,
or have,
then am I? Who is
possessor and
possessed?

Why am I?

# RESPITE OF THOUGHT

Joshua Sorensen

I don't understand it.
Why do I think?
    The way I do?
Why do thoughts form in the head?
Then, flit away like so much sand
Blown by a summer breeze?
My feet stuck
In so much mud
The water
Freezing me in place
    on a winter's night!
I can't shake this feeling.
I can't shake this thought.
I should rid myself
Of this apprehension.
    This anxiety.
This haunting note,
About to enter
A situation
A time
A place

At my own peril.

This dreadful thought

Rolling

Steaming

Percolating

In the back of my mind.

Still

I dive into the unknown.

Is it madness to drive full steam

Ahead into imagined peril?

    Or Greater

Madness to sit idly by

Letting the world pass,

Unwilling to act out of fear.

Feelings are faults.

Apprehensions are facts.

Every past traveler on this way has never returned.

Is it success or failure,

Holding them away?

    I drive on.

Into the darkness.

My thoughts slip.

I find myself again

    Frozen

My feet stuck in sludge.

All I want is respite.

# SNAKES

Brian Mealing

There are snakes inside my belly
The snakes warm my body
It is not warm from radiation

Poisonous snakes inside my body
They create the heat
Venomous snakes of fire

They are like giant worms
Dangerous venom
Dangerous snakes

I got rid of these snakes
Got rid of them a long time ago
Years ago

Giant wyrm-thing
It is a big snake
Still inside my body

Creates this heat
Like radiation sickness
It burns

These big giant worms, radiating
Stuck inside my body,
This kills me

It is a nightmare

# PSYCHOSIS

## Part III

Short Fiction

# MY METACOGNITIVE DEATH

Michael S. Glassford

My moment comes at my death. Lying in the street, broken and bleeding, I know it's boasting, but I'm nailing this. Sophia's tears rain down upon my face. They mix with my blood, a unified confluence of our humanity. A strand of black hair escapes her tightly wound bun and streams across her face like a Chinese Dragon on New Year's Day. She brushes it aside.

"Concédenos un milagro," she repeats. Her lips work over each word like a devout Catholic solemnly fingering rosary beads. Her gentle face remains just out of reach of my outstretched fingers.

"Rosebud," I whisper.

"Qué?"

The surging wind mutes my pronouncement. She lovingly inclines her slender neck nearer to my mouth.

"Rosebud." Her brow furrows with confusion. My beloved Sophia is too young for *Citizen Kane*. It's true I like younger women. If I wasn't dying, I'd make sure my next girlfriend was better versed with older movie references.

Speaking of regrets, there's the issue of her name. Why did it have to be Sophia and not Stella? If it were Stella,

I could bellow, "S-t-e-l-l-a!" expelling every last bit of air in my quivering lungs to warm the cold Nebraskan night. My delivery would rival Brando's.

The more I think about it, her name and her utter lack of silver screen knowledge disappoints me almost as much as she does. The feeling encapsulates our entire relationship, which, if you count the last precious moments of our time together, totals all of about six minutes.

Perhaps we aren't an epic couple. Not everyone has the chops to play *Romeo and Juliet*. Well, at least I do. But there's a glint in her chocolate eyes that affirms we could have been something more, we could have obtained classic romance status. At least her pain for me is real. Words fail her and the silent prayer ceases. She must sense my end is near. And I can feel Death's icy fingers steeling away the remaining warmth of my heart.

It's actually charming that Sophia is unable to say my name. I wait for a moment, for her to collect her thoughts. Nothing.

"I'm Scott," I stammer.

"Que´?"

It's times like this, as I lay dying, that I question why I even bother. Why am I always the more attentive one in my relationships? I listen too. I'd listen to Sophia if we ever really talked. I care about details. After all, I took the time to read her name, Sophia, sewed onto the front of her uniform. It's hard to miss, curved over her large breast. I recognize the uniform from the slummy diner, close to my office. I refuse to eat there because my co-workers love it. That and the owner refuses to serve me ever since the spinach incident.

In a way, I count myself fortunate. We wouldn't have

met, Sophia and I, had the reckless car not cut me down in the prime of my life. The driver didn't even stop. I hope my hip put a permanent dent in his fender. But it wasn't the car that brought me to this point, that brought Sophia and I together. It was really a chain of events.

First, my car didn't start after work. Well, that is not entirely accurate. The engine purred to life, but it wouldn't shift. Odd. I baby my 1987 Ford Mustang like a Tesla. I restored her to her current glory in high school and have maintained her ever since. She stays in a luxurious two-car garage every night. I don't allow anyone to park near her, including mother.

"It's my house!"

"Maybe, but I have the only key to the garage, Mother."

But I'm getting off track. It was dark after work; daylight is fleeting this time of year. And I needed a phone to call road-side assistance. My cell was dead. Well, not dead, the battery was full. I just stopped paying the bill months ago. The company wanted me to return the device, but why? What would I do without Candy Crush? Who were they to try and take it back?

I could've gone into the office to make the call, but it wasn't worth it. It would have been warmer but I was upset with my co-workers. No, I couldn't do it. I had left for the day. I'd already dealt with all the office politics, memos, and emails I could handle. Returning was unacceptable.

I opted to use the payphone adjacent to my premium parking space. I didn't know they still existed or worked for that matter. But there it was, glowing iridescently blue in the night. I fumbled through my wallet for my insurance card.

My quarter dropped into its innards with a metallic jingle. The sound reminded me of simpler times.

"To make a call, please deposit twenty-five cents."

"How many quarters does it take to make a call nowadays?" I said to no one in particular, or perhaps to Big Brother.

I inserted another quarter and dialed the number. The buttons crunched beneath my fingers and were slow to decompress. God only knows why.

"Road side assistance, how may I help you?"

"Yes, my name is Scott Anderson. My car doesn't drive."

"I understand."

No, she didn't, but that was part of her script.

"Do you need a tow truck?"

"No." I was annoyed. Even though she was reading from a required operations list, I wished just once I could get someone to exercise a little common sense or, if not that, empathy. "I don't need a tow truck. I need it to drive. I want to go home."

"Sir, we can send help to change a tire, unlock a door, or tow your vehicle to a destination of your choosing. That's about all."

I squeezed the receiver and held it as close to my mouth as possible without touching it with my lips. "I just need the orange boot removed from my wheel. Then I can drive home."

Silence.

"Hello, miss? Are you still there?" Maybe she went to

get a supervisor.

"Yes." The voice cracked through the receiver. She was holding something back. Was she laughing at me? Damn police. They'd gone too far. We had an unwritten arrangement. They left tickets on my windshield. I threw them away.

"I'm sorry, but we can't help with that. You need to call the police agency that booted your car, sir."

"Well, what good is paying for roadside assistance if you can't—?"

"I'm sorry—"

I slammed the receiver down. "This unit is out of order!" I spun around to my car and almost stepped on a stray cat begging for food. "Shew," I yelled. I'm more of a fish guy; I've had several blue bettas on my desk for years.

My frustration boiled over. I refused to be laughed at me. I would Yelp her customer service later. No one laughs at me. Not her. Not my co-workers. It never was a problem. Not until Darla.

Darla Jones. Ms. Jones. The ringleader. The Devil. No, not the actual devil, more like his evil step-sister. She had it out for me.

For the last year, she had gone out of her way to make fun of me. She was the Jim Halpert to my Dwight K. Schrute. Like Jim, she never tired of leaving little presents for me to find. She proved once and for all that you really could encase a stapler in a mold of gelatin.

Once she placed a whoopee cushion on my chair. A simple but elegant prank. You would think that I would have noticed something like that. I'm still not sure how she did it. I suspect that my cubicle-mate, Craig, was in on the gag. He and I were talking about the inner-office memo after we got a fresh cup of coffee. We came back to our desks and fffrrrttttt.

The entire office erupted in a euphoric tidal wave that made me want to go postal. I sat in my chair and drank my coffee like nothing had happened. Every time someone walked past my desk for the next month, they would make a fffrrrttttt noise and laugh.

I didn't let on that any of it bothered me. That's when my fish went missing. At first, I thought it was just a prank. But he's been gone for two weeks.

Darla Jones.

That wasn't the worst of it, though. Not by a long shot. The most maddening of all her pranks were the inner-office chain emails she insisted on forwarding to everyone. They filled my inbox like a perpetual plague without a cure in sight.

"Send this to the ten people or..."

"Forward this message..."

"We are having a company party on Saturday. Please bring..."

It was a ritual of mine to strike the delete key any time her name appeared in the header or subject line. I don't think she ever sent any relevant messages. She was the company's Human Resources Officer, but like I said, she never sent any relevant emails, so I was safe to erase them all.

This afternoon I received yet another one of Darla's infamous spam-o-grams. I glided my cursor across the monitor to hover over the trash can icon, a magical button that made all things Darla vanish into the digital void.

As my finger was primed to apply pressure to my mouse and click on the icon, my phone rang. The caller I.D.

indicated it was an inner-office page. I looked around. There weren't many of us left working so late in the day.

I hesitated. I was tempted to delete the email before dealing with whoever was on the other end of the line. Something made me stay my hand, and I answered the call.

"Don't do it."

It was Darla. I'd know that voice anywhere.

"Do what?" I wasn't going to give her the satisfaction. She would have to spell it out for me, and I doubted she would.

"Don't delete it."

"Sorry, Darla. I'm afraid I can't help you. I don't know what you are talking—" I hung up. A smile spread across my face, like Tim Curry in *Clue*.

I looked down at my computer screen—and the horror! What had I done? My Tim Curry smile contorted into something more akin to a Jim Carrey—my face frozen in a paralytic sneer. Somehow my cursor drifted from its previous spot and I had opened the email, its pernicious contents displayed for all to see. What had I done?

There it was, ugly and base, in bold letters, scrawled across the accursed communication: **DON'T DELETE THIS EMAIL OR YOU WILL HAVE TEN YEARS BAD LUCK.**

The words burnt my retinas. To add insult to injury, the email had a return notification feature. Darla knew I opened it. This would not end well. How hard would it be to procure porcupine quills by tomorrow morning? Revenge would be sweet. It would be mine. Ten years of bad luck. Ha! Try a lifetime of bad memories. What was ten years to that?

I stood to search across the sea of cubicles, flashing a mirthless smile in her direction. I could just see the top of her red hair bobbing up and down. She was laughing at me. Laughing! But I would have the last laugh. I slid the mouse to the right and erased her digital garbage with finality.

My Tim Curry smile returned to my face as I lay dying. *Bring it on*, I thought. I will have the last laugh, literally. I will defy Darla's email and not be subject to ten years of bad luck. It's not possible when I'll be dead in less than thirty minutes.

Sophia leans ever closer to my face. I haven't spoken in minutes. She may think I'm already gone. Her perfume washes over me like lavender in a spring meadow. I have her attention. This is my moment. She's ready to hear my dying message. The word that will immortalize me.

I whisper. Malice drips from my tongue. It's sticky, metallic like blood, but satisfying. My word is appropriate, accusatorial, triumphant, and much more.

"D…" But I succumb to the waiting Reaper as I speak. He and I float away from the scene, from my beloved Sophia, from my miserable life. Hand in hand.

The story of my death will sting my coworkers. But it will hurt Darla most. As the human resource officer, it's her responsibility to disseminate the news. I dare any of them to laugh. They will assume my last word was an attempt to say her name, Darla. The thought tickles me to death—pun intended. It will only add to her regrets. And there will be plenty for her to drown in:

"I shouldn't have cheated on Scott with his best friend."

"I shouldn't have encouraged my new husband to taint

Scott's spinach."

"I shouldn't have fed his betta to the stray cat."

"I shouldn't have called the police every time Scott parked in the red zone."

But the one that will haunt Darla, and the one I love the most, will be: "I shouldn't have sent him that chain email."

She will suffer. If I know her at all, and I do, it will torment her till her dying days—or at least for the next ten years. She will never know the truth. She will never know my dying word was…

D…ELETED!

## PAST LOVE IN A TRAIN STATION

Steven F. Craner

I morosely pondered the irony of my present state of affairs working as a night watchman, barely making minimum wage in one of the most opulent buildings for its time and location that I had ever seen. A student of historical architecture, I marveled at the restored workmanship of the Station. Constructed here in the early 1900's, it stood as a testament, or more appropriately, a warning to the pale fruits of hubris, extravagance, and ambition that had been so much a part of the life of its founder George Gould. Good ol' George and I would have been well matched drinkin' buddies had we lived in the same time period. I had had it all, the travel, the parties, the position, the money, the success, even the 'golden parachute' until I pulled the rip cord and ended up flat on my face.

I can't say as I blame Bethany. We had met in high school, married before we both completed our MBAs from the "U" and were well on our way to livin' the American Dream. At first it was wildly intoxicating, rubbing shoulders with the "best of the best" in the world of high finance. We attended the parties together, danced the night away, and ate in the best of restaurants in all the major cities of London, New York, Paris, Los Angeles, Hong Kong, Tokyo—tipping the poor slobs who had to put up with our excesses and insolence. Life was great and I was at the top of my game.

The pregnancy was not planned. Beth was supposed to be taking care of that side of the relationship. The arguments about ending this unwanted interruption to our life became the proverbial knock-down-drag-outs you could see every weekday on the Soaps. I thought we had been soul mates, with the same goals and desires for success. Work hard, play hard had been our mantra; now my wife was chanting on and on about a home with lawn and an upstairs nursery. The nesting urge had grabbed hold of her and would not let go. What then was I to do? Someone had to bring in the income that we had become so accustom too, so as she picked out paint and made regular visits to the OBGYN, I continued to work, and of course the parties and flirtations were all part of the role I needed to play in order to land the big contracts and keep the machinery of upward mobility well lubed.

As I shuffled through the dim and gloom, I wondered if Railroad tycoons had had the same problems in 1905. Weren't those the times when men ruled and women took care of the home, kids, and whatever else needed doing to keep up appearances.

So here I was in a cheap uniform, totting around a gun, pepper spray, and a flashlight big enough to brain a would-be felon and bright enough for a Las Vegas floor show. One week on the job and I was bored enough to hallucinate my way into heaven or hell—any place that would take me away from here.

I was on my third cup of coffee for the evening and headed towards the bathrooms when I heard the sound, faint at first, almost like the sigh of a breeze rustling through crisp satin curtains. No, I thought, my emotional ramblings were causing some sort of mental exhaustion. I would need another cup and maybe something stronger to stay alert. As I exited the men's room the light coming from under the door of the women's facility was unmistakable. *Do your job Bret, go in and investigate, turn off the light someone's left on or report the short to maintenance.*

Time to earn my pay, but when I placed my hand on the door to push it open, the chill I felt was unmistakable and the smell of roses more compelling still. I was a grown man and hadn't been afraid of the dark for decades. As the door swung open the sight caused such a reaction I would have relieved myself right then and there had I not just emptied my bladder. A faint purple glow greeted me in the shape of a slender young woman gazing out of the window, her back turned towards me and I swear I could hear her crying.

"Ma'am", I said before I realized I had opened my mouth—rational thinking seeking to supplant stark terror— "are you alright, you shouldn't be here." At the sound of my voice she turned around and looked me straight in the eye. This new sensation touched places in my emotional psyche that I didn't even know existed. She smiled and then vanished.

The rest of the night was a blur. How on earth do I log this in the report book? Faulty wiring, open window, weather balloon? Was this why the security company was having such a hard time keeping guards at this location?

I decided to log it as a possible short in the lighting in the women's bathroom to cover my butt and tried to forget all about it. Medication, or better yet a night at Jose's with some Tequila would cure this bout of self-depreciating insanity.

The bender seemed to have done the job and several boring weeks went by. The divorce was finalized. Beth had gotten everything, even the golden parachute and I was lucky to get a two hour visit once a week with my seven year old daughter. The fix of that wild red hair and dancing blue eyes seem to be the only thing left that kept me going.

The next visitation took me completely by surprise. I was just finishing up my midnight rounds when the singing just floated into my consciousness. The notes were so sweet and melancholy they made my heart ache with longing for my ex-wife. What a name to call a person I thought I had loved so much, so long ago. Before my mind could think otherwise, I found myself heading in the general direction of the singing, but it didn't seem to have a direction, it was everywhere and nowhere, which is where I was going to be if I didn't get a firm hold on my sanity.

I turned to head towards the coffee pot and there she was standing in front of me, close enough to reach out and touch, eyes as dark and deep as pools of obsidian. She smiled a crooked little smile that had the promise of breaking into a laugh, then tipped her head in my direction and disappeared.

What had just happened? Yes I had just been thinking about my little girl Daisy, she had that same way of smiling that looked like the birthplace of a glorious laugh. Yes, I was emotionally distraught and had every right to be. No, I was not crazy. Yes, I needed more Tequila.

This went on for well over a year. The slender young woman would appear every couple of weeks, but never at regular intervals and never in the same place. She was always dressed in the same light purple dress that shimmered with its own light and a stylish hat with a wispy white feather to the left perched atop a bun of raven red hair. Sometimes she would be crying, often singing a tune I didn't recognize, but she always ended the encounter looking directly into my soul with those hauntingly dark eyes—offering up that promising smile—then tipping her dainty head towards me and disappearing.

I had decided after the fourth visit that I was not going to talk to anyone, especially some high priced therapist. Whether this was the result of emotional stress, psychosis, or a real ghost-buster's haunting, I no longer cared. Here was something, someone I looked forward to seeing. Here was a bright, or should I say a pale shade of glowing lavender, spot in my life and it seemed to give me hope.

- - -

After about a year I decided to write this all down. If I was sliding into the spooky side of insanity I thought the least I could do is record the process so Daisy would know what happened to her broken down MBA failure of a father, even if she was now living 5,000 miles away in Amsterdam.

When the bank teller handed me my new savings account book the figure looked pretty insignificant. At this rate it would take me three years to save up enough for even a one way ticket to Amsterdam. I knew Bethany was bitter, but I never thought she'd stoop this low to take Daisy so far away I might possibly never see her again. I was still able to talk with my little princess once a week on a friend's international video link, but it just wasn't the same. I would miss so much of her growing up. I knew I had to do something or I would become as miserable and lost as so many of the street people I saw in my daily walks to and from work.

Life has a funny way of showin' you things when you least expect it. As I was walking home tonight I noticed the family shelter on fourth and second. Strange, I had walked by this place twice a day and never even paid attention to the broken people gathered outside. Maybe it was the sight of the little red-haired girl crying while her mother was trying so hard to comfort her? I wondered where her father might be, where was the rest of her family? I decided then and there if I couldn't be there for my little girl maybe I could make a difference in some other child's life. I had thought to try and get another job during the day to help earn money faster for a trip to see Daisy, but somehow volunteering at the shelter just felt like the right thing to do. Imagine that, Bret Hollaway doing something for someone else without a price tag attached. Would miracles never cease? A lonely young lady in the form of an otherworldly spirit had taken a shine to me and now this. It became clear in that moment that there were a lot more important things in life than money and success, and I have earnestly decided to find out what they might be.

I would never have imagined that helping could bring so much joy. I am so tired from serving in the chow line at the Family Center that this is the best I can do to write anything down. I'll change and shower when I wake up, just before I go into work at the Station.

Being around all of the families, even broken and penniless as they may be, has begun to heal some of the pain of being so far from Daisy. I really don't even miss the money and the clothes and the travel. It also seems I have a new perspective on the mysterious young lady of the Station. I have finally accepted this "relationship" as also being an important part of my life.

I did a short internet search and it seems the "Purple Lady" has been haunting the Station since around 1945 after her fiancée threw her engagement ring onto the tracks in front of an oncoming train. The young woman was so distraught from the argument and the rejection she jumped onto the tracks to retrieve the ring and was killed instantly. I guess she is still looking for her true love. I think I am too tired and cynical to ever look again.

The visitations of my special friend at the Station have become more frequent ever since I have let go of the anger and desperation. I do look forward to seeing this sweet lost soul. Call me crazy, but there is a connection, and the shift has become anything but boring. I write in this journal, read a little history, study the architecture in more detail, and dream about seeing my little girl again, hopefully, someday.

Spending more and more time at the shelter—so much to do, so many great people who just need a break—if only I had access to the resources I once had, I would put them to far better use than a new car or a thousand dollar suit. I know a couple of young people who could use just a nice suit of clothes so they might have a better chance landing a decent paying job.

- - -

So tired this afternoon, not much energy left to write.

- - -

Just time for a few hours of sleep before my night shift at the Station.

- - -

I have noticed that the young lady's visitations have become more frequent.

- - -

Once a week now, just like clockwork, on the first day of my shift after the weekend.

- - -

Now twice a week, first and last day of the shift. It almost seems as if she looks forward to seeing me as much as I look forward to seeing her.

Now several times during my five day shift. She still seems to like to surprise me. I had always heard that women like to be mysterious, but a woman who can appear and disappear at will is something else entirely. I have to stop and smile as I write this down and think about how thoroughly insane it sounds to my rational mind. I have come to the conclusion that logic has been highly overrated, after all where did it get me in the past. I wonder if the weekend guard ever sees her?

Oh Daisy, my precious little princess, I miss you so very much. Every moment of everyday. I would give anything, anything to be able to hold you just long enough for one of those special hugs of yours, the ones that make the world seem brighter and wash away all the fears and pain.

I meet with the purple lady every night now and it seems she stays longer and longer. Though I can hear her sing and occasionally cry, she never speaks a word, just looks at me with those eyes, those sad inescapable eyes…and smiles.

Daisy will be starting school soon, her summer break is over and she will need to find a way to adjust in a strange new city. Oh, how I wish I could be there to walk her to school on her first day. I miss my little princess so much that the pain, at times, feels like it will swallow me up. I was such a fool, to think I wanted Beth to end the pregnancy. Life is so very precious, and some of us have a very hard time letting it go.

This evening "she" touched me for the first time. As I sat at the break table drinking my coffee I heard the clock chime midnight and there she was sitting in the chair across from the small round wobbly table. She reached out and took my hand. The chill went through my hand, up my arm, down my spine and frosted my toes, riveting them to the old hardwood floor. She just sat there for several minutes looking deeply into my empty soul. Then she laughed; more a giggle that spread over her face and lightly shook her entire body. And then, she spoke just one word, "Tomorrow."

The next night at the stroke of midnight, I again sat at the table. There was no pretense that I was here to drink coffee, and again there she was.

Eyes, smile, laugh, and the final word, "Tomorrow."

This second night has changed me. I wept for several minutes after she had left.

I haven't cried for years, not since my mother died when I was ten. Not even when Beth served me papers. But tonight, I wept uncontrollably, and I feel spent and clean and free. Finally free!

Walking up to my fourth floor apartment tonight I heard old Mrs. Reilly playing her phonograph. I recognized the tune as the one the purple lady had been singing before. It sounds like a party of angels when her grandkids visit her. Every Sunday rain or shine. I wonder if someday I will have someone who cares that much about me.

Each night for seven nights in a row now, her visit has ended with the one word "Tomorrow." I even took the weekend shift so I could be here. On this, the eighth night, she spoke the words "At Last," with a deep sigh.

Whoever finds this journal, please make sure that my ex-wife Bethany gets this, so she can give it to my sweet daughter Daisy. Of all the things in this world, I think I will miss her precocious smile the most.

- - -

"Harold, did you ever hear from Bret?"

"Nope, the jerk just left his flashlight, gun, uniform, and this journal, and that was it. Never called in, never quit—just plain disappeared. It took the janitor all morning to clean the smell of some kind of rose perfume from his locker."

"Do you think it was because of his daughter's death, he talked a lot about her. Seemed to be about the only thing that kept him going after everything he had lost."

"Not sure. Maybe he got a message from his ex-wife that night about Daisy being hit by a commuter train on her way to her new school. The difference in time zones would have made it around midnight here."

"Sad really, he started out as a real lousy jerk, but became the nicest guy over the last few months. When the director came looking to find out what had happened to him, I found out he spent his days helping with the homeless families that gathered at the shelter down the street."

Harold took the shift that night but never told anyone about what he saw, the ghostly shapes of a young woman in a purple dress and an old-fashioned hat walking hand in hand down the tracks with a broad-shouldered man and a red-haired little girl. They were well past the platform when the lady turned and looked right at him—was that a smile he saw on her face? Funny how much the man resembled Bret. Oh well, he had worked this job off and on for over 20 years and ghosts in this old building were nothing new. He just wished he could get that old tune out of his head.

### DISSOCIATING MERCY

K. Scott Forman

It was a small request.

"Will you boys promise to take care of him?"

"Yes, Papa."

"You'll need to feed him, clean up after him, and spend time with him every day."

"We will."

My brother and I would agree to anything, just to have a dog. And this wasn't just any dog. This dog could communicate—could make a child feel good when they were sad—would always be there. Bingo was a ball of black and white fur, a sheepdog mix, and would be our third brother. Bingo, just like in the song. *B – I – N – G – O and Bingo was his name, oh!*

There were many days spent in the company of Bingo, more than in the company of humans. Bingo went everywhere we did, although most of the time we didn't go anywhere. We had a large lot on the edge of a bedroom community in the middle of the Mountain West. There was a large garden, an old, rotting foundation from a barn, orchards, and trees of every kind. This magical place we called the "Jungle." In our minds, and in the games we invented, it was a place within a place, a portal to another world, and Bingo was our constant companion, our protector, our friend.

Then came the day when Bingo would no longer be able to fill the large paws he had created, or that we had created for him. He loved bones, and he loved to run from us and tease us with the bones he acquired. This would be his downfall.

There's something about cars and dogs that just don't go together. Even dogs as passengers just feels wrong—yes, it's cute, entertaining, to see their addiction for wind, a strong breeze to blow their lips back, to wave their tongues against their cheeks, to even make wings of their ears. It might be endearing to see a dog in the back of a truck, running back and forth, side to side, to see where the wind is the best.

I was always a little uncomfortable seeing a dog in the back of a truck. I feared the dog slipping, falling to the hard pavement, a flying furry object at 35 miles per hour, 55 miles per hour, or worse. A bouncing ball of red fur—each damp mark on the pavement—a part of the dog's soul lost forever. If anything was left when he or she came to a stop the cars following, surrounding, would likely grind the bones and coat into the asphalt, the blood and fur atomically fusing with the petroleum and gravel.

Bingo was lucky, in a sense: he just ran out into traffic—he evaded the metal and rubber monsters—but the fear that he felt, or possibly the kiss of a radial tire, caused a slight loss of control of the pork chop bone in his mouth. The bone with its three sharp points found itself lodged in his throat, and with it the inability to swallow, difficulty in breathing, and pain. Bingo's fate was sealed.

Although my brother and I did not know this until we

were adults, our family was poor, dirt poor. We always had food on the table and a roof over our heads, but sometimes that food was scarce—sometimes we had the infamous blue milk on our cereal, and sometimes the roof leaked. There was no money for a visit to a veterinarian. There was no one to save our dog.

In those days, the single shot of a .22 caliber rifle was nothing unusual on the edge of town. Our father had grown up on a farm. When animals were hurt or suffering there was on-ly one thing to do. To two young boys, it would become the worst sound we would ever hear. It meant that our constant companion, our friend and confidant, our beloved brother was leaving this earth. The shot rang out, the report, jarring our hearts, and Bingo passed beyond that great wall of sleep.

We could only hope, hope to meet up with him again when our own lives had reached their ends and we would travel through the great unknown into another life.

"That must have been traumatic for you, Mr. Os-bourne. Do you think about it often?"

The voice, familiar. The question, silly. I could feel the tears on my cheeks. My eyes must have closed somewhere in the memory or the retelling of it. I opened my eyes, looked at the voice, a man in a white lab coat, a doctor? The question was still silly, even if he really was a doctor.

"Of course, I still think of it! The loss of a loved one stays with a person. Haven't you ever lost something, a pet, a friend, a parent or grandparent? Do you think about it often?"

These shrinks, if that was still a term used to refer to a psychiatrist, were all the same—talk about your feelings—let's find out why you're having problems now; it must be something from your childhood.

"Yes, of course, I didn't mean to sound—"

"I know, I know, you're just trying to help me. You wonder why this story, why I would choose it, why I would tell you about a dog, what the story represents, or the dog, or the .22 rifle, or the sound. Or maybe something else entirely—your Freudian dreams, Oedipus, memory interpretations—all mixed up and ready to go."

"Actually, Mr. Osbourne, I do see some similarities between Bingo's story and your own story."

"Why do you keep calling me Mr. Osbourne? I feel like I'm someone else...when you checked me in, did I have longer hair?"

"No, your hair has been like this since you arrived."

"Did I sing a lot. You keep calling me Mr. Osbourne. Am I a singer?"

"No, you are not a singer, at least not that I know of, but you were talking about your dog, Bingo, and how your father showed mercy."

"Was I? I thought you were talking about my dog and a connection to my memory loss, Doc. Did my dog lose his memory because of a traumatic event? Are you going to put a bullet in my head, so I don't have to suffer? Is this how you deal with this condition, what was it called, dissociative amnesia?"

"No, it's nothing like—"

"Like what, Doc? What's it like, this amnesia? I don't even remember your name."

"Dr. Hyde."

"Hyde? More like Jekyll."

"Yes, and as you can see, your long-term memories are still there, but you've blocked some of the short-term, some of the people in your life."

"So, I remember a book I may have read thirty years ago, but not my own name?"

"Yes."

Dr. Hyde, if that was his real name, was kind of irritating. If I had two tickets to a ball game, he would not be the first person I asked to go with me. I wasn't sure, but it felt like this conversation had already taken place, just like Bingo had already happened. I was lucky if I even remembered Dr. Whatever's face from day to day, much less his name.

"You've suffered a serious trauma that has affected your memories."

"Thanks for the diagnosis—I think I've got that—tell me something I don't know, like what I supposedly suffered?"

"I don't know if we're far enough along in our therapy to—"

"To what? Help me remember who I am? You call me Mr. Osbourne, and that hasn't helped. What's the danger in telling me what happened?"

The doctor sat there, jotted some things down on his clipboard.

"Dr. Hyde, Dr. Jekyll, what do you turn into when you drink your magic elixir? Do you turn into a monster? How about you give me a magic drink, so I can remember who I am?"

"Relax, Mr. Osbourne. I know how frustrating this can be and—"

"Really? So, you've had memory loss, have you, and you can be empathetic?"

"No, and I can't imagine what you're going through, but I'm here to listen."

A lot of good that was going to do. I just wanted my life back.

"Why don't you just lay back and tell me more about Bingo."

"That's all there is to tell about Bingo."

"Do you have any other thoughts associated with your dog or your father?"

"No, but I have another bullet story, and this one has a cat in it, if it will make you happy?"

"Just hearing you talk makes me happy. You've had a rough couple of weeks recovering from your accident, and we want to help you get back to a normal life."

"Who is this we? You mean you and the nurse that makes me take a sedative every day?"

"They aren't sedatives, they are for anxiety and depression."

"I'm not anxious or depressed."

"Why don't you tell me the cat story."

"Okay, whatever you say, Doc."

I reflected. I could still see Bingo. The small grave we had dug, my mother saying a prayer, and the fake plastic flowers. I would return to that grave for many years. It was in the remains of a chicken coop, the dilapidated leftover of a barn that had become a garage. My mother and father inherited it with the house and property they purchased. The weeds eventually overtook the Bingo's grave, the plastic flowers faded, but survived, just below the tops of the weeds. Years later, my parents would build a new house on that property. They tore down the old garage and built a large rambler right on top of Bingo's grave.

"Mr. Osbourne?"

"Sorry, I was still reflecting on Bingo, but a cat story, right?"

"We had several cats growing up, all transients, and all outside cats, cats that would live and hunt in the *Jungle* of our childhood. I think one of the reasons cats stayed outside was because my mother was deathly afraid of them. She was also afraid of birds, especially chickens, but that's another story. Goldy, the cat in this story, would end up in much the same state as our beloved Bingo.

"Goldy was an average-sized tabby and, as one might infer, was gold in color. He was very friendly and was the side-kick to a larger cat we called O'Malley after the more famous feline in Disney's Aristocats, a feature we had recently seen at the Bountiful Drive-In Theater.

"Do they still have drive-ins, Doc?"

"Yes, I believe there are one or two left, but please continue with Goldy."

"Yeah, Goldy and O'Malley."

"O'Malley was a little larger than Goldy and had more fur. The summer heat did not seem to bother him much, but when fall and winter set in, it was clear that he was much more comfortable in the cold than Goldy was.

"Evenings and morning would find Goldy snuggled up

against our kitchen windows trying to absorb any heat that the glass could radiate from inside the house. He liked the shed attached to the garage, not just because of the shelter from the storms of fall and winter, but because our father would routinely leave a small heater running to keep the place warm.

"One day in early fall, a Saturday, our father had returned early from some errand, some activity, maybe even work. The point was, he wanted to take us somewhere, take us to lunch, a movie, I don't remember. That's not the part of the story that is important enough to remember. This is Goldy's story, after all.

"The car was parked in the driveway, the fall sun heating the glass and metal, the warm engine radiating and making crackly-clicky sounds as it cooled. My mother needed 20 minutes to get ready. We all piled into the family car, anxious for whatever the activity was and where our father was about to take us. The key was in the ignition, the key turned, the starter engaged, the engine began to turn over, and"

"Meow!"

"Something was wrong. The motor didn't sound right, it was slow to start, and then it was running and Goldy was running with a trail of fur and blood following close behind. Goldy had somehow climbed up into the fan assembly of the car, up near the radiator full of hot, cooling water, to get warm. The fan couldn't tell the difference between air and cat flesh—it sliced either with the same indifference.

"There was really no point in getting out and chasing Goldy down. He had disappeared, an injured animal, especially a cat, would not be easy to find. We were late for whatever excursion we were going on. Again, our father's farm-life mentality did not pause or worry about an injured barn cat, especially since Goldy would not want to be found for some time.

"When we returned later that day, Goldy was there, in the *Jungle*, clearly injured. He had cleaned himself up somewhat, but his hind leg was cut to shreds, his tail not much better. It was time for the .22.

"The sound was not as traumatic for us as it had been for Bingo. Goldy was clearly worse off than our beloved dog, and Goldy, like most cats, had not developed that loyal bond a canine does with those it associates with. That said, Goldy was suffering and a bullet was the quickest path to relief. We expected the report of the rifle.

"I remember my father digging a grave in the *Jungle*, picking Goldy up by the tail and dropping him into the cold, dark tomb that would know no sound. In that moment, my father demonstrated kindness, mercy, and even sacrifice. It was hard to see an animal suffer, even harder to end its suffering.

"Years later, as I reflected, reflected from a position of financial security that would allow for veterinary visits, say to pull 100 porcupine quills out of a Siberian Husky or fix kidney stones in a Dalmatian, I think of Bingo and Goldy. Bingo we could have probably saved, Goldy was beyond repair, he could not be fixed, he was going to die, like a…"

My mind went blank and then something I recognized appeared at the fringes of my memory."

"Go on, Mr. Osbourne."

"You know, Doc, Goldy reminds me of something."

"What do you mean?"

"A lost cause, someone with nothing left, someone

with a terminal condition."

"A terminal condition? Someone you know?"

I thought. For a moment, a ray of sunlight filtered through the memories that had been covered in mystery, a shroud of trauma, and I saw a familiar face, a face with a name. Emily. Who was Emily? Was Emily my wife? Something was wrong? Emily had something wrong with her. She was suffering.

"My wife, she was suffering"

"Do you remember her name?"

"Emily."

"Do you remember your name?"

"Osbourne."

The light seemed to rush in, to gush in and out of every fiber of my body, to open my vision on something I could have never imagined, something that was reality, something I was sure of, and then the clouds started to swirl and threatened to blot everything out again. One thing stayed in the middle of the maelstrom, something that made me feel guilty, sad, something that couldn't be true.

Tears ran down my cheeks, down my neck, wetting the collar of my shirt. I couldn't speak. What had I done? I knew it was true.

"Do you want to talk about it?"

I looked at the doctor, at this Mr. Jekyll and Dr. Hyde, this duality of man, good and evil. My soul bared itself in all its glory of pitch and ebon, a stained soul, so dark it would never see light again, never even set foot in God's kingdom, not even at the foot of God's judgment seat to be judged. It was damned. I was damned. What had I done?

The light was gone. I remember a cat, a dog, and my name. Then the mist swirls and it's all gone again. There is a name.

"I don't remember having a dog named Emily."

"Mr. Osbourne?

"When animals are hurt or suffering there's only one thing to do. My father taught me that."

"Mr. Osbourne, do you remember your wife, Emily?"

That name—it made my chest ache, like I was going to have a heart attack—it was familiar. It made me feel empty, like suffering a great loss.

"I'm not sure. Who is Emily. Is she all right?"

What had happened. Something tragic, something unforgiveable had happened. This Emily, this fellow named Osbourne.

"Mr. Osbourne?"

"Osbourne, I remember."

"What do you remember?"

"What Osbourne means?"

"What does Osbourne mean?"

"The mercy of God."

# THE LODGE

Johnny Worthen

"The trappers had built their cabin over an old Indian camp."

"You're going there? Seriously?"

"It's a good story."

"Kyle, this is the kind of shit that happens with humanities majors. In STEM we don't make shit up."

"I didn't make it up. I'm telling you what the professor told me."

"But with embellishments?"

"Of course. I'm a writer, baby."

"And it was Rouke who told you this?"

"The NIMBYs asked him to do a historical survey."

"So he's on the other side?"

Kyle nodded. "He didn't get it. He practically busted a gut to tell me, even after I told him he was working against my dad."

"Another example of flutter-brained arts majors."

"Humanities—history professor, with a doctorate."

"That's what I said."

"Do you want to hear the story or don't you?"

"Fine, fine." Brad fanned a paper plate over the budding fire. Smoldering newspaper flared in a flameless orange glow then caught and spread to the fire-starting sticks they'd brought with them.

"Make sure the flue is open," said Kyle.

"It is."

"Then why is the room filling with smoke?"

Brad gave him a look and then peeked up the chimney. He reluctantly reached inside and pushed the lever. The flannel on his sleeve flared and balled as the hot smoke was sucked out and into the cold mountain air and the sticks glowed blue with chemical fuel and new air.

"Don't put the big logs on until the medium—"

"Tell your damn story," Brad said.

"Maybe I should save it for the girls," said Kyle.

"You do have more than one story, right?"

"Har har."

Brad fiddled with the grate, and jabbed a poker into the fire to shift things around. "An old Indian burial ground," he said. "Got it. Go on."

"Not a burial ground, a campsite."

"Ooooo, a campsite? That is so much scarier."

Kyle wiped meat off the end of his knife and waved the blade at his friend like an accusing finger. "Enough of your sass, young man."

Brad gave him the finger and they both laughed.

Outside, through the window over the sink, Kyle saw the sky was ashen slate and the little light that found its way through the cabin windows was low and murky. The snow cover outside, though icy and old, had not light enough to sparkle the frost. A storm was coming. Ski reports offered a thirty percent chance of flurries by the late afternoon to finalize the cloud cover they'd had all day.

It would be great cuddling weather and Kyle chopped and cooked with warm expectations of holing up for a few days with his best friend and their best girls. Roughing it in luxury. Season passes and just a hill between them and a black diamond mogul run. He looked forward to the shared solitude and was glad that his father had been unsuccessful turning the cheaply bought land into overpriced condos.

Ski-in condos had been the plan when the resort announced new boundaries. Kyle's father, however, had been unable to get past the planning commission. He needed permits for a road, sewer, and water. And now there were the neighbors, the NIMBYs—Not In My Back Yard—complainers who promised to battle him until the next century; and this one had just begun. In the meantime, more as proof of concept than long term investment, Kyle's dad had built this great underutilized ski retreat. Kyle had every belief that he'd inherit the zoning fight along with this lodge when his father died. He was an only child.

"It's a natural campsite," Kyle went on. He pushed the meat and carrots into the pot, put it in the sink and pumped water up from the spigot.

"And so convenient," Brad said, his sarcastic gaze aimed squarely at the antique water pump.

"It is, actually. Dumbass," said Kyle. "It's flat. There's a spring. Lots of sheltering trees."

"Great powder."

"The trappers didn't have the same appreciation for that that we do. I can't speak to the Indians."

"It's choice."

"There is something about this place," he said.

"I'll stop dissing it."

"You can put on a big log now," Kyle said.

"I know how to build a fire."

"Tell that to the flue."

Kyle turned the stove on and a blue propane flame leaped up to meet the heavy pot. The smooth spicy smell of pepper and chives, chicken and broth, made Kyle's stomach gurgle. Though power came from generators, heat from a fireplace and two wood stoves, and water from the antique pump, the cabin was otherwise a modern house. It had a full kitchen, three comfortable bedrooms, two bathrooms, and art on the walls—water colors of elk and cowboys, Indian squaws smoking meat, a trapper with a mule. One was of a clown with big eyes painted on black velvet. Supposedly that one was valuable.

The wind blew a gust and the door rumbled pulling Kyle's attention to the big mudroom where he could see their skis set against the wall, their coats hanging on hooks, but not the entrance.

"You closed the door right?" asked Kyle.

"Do you see a snow drift in here?"

"No."

"Then I damn well closed it, didn't I?"

Kyle stirred the pot, added a soup mix for flavor, a touch of salt. "The girls are what...an hour away?"

"Closer to two, I'd bet. They'll wait to be sure the house is good and warm before they even put on their parkas this time. We won't see them before four."

It takes about an hour to get the house awake and habitable after sitting empty for a month. The last time they'd come, the girls were wet from a drizzly storm, cold from falling in the deep snow, short-tempered and hungry. When they finally got inside, they complained and sulked together until the fire was lit, not taking off their coats until the cabin was a sauna and they'd each had a bowl of soup and two margaritas. This time the boys arrived early to get the place cozy and warm for a good long weekend break between semesters.

"Trappers," said Brad. "Trappers—remember? Man, even in your bullshit stories, you wander. Your mind ain't right."

"There were two of them—the trappers. French. Axel Fournier and Theodore Durand."

"You know the names?"

"It made the papers."

"What did?"

"I'll get there."

"Then do." Brad closed the fire grate and flopped on the couch. He unzipped his Tau Sigma Phi jacket and put his feet up on the coffee table.

Kyle remembered Professor Rouke's excitement when he'd told him. He'd been full of dates and references, myths and folktales. Kyle decided he would add a bit of drama, use his humanities chops, theme, parallel and malaise. If it played well on Brad, he'd tell it to the girls even better.

"It was toward the end of the fur trade," Kyle said stirring. "The two men had trapped together for years. They were the best of friends." Rouke hadn't told him that, but it felt right and so he went with it. "They'd trapped across three states and ended up here in the Wasatch Mountains chasing the last few beavers in the area before civilization came in and the hat fad went out."

"My friend the author," said Brad.

"Humanities, baby. Where the mind is free."

"Where the mind is warped," said Brad. "Come on. Crack a beer, Shakespeare. Sit down. We got time."

Kyle adjusted the stove and snapped a couple of cans from the case before sitting down across from his friend. The fire was bright and warm, already heating the room to a tolerable level, and like his friend, Kyle unzipped his jacket and relaxed.

"So they were best friends," said Brad. "Known each other since grade school? Lived on the same street growing up? Roommates in college?"

"The were from Quebec," said Kyle, unfazed. "There are mentions of them both in the records of the rendezvous."

"The big drunk mountain man party?"

"Yeah."

"Cheers!" Brad tilted back his beer with a grin.

"Bridger also recorded—"

"From Quebec. Hunted three states. Came to Utah.

Stay on target, Red One."

"You're fun to talk to."

"Just keeping your wandering mind on course, old buddy."

"Axel Fournier scouted this place and built a rough cabin, staying a year alone in it while Durand took their furs to St. Louis. They met up in late summer at Fort Bridger."

"Durand is Teddy?"

"Theodore, yeah."

"And the year was?"

"I don't remember."

"Rouke would be disappointed."

"I know, right?" said Kyle. "I can't believe I don't remember that kind of detail when no one was interrupting him."

"Fine, fine. Go on."

Kyle smirked and sipped his beer, it was cold and icy, but warmed him inside. The house was cozy and intimate. The fire crackled and cast orange tinged shadows over the carpeted floor. While the food cooked and the cabin warmed, Kyle told his story.

- - -

The trappers should have had good time to make it to their winter cabin. The hard part, the long journey was behind them—Durand's trek from St. Louis across great plains and sullen rivers, but early snow found them still packing in Fort Bridger Wyoming.

It was a quick squall, blew in and out, and left only a

few inches of snow, but it promised a long and hard winter. The men set out at once.

Carrying all they had on their backs or pulling it in wide travois, they set left the fort aiming west and south over Indian roads and deer trails. Soon the Wyoming plains turned to low hills and then high peaks. Following a river gorge, they came out into a wide empty valley.

"Our place is up there around that second canyon," said Fournier.

"That's the Great Salt Lake there?" asked Durand pointing to the water in the far distance.

"It is," said Fournier. "It's a poisoned hole. There's a better lake in the south, fresh water there, but the area looks like to have been trapped out. And there are Indians."

"And the place you found is good?"

"It is a great place to overwinter," Fournier said. "High and sheltered. There's water. The Indians won't bother us."

"Why's that?"

"Long story."

"Can't wait to hear it."

At the mouth of their canyon, the snow began. It took them a day and half to reach the shelter. The slope was mild but made hard by the deepening snow. When they broke out of the tree line Fournier was pleased at how picturesque and pleasant the little meadow was, and their cabin nestled within it. It was short lived. Tired and sore, sleep deprived, the men threw themselves onto the frozen dirt floor and rested the moment they were inside.

Fournier woke before his friend and set the cabin right. He stored their supplies and rolled out buffalo furs for bedding over the floor. He set a pot of meal to boil and another for coffee while Durand slept.

All the while it snowed outside.

Durand woke to the smell of hot food and coffee and smiled with relief and gratitude.

"I thought I was dreaming that," he said. He looked around the space, peering into the corners and low ceiling by the light of the fire and a single lamp. "Is it night?"

"I think so, but I can't be sure," said Fournier. "We're already snowed in."

"What?"

Fournier went to the rough door and pulled it open to show a blocking wall of white beyond. "We've been here a day and it hasn't stopped for a moment. It could still be snowing."

Durand nodded his head and grimacing, having scalded his mouth on a cup of boiling coffee.

They'd expected this. This is how one wintered in the high mountains. They made to be bears, holed up and fed, waiting for conditions to change, for spring, for the sun to come and the snow to go. This year it had come earlier than expected, but they were ready for that, safe in their hole.

The men stretched out on the furs and ate stew in a silence that bespoke their long friendship and deep understanding. Fournier was pleased when Durand produced a new deck of cards and they had their first game of the season.

They did not know how long the storm lasted or the next or the next, nor how deep the snow had become. "Less than twelve feet," was what Fournier said because that was the height of their chimney. "Then again, it could be more and the heat has made a tunnel."

Durand thought that was unlikely. "If it's much taller, it'll cave in eventually and then we'd know it."

That first week, they dug a tunnel from the doorway to the woodshed and kept the piles high in the cabin, making it their daily routine more as a way to keep time than by any immediate necessity.

They played cards, rationed their coffee, and waited.

Weeks went by. Months.

They spent most days in silence, comfortable and enduring. They'd known each other since childhood and had nothing new to discuss and were comfortable in it; like the little cabin itself, insulated and safe.

It was some time before Durand finally asked Fournier about the Indians and the tale he promised on the trail.

Axel was shocked to remember he hadn't told his friend the story. "Oh it is a good yarn," he said.

"Do tell. I'll make time. Message the baron, I will be busy this afternoon."

Fournier threw a log in the fire, preparing to speak more in the next hour than he had all month.

"The story as I understood it was about two friends who stayed here. In this very spot. In this very meadow."

Durand lay back contentedly. Fournier saw the excitement in his face. A new yarn was a thing to rejoice. He cleared his throat and embellished.

"They were best friends and had been warned of this

place."

"Oh?" said Durand.

"Yes, the older peoples had warned them."

"What's wrong with here?"

"I'll get there, Theodore," said Fournier. "Sit back and listen."

"Very well, very well."

"So even before the Indians there was—"

"Is the door closed?" asked Durand.

Axel turned and felt the draft. How air could move so fast through the tunnel to shake the door, he was uncertain. He could see though that the door was closed. He pushed a shirt into the gap at the bottom to stop the breeze and returned.

"Who told you this?" said Durand.

"An Indian woman—a shaman," Fournier hoped that his friend wouldn't recognize the obvious lie there. Utes don't have female shaman.

"Go on."

"So the Indian braves knew the history, knew the curse of the place."

"A curse now?"

"Yes, why not?"

"You read too much, Axel," said Durand.

Fournier ignored the comment. He was never sure if he was being teased or complimented. Theodore often chided him for wasting his mind on fantasy and imagination, but then again, he never complained when Axel found a new novel and read it to him at night after a long day's work pulling glorified rats from steel traps in icy rivers.

"So the braves…" coaxed Durand.

"They knew the stories, but the place was so amicable that they chose to build a hunting lodge here. There was much game nearby. Deer, elk. Beaver. They made a smoking rack and a lean-to and planned to spend a week or so before heading back to their village, big men for all the meat."

"Let me guess," said Durand. "It started snowing?"

"Yes. Exactly."

"So goes the legend."

Fournier winked at his friend. "They holed up in the lean-to but the snow was so heavy they soon found themselves trapped and running low on food."

Fournier saw his friend's eyes flash over to their food supply and return to him contentedly. Fournier glanced too and counted three full crates of provisions. Coffee, sugar, meal. Smoked meat. A year's worth.

Getting back in the mood, he said. "It came up on them suddenly."

"What did?"

"The woman wouldn't say. When she came to the name, she fell silent, the gap being the name. I didn't know if she meant a curse, or a devil, or a madness." He paused for effect, the fire crackled and the pot steamed.

"The one leapt upon his friend," he said. "He drove his flint knife into his throat and ripped it open. A stare of horror and surprise met the attack as the Indian drank the gushing blood like it was a desert spring and he'd been wandering the sands thirsty for weeks."

Durand stared at him, captivated.

Fournier pulled his knife off his belt for effect.

"While his friend still lived, sucking breaths—his last ones, gurgling and disbelieving, the killer butchered him into strips of meat."

Fournier paused for effect holding the knife over his head dramatically.

"When he got to the liver he took a big bite out of it, savoring the flavor—food to a starving man. He slurped and sucked and moaned in delight. He stuck the leftover liver on a spit and cooked it in the fire while he prepared the rest of the meat for the smokehouse."

Fournier's eyes unfocussed and he felt ill.

The draft was back and he looked to see if perhaps his friend had left to relieve himself, or more hopefully, vomit for the terror of the story. He thought it'd told it well.

The door was shut.

Turning back to Durand, he saw the mess. Durand was cut to pieces. A piece of meat sizzled in the fire place, the room smelled of wet metal and roasting game.

He had no recollection of what he had done, but looking at his hands he saw his own bloody knife. Licking his lips, he tasted thick congealing rust. Sucking his teeth, he found shreds of raw meat, gamey, spongy, and fresh.

"The old trapper, Fournier, screamed. It was all he could do. Scream. He screamed and screamed. For days they say he screamed, until a passing—"

A gust of wind shook Kyle out of the tale and he turned to looked down the hall. Melissa and Anne stood in the doorway, their pink and purple parkas wet with new melting snow.

"Thanks for getting the place ready for us," Melissa said. "Feels warm. Smells good."

"Is that barbecue?" asked Anne. "I thought we were having stew."

"What's on your—"

They paused a step farther in. Their eyes grew big. They stared and stumbled.

Slowly, Kyle turned toward the fire, to where Brad had been. The blood was black in the carpet, pooled on the couch. Meat—clean cut pink strips of it, lay on coffee table, ready for the smoke house and a half-eaten liver sizzled seductively in the fireplace.

# THE SIGN

Joshua Sorensen

*Monday*

James Madsen sneered at the sign on the hobo's lap. "Veteran; Please Give." Doubtful. These homeless beggars all had the same sob story. James didn't seriously believe any of them really were veterans. He wasn't even certain why he had stopped to pay attention today. He was certain that he had walked past this same beggar dozens of times and not paid him a second notice. Maybe it was the stiff winter wind that hit him in the face and flung open his coat. Or maybe it was the way that the homeless man smelled of his grandmother's oatmeal cookies, not the delicious ones of his childhood but the ones she made once age and dementia set in—horrible overcooked concoctions of uncertain ingredients.

"Get a job, you waste," he crooned.

A sudden urge tempted him to kick the other man's boots as he walked away. Then, half-guilty at his revulsion, he pulled some change from his pocket and dropped it in the proffered fast-food cup.

Just a few short minutes later, he reclined in his big leather chair, in his big corner office, soaking in his big city view. It was good to be the king. And king he was. President and CEO of AssureInsure, one of the biggest insurance reinsurance reinsurers in the nation. There was big money in insuring the guys that insured the insurance companies. One of those back-channel money trains laying hidden from the eyes of most normal people.

He rose and walked to the window. Down on the street below, he could still see the beggar perched near the train stop. The TRAX light-rail made his morning commutes easier than he expected and, also, gave him smug satisfaction at how environmentally conscious he was. His eyes darted back to the homeless man.

Why did the beggar occupy his thoughts? It was abnormal. He shouldn't give the man another thought. Sure, his wife took the kids to church, but James hadn't been an active member of The Church since college. His wife might hammer on about Jesus, being charitable to those less fortunate, and the state of souls; but James wasn't a believer. It wasn't that James wished anyone ill will or anything. In fact, his company regularly gave to several charities. And he didn't begrudge his wife any of her activities or donations to The Church. He decided to put the slovenly man out of his mind altogether.

His day was filled with a deluge of meetings. The holidays were over, and they were starting a new quarter. Time to start the year off with a bang. But, no matter how engaging the conference or meeting, his mind kept wandering unbidden back to the homeless beggar.

The day progressed slowly. It was long after sunset when James Madsen took the elevator down to the street and walked to his train stop. That same disgusting hobo perched on the roadside. The same disgusting cardboard sign lay across his lap. James had wasted enough time and energy thinking about the man. He gave a wide berth to the sitting figure, proceeded to the train platform, and headed home.

*Tuesday*

Another chilly day, another commute on the TRAX. A light snowfall floated out of the sky, dusting everything with a fresh coat of whitewash.

The doors hissed open, disgorging the stream of passengers onto the platform. They moved in droves, each to their appointed place for the morning.

James Madsen hesitated on the platform. He spied the beggar in his customary spot. He debated reboarding the train, getting off at the next block. The doors hissed closed and the train sped off northbound, ending that possibility.

"What are you doing?" he chided himself. "It's just a homeless person. You've walked past him or those like him so often, why should today be any different?"

He stepped into the crosswalk and strode confidently towards the man. His steps faltered slightly as he saw the sign had changed. It no longer declared some status to elicit sympathy, instead: "The End of the World is Nigh" was scrawled across a torn piece of pizza box.

"That's original. You don't see that much here in Salt Lake City. But I already gave you something, yesterday, don't expect any more free handouts from me."

The beggar didn't look up, didn't even acknowledge his existence. With an annoyed huff, James Madsen headed towards his office and another day of boring quarterly meetings.

It was easier, today, to put the beggar out of his mind. He only thought of him during moments of silence, which were near absent during the busy course of his day.

James concentrated on the day's conferences. His staff

presented data on quarterly earnings, expenses, and profits. He reviewed the presentations, running it through his mind. His assistants and vice-presidents had done well.

Tomorrow, he would have to submit the quarterlies to the board. It was merely a preliminary to next week's annual review, but still weighed heavily on his mind.

By the end of the day, he had nearly forgotten about the lazy slob or the anxious feelings of the previous day. He took the elevator and exhaustedly, half-stumbled his way to the train stop. He was glad he didn't have to drive home.

"The End of the World is Nigh. How's Your Soul?"

The changed sign beat him in the face without moving an inch from the man's lap.

"How's my soul?" he roared at the beggar. "That's none of your business!"

Once again, an urge to strike out at the silent form. Once more, curbed-in by half-guilty afterthoughts.

James Madsen stormed out into the street without looking. A car slammed on its brakes, skidding on the icy concrete towards him. James darted onto the platform in the middle of the road. The driver slammed on his horn as well, shooting an icy glare at the careless pedestrian.

"How's my soul? How dare he ask that?"

James' wife, Shera, had asked him that several times over the holidays this year. "How's your soul?" she would nag.

She had become particularly shrill these past few months. Demanding that he go to church with them. Spend time during Christmas "with Christ." Even his three kids had joined in the cajoling, roped into their mother's ploy.

He spent the rest of the evening in a funk. Ignoring his wife and children. Finally, going to bed early for a night of restless sleep.

*Wednesday*

James Madsen grunted as he stepped across the crosswalk. That same useless scum sat at the same useless piece of concrete, the same useless cardboard sign across his lap.

But it wasn't the same. "How's your soul, James?" blazed in his eyes in flat letters on stale brown cardboard.

He clenched his fists in anger. Snorts erupted from his flared nostrils. A scream of rage boiled up from his gut. Before it shot forth, he stormed off.

"That's it. I lost one night of sleep thanks to that man. I won't let this get to me. I won't let this get to me," he repeated that mantra over and over in his head as the elevator ascended to his office in the heavens. This far up, he was safe from the beggar and his incipient sign.

He paced the window of his office, the mantra chanted under his breath. Glancing down at the sitting figure so far below, he was certain that the beggar watched him back. Piercing eyes, like a vulture, staring at him. Staring at his anger. Staring at his soul.

"Mr. Madsen," Travis, his secretary, buzzed him. "It's time for the..."

James shot him a glare that froze Travis in his words.

"The teleconference. The quarterlies," Travis stammered.

"Thanks, Travis." His urge to yell broken off by a moment's quick thinking. "I'll be right there."

The conference room was as inviting as any other meeting room. His staff was jovial, but serious. The board members stared from screens at the end of the table.

Fortunately, James' participation in the meeting consisted of sitting there and looking serious. His hardened face hid his inner turmoil. No matter how hard he tried to focus, the beggar invaded his thoughts and danced about the stream of his concentration.

As soon as the meeting finished, James stormed back to his office. A warm flood of wrath poured across him. Nostrils flared. Blood pooled in his cheeks, turning skin to crimson.

He caught his breath. Thoughts churned in his head until they congealed like sour butter. He tore through door and headed for the elevator.

"Travis, hold my calls. Bob Young can handle anything big that comes up."

The descent was interminable. The doors mocked him as they crept open. His entire World slowed to a crawl. He nearly slipped on the frost covered sidewalk as he stomped towards the man.

"I'm talking to you, James Madsen!" declared the sign.

James tromped up and laid a right hook across the tramp's jaw. The beggar flung over backwards. His meager possessions sprayed in all directions. A squeal of surprise escaped his lips. James closed in, kicking the prone form.

"You maggot. You filth. You waste of oxygen."

Insults and expletives escaped James' mouth. A barrage of words and blows rained down upon the feeble target.

Crowds of people gathered around the altercation.

It didn't take long for the police to arrive. They hand-cuffed and arrested the beggar, assuming he had started the altercation and attacked James, but witnesses informed the police that James have been the attacker. He found himself restrained in the back of a police car. The beggar went free. The police transported him back to the station and booked him on assault and disturbing the peace.

Late that night, his wife arrived and bailed him out. The beggar had declined to press charges, but James still had to worry about a disturbing the peace charge.

On the way home Shera continued to nag him about his behavior.

"James, I'm concerned about this. How's your soul?"

"How's my soul? Why do you keep asking that? Never mind, I don't want to talk about it."

She continued to yammer on, but James didn't hear. He fumed with anger. All the rest of the night, James ignored his wife's comments and nagging. He even slept on the couch to avoid her.

*Thursday*

Yesterday's outburst should have burned off some of the steam, it did not. Anger flushed through his veins. It threatened to boil out when he saw the unmoving form of his foe, still occupying his ever-present vigil.

"I'm watching you, James Madsen," greeted the sign.

Barely controlled ire threatened to overcome James. He flew from the beggar. Fear and fury drove him onwards.

He deflected questions and comments as he stomped

through the office. James spent the day locked in his office. Ignoring calls and barely responding to email, the day passed quicker than expected.

"You can't escape." The sign mocked him as he headed to the train in the falling winter snow.

Something had to be done. This had to stopped.

The train ride home was a flurry of emotions.

*Thursday Night*

James Madsen pulled his car into the company garage. He parked in his reserved spot. The night air blew cold in his face, but he didn't notice as he stepped onto the street.

It was late. The street was empty of pedestrians. Friday or Saturday might be crowded, today was Thursday. Not a night of busy foot traffic on a cold, snowy, January weeknight.

Despite the weather, the beggar remained in his daytime spot. James made a beeline for him.

"Hey, slob! Get up!" James pointed a pistol in the other man's face.

Angered by the slow response, he grabbed the hobo's shoulder and hauled him to his feet.

"Get moving!"

He threatened and shoved the homeless man up the street to the parking garage. In the darkness of the parking spaces, James kicked him in the butt. The tramp sprawled onto the concrete.

James popped open the trunk of his Lexus.

Grabbing the greasy, unkempt mop of hair, he pressed

the muzzle against the bum's forehead. He pulled the vagrant to his knees and flung him against the bumper. James tore the decrepit coat off the beggar.

"Get in!"

The beggar crawled into the trunk like some slow, dumb animal. James unceremoniously slammed the lid down, locking the other inside. He was surprised how easy it had been.

Exiting the garage, James headed south. A half-hour later, he found himself driving up Big Cottonwood Canyon.

At first, noises emanated from behind him. Knocks and moans from the trunk slowly faded as the cold took its hold on his captive.

Sliding around a sharp, left turn, the car skidded into a roadside snowbank. Cursing, the driver jumped out of vehicle and slipped in the slush.

James pulled himself out of the wet muck. He slid towards the trunk. Flinging it open, he grabbed the shivering form from within.

"Get out here!"

The beggar's skinny, half-starved frame emerged. James pushed him up the snow bank.

The pair of them trudged through the waist deep snow. Their legs sunk to the crotch with each step. They left the road behind and were soon surrounded by pine trees, cut off from the World.

James was surprised that the man continued to comply. There was no way the man didn't know what was about to happen. Yet, he still followed James' barked commands. There was no resistance, no fight, left in the destitute scrap of a human.

"That's far enough," he hollered. "Turn around."

The pair stood in the snow, giant flakes falling around them. The World was silent.

"Tell me what you know."

The beggar just gaped at him.

"TELL ME!"

Still no answer.

James shook the gun violently in the other man's face.

"You tell me how my soul is, you sorry excuse for life!"

The homeless man just wept. The tears froze against his skin in the bitter cold.

BANG!

His body jerked as James pulled the trigger.

BANG!

He fell backwards into the snow. Red blood stained the white covered ground.

BANG! BANG! BANG!

James continued to pull the trigger, emptying the magazine into the prone corpse before him. An uncontrolled laugh broke forth from his mouth.

He turned his face into the wind. His laugh echoed from the canyon walls and died in the boughs of the trees.

Suddenly, the echo came from behind him, on the ground. A hissing, burning sound filled the air.

James turned. The snow sizzled and crackled, creating

a steamy mist. Slowly, the dead body of the hobo stood.

This time James gaped at the other man. The mouth of the decrepit vagabond elongated unnaturally. Sharp teeth ripped forth from his gums. His eyes glowed with amber malevolence. His bones contorted; his flesh rippled. His skin turned a pale aqua. And he grew.

Extreme cold wafted from his body. Cold so extreme that it burned all around it. What remained of his clothing froze, cracked, and splintered into thousands of tiny shards. Great black wings sprouted from his back and stretched into the night air. The demon continued to laugh at James as a he stood there, paralyzed like a dumb animal.

"You poor dumb mortal," it chided. "You never make it more than a couple weeks, but, this time, you didn't even make it to the first weekend."

A great hoofed foot kicked James over onto his back.

"Since you seem to have forgotten: Welcome to Hell. Abandon All Hope, Ye Who Enter Here."

- - -

*Monday*

James Madsen sneered at the sign on the hobo's lap. "Veteran; Please Give." Doubtful. These homeless beggars all had the same sob story.

# GHOST OF THE OLD MAIN

Sariah Horowitz


Stephan smiled rigidly at the camera waiting for the flash. He could feel his wife, Mary's, hand twitching on the back of the chair. He hoped this wouldn't take much longer or his joints would freeze up. The large window of the studio kept drawing his eye. The eastern facing windows showed a hint of the mountain of red rock on the edge of Cedar City. Stephan wanted to turn his head to look but didn't dare.

Setting up for the shots had been long enough. He remembered when taking a photograph was worse. From the structure, this building must be from back in the day with the flash pan. Natural light must be for the cameras but it didn't help the lack of airflow.

The flash split the room adding to the stuffy heat in the room. Finally, Stephan allowed himself to relax. Mary was already walking around the room looking at the other paper windows of stiff people posing for pictures.

The photographer disappeared into his dark room.

Stephan wondered to the window. Cedar City had grown since the last time he'd been here. Paved roads and real street lights replaced the scorched dusty city he'd left. More cars passed no longer plagued with fuel rations from the war.

He'd heard the college had grown too. More buildings

but the originals were still standing. His skin prickled at the thought of the brick building he'd help build. The peaked roof and large windows could be seen above the smaller houses.

"Here it is." the photographer appeared with a large piece of paper in his hand. "It turned out fabulous."

Mary picked up the picture. She commented on the way they looked so clear and almost lifelike. Stephan thought they looked stiff and more like puppets. The black and white made him look more like a corpse, but Mary seemed to like it so he didn't voice his thought.

- - -

Mary insisted on placing the picture in a prominent place on the mantle in their new house. He didn't mind but found himself often glancing at it from a safe distance across the room. There was something odd about it. Silvery things on the side of the picture seemed to flicker. It must be a flaw in the glass messing with him.

That evening, their nightly walk brought them near the campus buildings. Some students lingered by front stone steps. The bleaching of the sun barely seemed to have made an effect on the bricks.

"Amazing," Mary said. "And to think you helped build it."

"I just helped with the bricks." Stephan smiled.

For a moment he thought he saw a familiar face of a woman at one of the windows. But that was impossible. Christine was dead. He stepped closer but the window was vacant.

"What is the matter, Dear," Mary asked.

"Nothing." He turned away. "We better head back. It's

getting dark."

They walked home. There again the picture drew his attention. There was something off about it.

Mary touched his arm making him jump.

"What's wrong?" she asked.

"Nothing."

"You've been acting odd for days. What's the matter?"

He looked out the front window. "Maybe we shouldn't have moved back here."

"You were alright with the move."

"I didn't realize it would affect me like this." Of course, it was stupid to think coming back to their home town wouldn't bring back the memories.

"It's been years. It was an accident, not your fault." Mary touched his arm.

He nodded. He should have realized returning would bring everything back up again. The construction of the college buildings. Christine. The rickety scaffolding. The kiln.

- - -

The next morning the photograph stood illuminated on the mantle in the beam from the front window. Being in the light couldn't be good for the picture. He reached out to move it, but he froze. There was something else in the picture. A third figure stood in the picture. Faint, but clear enough to make out the features of a young woman standing behind him. Her hair pinned up in a bun and wore a long skirt. He hadn't seen her for fifty years ago.

"Christine?"

Mary's footstep behind him made him stagger back and into the sofa.

"Darling, what's the matter?"

"There!" He pointed at the picture. "You see her too?"

She studied the picture and frowned. "What are you talking about?"

"There." He went up and pointed at the figure with his fingers brushing the glass.

"Don't touch it. You'll get your prints on it."

"Don't you see her?"

She readjusted the frame. "Stephan, I only see you and me."

Chills ran down his skin.

"Why don't you go back to bed. You're seeing things." Mary took his arm and lead him back. The picture's eyes seemed to follow him as they left.

- - -

The next day the image was still there but he didn't bring it up again. Nothing else in the house had changed beside the picture and his nerves. For days he tried to avoid the picture. A shadow appearing in the corner of his eyes. Watching him. Even in his dreams he couldn't escape her gaze.

He hid the picture in a drawer. It was a type of release.

Everything seemed to go back to normal. The nightmares ceased and he was able to block the shadowy presence preying in his mind.

Then Mary got sick. Coughs at first but progressing to rashes and then a coma. The doctors had no answers. Stephan was frantic. Unexplainable diseases were of the past. He remembered living in the age with no answers. Those days were supposed to be solved by science.

He returned home for fresh clothes before he returning to the hospital. He passed the drawer where he had put the photograph. A nagging suspicion made him open it and pull out the picture. Christine was still there, but she had moved. Now she she stood over Mary as if trying to replace her.

- - -

Fifty years ago, felt like yesterday. He had lied about not knowing Christine when they worked at the construction. He remembered that night he had invited her to the brickyard.

The others had gone home. Stephan had paced back and forth in front of the kiln, trying to find a way to tell her it was over.

He was already married by seventeen. His mother insisted it was for his salvation. Mary wasn't a bad girl, but a bit naive. Then he met Christine at a church social. She was interesting, smart, and fiery. She would have made a perfect wife.

They met in secret. The building of the college gave them an excuse to be together daily. She helped with the bricks, and that was his trade. They planned to and run off to California together.

Then Mary inherited a small fortune from her uncle back east. Now she had the option to have a real life, with money, get him a job in a proper place. Move to Salt Lake City or Ogden, or somewhere far away from sagebrush and rust filled rocks. Not only leave but have money to live on. The fortune was too much to ignore. In the brickyards at dusk, he was going to end his sinning.

Christine appeared like the angel she was. In the sunset light, her blond hair seemed to glow red. She tried to kiss him, but he pushed her away

"I'm sorry. I can't do it." he said.

"What?" she laughed thinking it was a joke. Again she came for him but he backed away.

Finally, she seemed to understand.

Her angel face darkened. "You're staying with her?"

"I'm sorry." Stephan turned to leave, but she grabbed him.

"I'll tell her about us. She won't want you then. She'll set you free."

"No, Christine, it's over." He tried to pull away, but her grip was vice-like.

"I'm not giving you up. Not to her or anyone."

The next events were a blur: He remembers pulling away again. He stumbled and as he fell and he pulled her down. Trying to regain her footing she tripped over him and fell against the kiln. The smack of her head against the brick wall resounded through the evening air. She crumpled onto the ground. He stood, panting, heart pounding. Christine remained motionless.

Panic set in. He'd killed her. He realized he was alone. No witness. Looking back at her body he realized how this was going to destroy his life. She was going to ruin it dead or alive.

Unless.

The kiln.

The coke was smoldering as he placed her body inside. Closing the doors, he waited for smoke to come out of the kiln.

Screams came from within it.

She was still alive! Horrified, he tried to open the door but stopped. If she got out she'd tell everyone and make this situation worse. But if she were gone..

He fled but the smoke and the screams followed him for miles.

- - -

Stephan grabbed a chair to reassure himself he was in the present. Beads of sweat glistened on his arms. The picture frame was cold to his touch.

He turned to the fireplace to destroy the picture, ready to burn her anew, but hesitated. That would be too easy. He sensed Christine's power, fury and rage from the picture. She scowled at him. He knew a simple fire would not destroy what he needed destroyed. It had to be somewhere special.

The brick walls gave him the solution. The school. It made sense. That was the place where it began. The place she died. Where he had seen her spirit watching him from the windows. If she was going to be put to rest he had to go where it began.

- - -

The door of the school was easy to force. Each creek of his joints seemed to shake the walls. Not daring to strike a light he followed walls to the basement. Among the boxes and exposed pipes, he located a metal pail. Allowing himself then to light a match, he saw where he was. Placing the bucket on the floor he retrieved the folded picture from his back pocket.

Christine's image nearly completely covered Mary's. He needed to work fast.

Holding the picture out over the pail he lit another match. He let it lick at the photo until the flames caught the paper and spread.

He dropped it in the metal pail.

Backing towards the door he waited for the fire to die, but it only grew. The flames rose to spill out of the pail onto the floor. Sparks flew, catching onto unseen fuels and starting new fires. The flames leaped higher.

Stephan pulled at the knob. It stuck. He rammed his shoulder again and again at the unrelenting door.

"Stephan."

His name crackled from the bucket.

He turned to see the shadows flowing around the walls. Red drops pooled from the bricks. Blood, he realized. The flames and the blood combined. The fusion popped and hissed, but the flames only grew. Sweat poured down his face, but the door would not move. Desperate, he began to claw at the door with his nails.

Again, his name sounded from the fire. The ghostly form he knew so well rose among the orange light. Flames did for her dress while her face was a blood red dripping mass.

She reached for him. He backed away, but there was nowhere to go.

She drew closer.

"I knew you'd come." Her death rattle voice gurgled in her throat. The smoke choked his own voice. Her hands stroked his chest. Flames erupted behind her loving caresses. He turned to run but there was nowhere to go.

- - -

The fire burned all night. Firemen did their best but not even the bricks survived. Crews cleared later found the charred remains of a man, his features completely erased. Beside him, were ashes, an outline of another human figure. More ashes surrounded them both like the mattress of a wedding bed.

# MOUSEHOLE COTTAGE

Laurie Heath

You run into the room and slam the door. It's a heavy, solid door, the sort no longer manufactured. A resounding thud reassures you that you haven't been followed. You lock the door with the antique key. It won't be able to get in.

In the silence of this old cottage you hear all sorts of things; the creak and groans that tell the entire life of a very cozy, serene cottage. It is serene, you know. A peaceful Cornwall cottage a stone's throw from Penzance in Mousehole. You know no one will believe that you saw a pair of very sharp teeth the color of the moon. The moon shining through the window that looks out on the boat-strewn sea far below.

Your heartbeat slows. "I know this is irrational," you say to yourself since (you assume) you are all alone—and then something hits the window. Something large; it was black or gray or maybe dark brown. Your heart races like it will tear a hole in your chest—which would be a pity since it is a very nice chest.

You rest your forehead against the glass. You don't see anything and the cool window feels good on your sweating brow. "A bird. Maybe an owl," you reassure yourself. You bury the notion that it could have been a bat. A bat that can turn into human form. You don't believe the lie you're telling yourself. .

You unpack the supplies you bought to fight it—if it comes to that. There's the cream tea from the café next door. You set the scones and the cup on the bedside table. You pull rope after rope of garlic out of your backpack. You'll never get the smell out of it, you know. "I'll burn it when I get home," you say. Home seems planets away from this tiny idyllic seaside village.

The holy water is in a small pocket. You filled an empty Evian bottle with water from a baptismal font—that counts, right? The priest had just christened some screaming baby ten minutes before you took it. Everyone was so enamored by the little bundle of joy that they didn't notice the tourist filling the bottle in the baptismal font.

You pull out an old mallet and an new wooden stake you found at a thrift shop. They call them jumble shops here, which seems more accurate and charming. The stake was more of the croquet variety rather than rosewood or fire-hardened oak, but it will have to do. You couldn't exactly ask around Mousehole or Penzance if there was anyone who would fashion a classic wooden stake of the vampire hunter variety. People would think you were crazy and you weren't crazy. At least, you don't think you were crazy.

You drape the garlic around the door jamb and the window casing. The smell of it is comforting; it reminds you of your aunt's kitchen and her spaghetti and meatballs. When you get home, you're going to make a big batch of spaghetti and meatballs and invite everyone you care about over. You won't take them for granted again.

Your eyes are burning with tears. Your nose is starting to drip. Pull yourself together. You're not going to die. You're too young to die. You have too many unfinished projects. You don't have time to die.

You are a fool if you believe that. You don't know the history of this cozy cottage in Mousehole. You don't know what lurks in the walls enveloping you. You don't know what is waiting for just the right time. But wait. You do know. Or you think you know. You think you can beat it.

"This is silly. I should go downstairs. Nothing is here. What am I doing?" Silence through the room in response to your question. It isn't very reassuring. You feel like the cottage is breathing around you, inhaling deeply, but you don't feel the exhales, the sense of impending relief. You exhale. You were holding your breath. Again.

You sit on the edge of the bed, eyes glued to the window—waiting for it to make itself known again. Nothing happens except your stomach rumbles. How can you be hungry at a time like this? Shouldn't you be preparing for the next encounter?

You nibble at the cream scone you slathered with Devonshire clotted cream and a healthy dollop of blackcurrant jam. Your personal research and taste informed you that this was the correct way to eat this delicacy. It wasn't the proper way according to Cornish folk, but folks in Devonshire would approve. A pity it tasted like metallic sawdust and you couldn't savor each tender morsel. A pity, really. It was, after all, a perfect tea-time scone.

The doorknob jiggles. Click. Click. It sounds like a key is inserted in the antique lock. You wad up the napkin and stuff it in the keyhole. You check the door. Still very securely shut and locked. You pace the room like a doomed tiger. Tigers are dangerous captives. Are you? Will you have the guts to attack when it makes its grand entrance? You study the stake. It seemed sharper in the thrift shop. Maybe you could sharpen it.

A knife! You forgot a knife! How could you be so stupid? You know you need to decapitate it to make sure it's well and truly dead and no longer a threat. There were knives in the kitchen. Maybe even a cleaver. But the kitchen may as well be back in Utah because you aren't opening that door until noon. Maybe later. Thank goodness the cottage owners renovated to make the room a suite, so you didn't need to worry about relieving yourself or getting a drink of water.

You need a weapon. You don't think a mallet and a dull stake will do the trick anymore. You wish you had a gun, silver bullets, a large sword that you wouldn't know how to use, but at least it would give you some sense of security. If you were armed, maybe it would leave you alone because you wouldn't be an easy target. Maybe.

You don't know about prior visitors who valiantly fought for their lives on their last holidays. You don't see those restless souls. You don't see Erik who fought with his martial arts skills. He was a magnificent fighter and delicious. He was savored over the course of a week, until his end. Now he ineffectively tries to protect those temporary inhabitants of Mousehole Cottage. He would attempt to help you, if you could see him.

Mary Katharine fought valiantly, for an old crone. Does she sound like a nun to you? She was Wiccan. Her New Age ways were no match for the ancient forces that battered and sucked her dry over two nights. Nothing is left of her. Her soul flew away as soon as she was released.

There were the newlyweds. They kept to themselves, cowering whenever they catch a whiff of it. They consummated their union before the wedding. She was pregnant, but they weren't planning to tell anyone until the honeymoon was over. Two against it, but he was a sound sleeper and the first course of the night. "My baby," she begged for mercy, thinking there was an empathic soul in the monster. If there was an empathic soul, perhaps that phrase would've saved the young widow. But you know what she didn't know—it doesn't have a soul and it won't be merciful. Fetal blood is a rare treat in this cottage in Mousehole.

Ah! If only you could savor and learn from these memories, you might have a chance against it! But you rummage restlessly through the scant supplies you brought with you. You futilely go through the washroom and look under the bed and in the closet for something that will help you in the upcoming fight. Do you really think a weapon would be left for your use? Do you think it wants a fair fight? That's laughable.

Tick tock. Tick tock. Tick tock. Is it the grandfather clock in the parlor or is it the timer in your head ticking away the seconds of your life? You shove that thought away. It's four in the afternoon back home. You could call your parents, but if you tell them what is going on they'd ask if you were taking your medicine and seeing your therapist. No need to listen to a lecture about that again. You know reality, and in this reality something is stalking you. Something wants to devour you.

You just need to hold out a couple days and then you could be on a train back to London and then it was off to Gatwick to catch the flight home. Utah never sounded like such a great place until it had left its mark on you last night. Until you felt its hot breath that smelled like a hundred rotting corpses on your face. The marks looked like a couple bug bites on your throat, but you knew better. You knew it would return. It was just a matter of when.

Fear is exhausting. It's beating you down. You wear

your fear like a perfume and it finds the smell intoxicating. After the frenzied search for a weapon besides the mallet and stake (which will likely be useless since it's so dull. Do you really think you have the strength to force it in an inert body, much less a fiend that is fighting you?), you sit in the straight-backed wooden chair.

You write what you're experiencing in your travel notebook. You'll never forget this, but when it's over, you'll want to be able to show it to someone, perhaps tell your therapist that this really happened to you, despite all your work together. No one would believe you. They would try to give you a logical explanation, but there isn't a logical explanation for what is hunting you. You write it down anyways. You know the truth. You know the truth almost as well as the cottage knows the truth.

You move to the bed. Your back cracks and aches from the chair. It seems quieter. You start to think it has given up on you. You start wondering if it is a figment of your imagination. Perhaps this is a delusion and the medicine needs to be adjusted when you get home. Nothing has attempted to force its way in for hours. The napkin you stuffed in the lock is on the floor. It wasn't packed in there tightly enough.

You didn't expect to doze off. No one ever does, but your caffeine ran out some time ago, and the paperback that sounded so interesting in the airport newsstand wasn't riveting or even well-written. It was bad enough to put you, the consummate insomniac, to sleep. You are lured into sleep so gently that you don't feel the book slip from your hands. You don't hear it drop to the floor, right next to the useless stake and mallet.

That's when it creeps mist-like, a fog rolling into the harbor, into your well-guarded room. It doesn't mind the garlic. It chuckles. It created the rumor that garlic would ward it away—the same sort of rumor about holy water—lies that mortals pass down for generations—all for naught.

You feel a cool finger on your cheek. Its finger. The contrast feels good. You were too hot but didn't realize it until now. You sigh. You wish you could shift positions. You try and fail. *Get up*, your brain urges. Your body doesn't obey your brain.

Its eyes are close to your face. You can smell its grave stench. You wish your smell receptors were as unresponsive as your limbs. It is close enough that the outline of its high aquiline nose is clear, and the moonlit ivory incisors stand out.

*Get up*! your brain screams again, more urgent and is just as ignored by your body. You wonder if it is keeping you in that state, if it has the power to command your body to act against its best interest. You've never felt sleep paralysis while you have been awake before.

You can't fight it. You don't know why you wanted to fight it before. This is what you want. You want to succumb completely to your fate. In this state—half awake half asleep—the room begins to spin. You feel heavier and heavier, as if lead slabs are being piled on top of you. You stop breathing, stop fighting for life. You feel your soul surge upwards and then you are looking down at your cold corpse bundled in its arms. It unlocks the door and leaves.

The cottage in Mousehole has another vacancy.

# MUCHNESS

Miranda Renaé

Alice grabbed a white, sleeveless sundress and blue tights from the closet, forgoing the heavy sweater and jeans her mom encouraged her to wear. Yeah, she'd freeze, but at least she'd chosen it, unlike moving here. She couldn't understand why she had to move here when her brothers got to stay with their dad. No changing schools, no making new friends and no snow. Her fingers brushed across the tops of the thick wool-lined boots that went perfectly with the outfit her mother suggested. It was one thing to be surrounded by cold, but cold feet meant she'd be freezing the rest of the day. She looked down at her legs; the gray wool of the boots would match the stars dotting the blue tights.

"Alice, let's go. We're already late," her mom called up the stairs.

She looked longingly at the boots. "I won't give her the satisfaction," Alice growled, as she snapped the rubber band on her wrist. She grabbed the lace-up sneakers that matched her tights, jamming her feet into their fabric confines. She stomped down the stairs, pulling her favorite jean jacket from the hook by the door, and met her mom in the car. *I will be cold, but it's worth it.*

The entire drive to the theater her mom didn't say anything about Alice's silent protest. She just talked on and on about the city, pointing out stores and landmarks as they went. Alice couldn't believe it. *How can she not say anything?* They drove around the parking lot in an older part of town near an abandoned storefront and still, her mother went on about how sad it was the town was dying but Red Queen Inc would bring in new jobs. Revitalizing the town. *And tearing families apart!* Alice snapped the rubber-band.

Alice opened the door before her mom had finished parking their new car. A perk of the job, her mom had told her. Looking at it added to Alice's anger. *A perk for who?* It wasn't like it could be her friend or make going to a new school easier. Alice took a deep breath and counted silently, one, two, three...She looked down at the broken pavement, remembering what her mom had said about the town dying. *I bet I'm the only one in my grade.*

Alice pulled the thin jean jacket close around her. "I want to go home."

Her mom slammed the car door shut, stopping to stand next to Alice. "I don't have time for this. We're already late."

*She never listens to me. It's all about her.* Alice started to shake, words wouldn't form. *The people who live in this crappy town don't even want to be here, why would I?* Alice didn't want to go back to the crappy apartment they shared. "I want to go home," she yelled.

"Alice Marie Smith, you wanted to go to this movie. Now you—what? Don't feel like it?"

Alice snapped the rubber-band on her wrist in an attempt to ground herself, but it wasn't working. She was losing control. A slow tide of fury that had been swirling inside since this morning threatened to wash her away. "I just... I don't know. Okay?"

Her mom's face fell, and she moved toward Alice. Alice backed away. If her mom touched her...

Alice clenched her jaw, "not yet" she mumbled.

In a smooth, calm voice, her mom reminded her to not only breath but that she was fine. It wasn't enough. Alice started to count. "One, two, three.." Her chest rose with each number, calming her, changing her. Her mom moved closer, a few steps at a time. The episode now over, Alice nodded giving her mom permission to pull Alice into her arms.

Stroking her hair, Alice's mom whispered. "We don't have..."

"There you are." Ms. Redding, Mom's boss, interrupted.

Alice stepped away from her mom to look at Ms. Redding. A teenage girl with a long ponytail stood next to her glared at Ms. Redding, frustration flashing across her face. She rolled her eyes at mom's boss before turning to Alice's mom with a smile. "We were worried you weren't going to make it."

Slightly embarrassed by her actions and what they might have seen, Alice flashed her "everything is great" smile and said, "Sorry, it was my fault." She motioned to her outfit. "I couldn't find anything to wear."

The girl giggled and Alice couldn't help but really smile. There was something about the girl that felt inviting and friendly.

"I completely understand. Love the tights." She held her hand out to Alice. "Name's Dinah, but I prefer DeeDee. Only family and people who have known me forever call me Dinah."

"Should we go in, then?" Alice's mom asked.

They walked together through one of the side doors to the theater. The door was actually an emergency exit that was held open by a bulky blond guy. Alice wasn't sure why they went this way. Was it because they were late or because of the Reddings? It didn't matter much, though; for the first time since coming to this town, Alice was excited about something.

DeeDee told Alice about this great, little vintage shop down the street and how they should go shopping next week. Before showing Alice to her seat in the full theatre, they exchanged numbers. Then DeeDee, Ms. Redding, and Alice's mom started their speech about the new product and the opening of the factory in town.

Alice only kinda listened while she arranged her contraband licorice around the edge of the complimentary popcorn tub. Focusing on the upcoming shopping trip, and the possibility of making a friend, washed away the last of her anger from the parking lot.

The speeches finished up and Alice's mom sat next to her, while DeeDee and Ms. Redding left the theater the same way they'd come in. Alice wondered why they weren't staying and made a mental note to ask DeeDee when she saw her next week.

Alice stared up at the screen. She'd been excited to see the movie; she loved comic book reboots. But, for some reason, this one wasn't catching her interest, and it seemed like the rest of the audience agreed. No matter how hard she tried to concentrate on the movie, there were whispered conversations that surrounded her.

The guy sitting next to Alice stood up, making her jerk

in surprise. He stared past her, the light of the screen reflecting off his black-rimmed glasses. He moved in front of her, blocking the screen, now staring down at her. He cracked his knuckles as he muttered something she couldn't quite hear.

She looked around the room trying to find a reason for the guy's unusual behavior. Something pink caught her eye, but before she could focus on it, Glasses Guy moved closer. She could smell the popcorn on his stale breath as he screamed, "Because I'm not."

Alice wasn't sure why he'd yelled at her, but she could tell he was angry. It was a kind of anger she had seen before and knew it was best to try and make herself smaller. She shrunk into the chair trying to disappear when her mom stood up and moved toward the guy. Comforted in the knowledge that her mom would save her—she always did—Alice moved in her seat.

Her mom roared and Alice slunk back down in her chair. *This isn't right.* She looked around the room snapping the rubber-band on her wrist. The pink that had caught Alice's eyes earlier moved toward her. A cloud-like fluffy cotton candy covered the room in a thick dust. It moved closer, hiding Alice from the scene playing out in front of her. Its sweet flavor clawed at her throat, dragging her into the depths of her fears and choking out the light.

She was trapped in a pit of her worst fears and there was no way out. Alice closed her eyes and started counting. The noise of people screaming floated around her, into her. Alice covered her ears, but she could still feel the woosh of the walls as they moved closer, crushing the chair that Glasses Guy had sat in. *It's just a dream.* She'd been here before. It wasn't real; she knew it wasn't real. *Twenty-one, twenty-two, twenty-three...*It wasn't working. The gurgled cries of women behind her drilled their way into her covered ears.

*Fifty-one, fifty-two...* There was a tug in the back of her mind. A voice pierced the hatred that engulfed her, lighting her way back to reality.

*Mom.*

Alice opened her eyes. The smoke was gone, and her mom stood over her. Glasses Guy was nowhere to be found. Alice tried to stand up, there was something wrong....Her mom grunted and the light of the screen lit up her face. Red streams moved down her face, dark lines from the corners of her eyes.

"Mom, are you okay?"

She didn't answer, staring down at Alice, a coldness in her eyes. Alice shuddered. "Mom?"

Her mom lunged at her, hands ready to clasp her neck, screaming, "My stars and whiskers."

Alice slid down the chair and away from her mother's cold fingers. Her knees hit the sticky floor of the dark theater. *It's not real. It has to be a dream.* Alice stood up and turned to face her fears. *None of this was real. I'm safe in my bed. Just face your fears.*

Ignoring the turning in her stomach telling her to hide, Alice took a step toward her mother. Well, not her mother but the dream monster that looked like her. It turned to face Alice; a hiss escaped from its stained teeth. *Just a dream.* Alice moved closer.

The blood that stained its face shone in the light of the movie. Someone screamed nearby, and the creature cackled. It lumbered toward Alice.

She intended to stand her ground. The monster moved

closer, and she knew she couldn't do it, so Alice ran, kicking up pink dust with every step. She pushed her way through the mass of people that blocked the door she'd come through earlier. A door that wouldn't budge. She was trapped.

A roar moved through the crowd. The people around her moved, some by choice, most by force. Screams filled the air. Alice moved to the right, dodging the large mass of bodies that threatened to engulf her in their terror-filled flee. Exposed, Alice turned in circles searching for the creature that looked like her mom. *Wake up, Alice, wake up!*

Something grabbed her loose hair, dragging her to the floor. It dragged her across the sticky concrete yanking out strands of her long hair with each tug. Unsure of what to do, Alice spread her arms, letting her hands feel for something to help her get free. Her hands no longer relieving the pressure of being dragged caused pain to shoot through her scalp. *It's just a dream,* Alice reminded herself.

Her hand slid across the remains of what felt like a broken chair. Alice wrapped her hands around the pieces of the metal legs still bolted to the ground, pulling herself free. She held back the scream that clawed at her throat as hair was yanked from her scalp.

Now free and with no way of escape, Alice looked for a place to hide. The nightmare had reached its height; the killers had found their victims in the people who had tried to escape and were playing out Alice's bloodiest fears.

Her sights landed on a dark corner of the room, free of gore, under the screen where the movie still played. Alice made her way to the spot and sat on the floor, wrapping her arms around her knees. *I'm fine.*

She counted, but it wasn't working, not like it did in

the real world. She looked around the room nothing had
changed. A loud scream echoed through the room and Alice
covered her ears. *Why can't I wake up?* Her eyes meet the fear
-stricken ladies who'd sat behind her, the women who talked
through the credits and most of the movie, they were tied
down to their chairs at the front of the theater. Lips sewed together with red thread. She blinked. *Wait...What?* She hadn't
seen that before.

Not only had the room changed from color to black
and white, but it was littered with spots of red. Alice stood up.
The fear she'd felt swirling around changed as the color
blinked out. A new emotion took over, one she knew well. It
bathed her in its warmth.

Her old friend anger, its hunger threatening to con-
sume her.

Those old biddies deserved what had happened to
them. Alice's only regret was that she wasn't the one to do it.
But there were others in this room, people who had wronged
her. But first, she needed…

A battle cry moved through the room, calling to Alice.
The creature that resembled her mother stumbled toward her,
a fist raised high above it. It held a long metal bar that glowed
red in the black and white world around them.

Alice wanted that bar. No, she needed it. It was the
perfect weapon to destroy her enemies, starting with the thing
that looked like her mom. The mom who had dragged her to
this snow-covered hell and told her to call it home.

The creature lumbered closer and with each step, Alice
saw all the wonderfully horrible things she could do with that
piece of metal. She could feel the vibration of metal crashing
into bone even now. She could see the delicious damage it

would cause. And the stupid creature was bringing it to her.

A heavy thud pushed Alice to the ground, knocking the air from her lungs and bringing a bit of color back to her vision. Glasses Guy sat on top of her, something large and pulsing clasped in his hands and raised above him. "I am not!" he yelled.

Alice tried to get away, but he was too strong. His arms came down and Alice knew this was the end. *If you die in your dreams, do you die in real life?* She closed her eyes, not sure if she wanted to know the answer.

Glasses Guy screamed and the weight holding her to the floor was gone. Guessing that the dream was over, Alice opened her eyes. She was still in the theater among the echoes and death.

Her mother, not the monster that looked like her, lay next to Alice, breathing heavily. "I'm sorry. I should have never brought you here," she breathed.

Alice had never gotten this far in her nightmare, always waking up before the end. It wasn't as bad she thought it would be. The one thing Alice had wanted since being brought to this town was for her mom to apologize for bringing her here. Maybe it would be enough if it happened in a dream.

Alice stood up and looked around the room, waiting for the dream to fade away. To wake up in her bed in the small apartment cocooned in her fluffy down comforter. The room didn't change. The remains of the madness that had consumed the dark theater marked the walls. She sat down next to her mom, the heartwarming end of the movie playing behind them.

Her mom looked at Alice confused. "Alice…"

"The dream won't end."

"Oh, Alice." Her mom coughed. "I'm sorry. This isn't a dream."

Before Alice was able to process what her mom said, the doors in front of her opened and men in white suits stomped in. Alice stood ready to fight when the one in front said, "We have a survivor."

# PARTNERS

Glenn Hammer

*You are great.*

*There is no one like you.*

*Others are taking notice.*

Marion woke up to pain. He lay for a moment to sense where it came from. At another burst he grunted softly and sucked in air through his clenched teeth.

His head, that's what hurt.

He let the air out through pursed lips. Where on his head did he hurt? His eyes? No, it was not his eyes. It was higher up and farther back. He flinched.

"Headache again, dear?" JoSelle asked. She rolled over, and the bed rocked gently.

"Mm," was all he could manage. He rubbed his temples with his thumbs where he felt the hammering of his blood, then massaged the crown of his head with the rest of his fingers. He waved his elbows in the direction of the screaming alarm.

The bed shifted when JoSelle got up and switched off the knife-like buzzing.

"Thanks." He smiled and racked his eyes open. The

room was dim, but along the floor, fingers of morning light tried to reach past the curtains.

"You've got to get up anyway." She threw open the curtains.

Marion rolled away from the blast of light and pain.

"You thrashed all night, you know," she said unsympathetically.

He listened as she moved across the floor toward the hall bathroom. "I didn't sleep well."

"I didn't get much sleep because of you." Her voice sounded muffled behind the partly closed door.

Marion slowly opened one eye to test the pain.

"It was 'the dreams' again."

She did not reply.

Marion opened his other eye, sat up, and stretched. The throbbing in his head lessened. He was tired of the poor sleep. He smiled to himself at the unintended joke.

"JoSelle!"

"What?" She stuck her head out of the bathroom.

He held up two boxes of frozen breakfast burritos and gently waved them. The plastic of the individually wrapped items crinkled, and frost from the waxed boxes sprinkled to the floor. "Sausage or bacon?"

She brushed her hair a few times. "Um. Bacon."

Marion nearly gagged with the overpowering scent of perfume. "That…" he started.

JoSelle brought her eyebrows together. "What!?" She tightened her lips.

"That's nice," was all he could think of.

- - -

*You need to show your greatness.*

*Take what you want.*

*The problems of others are not your concern unless you can gain something in fixing them.*

Marion chewed on his lips and wondered what was needling him in his dreams as he drove to work. Marion parked, entered the mountain-like building, and rode the elevator up until the black doors opened to the investment office. He smiled at Alice and wove his way through the low-walled cubicles to his desk.

His fund's past, current, and projected values appeared. He frowned and knew what to expect before he saw the important flagged email from Larry.

*See me*, was all it said.

Marion screwed on a smile and went to Larry's office. Arjun, another fund manager, was already standing in front of the desk.

"What are your plans for the upcoming quarter?" Larry asked both of them.

The meeting, or lecture, followed the pattern Marion expected, so he did not speak much. It was best to let Larry get out his frustration, then try and come up with a solution.

Marion looked sideways at Arjun. They gave each other sympathetic looks, then turned back to Larry and nodded and nodded and nodded.

Behind Larry was a painting of a forest. It was not a large forest but was more of a glen in a valley. There was a wisp of smoke from a hidden cabin.

"We have made excellent choices—" the dark-skinned Arjun started.

Marion shook his head, but Arjun did not see or did not understand.

"I'm talking about last quarter…"

The lecture went into overtime.

"Hmm," was all Marion could get over the next half an hour that did not involve telling Larry exactly what he thought of him.

- - -

*Why do you let people continue to treat you badly?*

*There must be changes.*

*Changes that he won't like.*

Marion ran his finger along the rim of his glass. He was working up to a nice buzz at The Time Out. He looked down the bar at Arjun and it seemed the other man was looking for inspiration in the amber liquid. Marion slowly spun his glass and watched the light patterns change.

"Another?" the bartender asked.

Marion only saw the waist of the man. "Uh-uh." He moved down to check the next patron.

"Marion?" Arjun called

"Yeah?" Marion finished his drink.

"Today was not a good day."

*Understatement*, Marion thought. The two men commiserated and drank another round.

"I need to get home."

Marion fumbled for his keys. "I can take you." He paid and looked for his blood red car in the lot. The yellowish sodium light and the orange lights from the bar created an infected-pus color on the roof and hood. He studied it and felt a little sick.

Marion unlocked it and sat. He loved the smell of leather. His eyes closed and rested, he did not want to go home—did not want to go anywhere. Marion looked out the window at the dark night. A portion of the moon visible past the mountain range-like buildings. There was screaming in the black of his dreams.

He tried to move, but the screaming followed him. It was somewhere off to his right and sounded like the call of a bird. Struggling to move his feet, he tried to run, but could not. Something was holding his chest, something he could not get free from. What was it?

Marion stepped on the brake. Still in the car, he blinked to clear his vision, but it did not help much. The passenger seat was empty, but there was a brick wall on the other side of the broken glass. Right on the other side. He had only driven about thirty feet, but most of that was along the side of a building. He could not remember starting the car.

Marion got a free ride to the local police station after a rather short officer confiscated his keys. He sat on hard a bench for some time before JoSelle arrived. He could not remember ever doing something so stupid. Would he lose his license?

- - -

*Others are holding you back.*

*You are surrounded by idiots.*

Marion arrived at work the next day with a headache. He was not sure if it was from the drinking or the poor sleep. He did research on the small cap stocks to sell and tried to confer with Arjun, but he was not at his desk. Marion dialed the other man's number, but only reached the office voice mail.

Marion walked over and talked to the office manager, who wore an arterial red blouse. "Alice?"

She looked up. "Yes?"

"Do you know where Arjun is today?"

"No, but Larry did call the number we have on file for him." She looked at her screen.

Marion did not want to talk to Larry if he did not have to. "What did he say?"

Alice looked back up at him and blinked. "I don't know, and it's none of your business."

OK, that was a bit snippy. "Can I have his home number so I can call and find out if he's OK?" Arjun was not in the accident, but Marion did not know how or if he had gotten home.

"That is private information. If Arjun did not give you his number, I can't. Besides, you know his kind, and we have such high turnover here anyway."

Marion felt as if he had been slapped. Did he hear her right? What did that mean? Had something happened to Arjun?

- - -

*That person is not very helpful.*

*You are not surrounded by many useful people.*

Marion stopped at The Time Out bar on the way home. He turned the engine off and looked at the wall. The long horizontal scratches from the night before traveled a straight line along the old stone colored brick wall. He took deep breath and walked to the door, nervous about what to expect. He entered and braced himself, but no one gave him a second glance. The bartender did raise an eyebrow, but that was it. Marion wondered how long he had worked here if a patron running into his building did not bother him.

"What can I get you?"

"Nothing. Do you remember the guy I was with last night?" Marion walked over.

"Yea, the dark-skinned guy?"

Marion was not sure how to ask what he wanted. "I was going to take him home, but he was not in the car…" He did not want to say any more, so he just pointed at the wall with his thumb.

"He wasn't in the car with you, but if you want some advice, you should've let him drive you home."

The tightness in his chest loosened. "Thanks." Marion nodded, relieved but still confused at Arjun's disappearance, left for home.

"You need to get something to help you sleep," Jo-Selle commented.

"Hmm?" Marion had not realized she was even at the table with him.

She dropped her fork with a clang. "You've not listened to a word I've said."

"Sorry. You might be right about the sleep." When did she get home?

"How's work?" She put a spoon full of something into her mouth.

What was he eating? Was it rice or cheese? "Work? Not that great." He ate mechanically.

JoSelle spoke around her food. "Want to talk about it?"

"NO!"

She leaned back and widened her eyes.

"Sorry. I mean, no. Crazy day. How about you?"

She looked down at her plate. "Catering's been slow this week."

Was *slow* code for something?

"I might be able to get Friday off. There's only a small party, and the entire staff's not needed."

Marion was not sure if he was supposed to reply.

They finished eating in quiet.

JoSelle stood and placed her dishes in the sink.

"Let me." He reached out with his hand. "I've not been very good company for the past few days."

She opened and closed her mouth as if to say, *you're right*, but said, "Thanks."

Marion washed the dishes and glasses by hand. With only two of them, it was pointless to use the dishwasher. He wiped down the counter and the table, even gave the refrigerator doors a quick polish. He looked around for something else to do, but the sterile room just stared back at him.

JoSelle lay under the covers and faced the wall as if she were asleep. Marion put on his soft cotton pajamas and fished his keys out of his pants pocket. They clinked on the nightstand, but he could not find his phone.

Marion rummaged through his coat in the front closet but found nothing. The counters were clear and it was not in the bathroom. He returned to the bedroom, and the black case was face down under his keys. He checked the alarm time and messages. There were no new messages, but there was one an hour old.

What?

Marion had been home an hour ago. How did he miss it and why was it read? He looked at JoSelle, but she still lay facing the wall.

"JoSelle?" he whispered.

She did not move.

He stared at her.

She breathed.

Marion placed the cold phone against his ear. There was a faint click as he played the message. It was forwarded from his work desk. Was it Arjun calling him back? No, it was Larry's voice.

"I'm reminding you that you better have plans in two days to compensate for last quarter's losses."

Larry was a jerk. Larry was an idiot. What did he think he was working on? Why did he call and leave a message? Marion clenched his teeth and squeezed his phone and his fingers turned white. Why was the message not marked as new? Marion looked at the dresser and back to the prone form on the bed.

Had JoSelle listened to his messages? Marion placed

his hand on her hip and gently shook.

"I'm awake."

She did not roll over or look at him.

"Why did you listen to my messages?"

"I didn't mean to."

He gripped her hip.

She sighed. "You've been acting strange. I didn't know what to do." She tried to brush his hand away.

Marion tightened his grip.

"Stop." She pressed her palm on his wrist.

His irritation grew. He was working on it. Larry was giving him grief at work, and now she was bugging him at home. He clenched his teeth and tightened his grip.

"That hurts." She tried to move her leg.

He looked at the wall. He hated his job. He hated his life. He hated JoSelle at that moment. His muscled clenched.

"Ow!" She clawed at him.

He felt pain and tightened his grip.

"Marion!"

Nothing made sense anymore. He was just trying to work. He was trying to provide for her. He looked back at her.

Her eyes were wide and filled with tears. "Marion!"

Was she in some kind of pain? He was the one with work problems. What was she upset about?

What was her pain from?

He thought.

He was causing her pain.

He released his grip.

"Sorry." That sounded lame, even to him.

"Ass." She pulled up the worn cotton T-shirt she slept in and revealed her hip. Dark red and purple lines wrapped it. She rubbed them and sucked in a breath. "What was that for? Just for listening to a few messages?" She glared at him.

Marion stood. He took a step back to the door without realizing it. "I didn't mean to hurt you." What could he say? He really did not mean to, but there were his finger marks on her for all the world to see. What was happening to him? Was worrying about his job and possibly losing his license pushing him over the edge? Could he seriously hurt her? He did not want to. She was important to him, but he was feeling strange.

"I'm sorry." He held up his hands in a pathetic plea for understanding.

JoSelle pulled her shirt back down. "Right!" She curled up against the headboard. "Get out."

"I told you I'm not sleeping well…" he looked around the room searching for support, "and work…"

JoSelle squinted at him and grimaced wide. "Humh."

"Why don't you visit your mother?" He was grasping for thoughts. What could he do to make this better? If she left he would have time to think and relax.

- - -

*People are hurting you.*

*People are keeping secrets from you.*

*Actions will get you respect.*

Marion awoke in the night again from dreams. He was taller than the couch was long, so he had to sleep hunched over, and that made his back ache. He entered the small bathroom and felt for the faucet and knobs. Turning on the cold and added just a bit of hot, after testing the temperature, he cupped his hands and splashed the warm liquid on his face. Again and again the water splashed. It spread down his neck and formed rivulets on his back and chest. He let out a breath and grasped the edges of the sink. What was happening to him? He closed the door with a foot and stretched for the switch.

Light.

Red.

Blood.

There was blood on his face and blood on his hands. His shirt was soaked with it. The sink was covered in it. He staggered to the door, fumbled with the latch and fell through the opening, hitting the cream-colored carpet hard. Where did the blood come from?

He looked up the hall.

The door to the bedroom door was ajar, but the dim light from the bathroom did not penetrate beyond the jam. There was no blood on the floor or the bedroom door. He patted his throat and chest but felt no cuts.

Was JoSelle injured? Had she hurt herself? Had he hurt her?

Marion did not remember anything after the argument. He had gone to bed, and that was it. Was JoSelle OK?—he did not want to look in the room. What if he had done something to her in his sleep?

Half crawling, half staggering back toward the kitchen, Marion felt the cold tile on his hands and feet. He rounded the corner and rested against the wall. What was going on?

Cold sweat ran down his back and mixed with the water. No, it was not water. Blood. He was covered in blood. He closed his eyes and felt the sticky mixture on his back and chest. Something moved.

"Marion?" A soft voice came from the hall.

His heart sped up. His palms started to sweat.

"Marion?" the whisper repeated.

What was it? He pulled at the hair on his head. Stop, make it stop.

The door to their room creaked. Something was coming out. Did specters roam near a body? Was this the ghost of his wife? She was coming to get him, coming to exact her revenge for whatever he had done to her. He had squeezed her hip, or was it her throat? Why could he not remember what happened just a few hours ago?

The something light brushed across the carpet. Marion imagined the phantom of his wife wafting down the hall toward him. He bit his right palm and covered his left ear with his other hand. It would round the corner any moment. He needed to move. He needed to get out.

*Click.*

The bathroom door closed.

What?

Marion's pulse slowed, and he started to think clearly. Why would a ghost need the bathroom? He stopped sweating and cold washed over his body as moisture evaporated.

The toilet flushed.

JoSelle was in there. She was not dead, but where did the blood come from? Why had she not reacted? She must have seen it.

The bathroom door opened.

Marion forced himself to his feet. His knees were weak, so he braced himself against the wall. "Are you OK, dear?"

"Marion?" she asked from around the corner. "Why'd you leave the light on?"

"Sorry. I'm... Are you OK?" He mumbled. *Did you notice all the blood in there? I thought it was yours. I thought I accidentally murdered you in your sleep.*

"I think I will take the day off. I need...I need space."

"OK." The scent of her lotion choked his nose, and he nearly gagged.

- - -

*You need to get away from him.*

*He is a bad influence.*

*There are so many things you can do without him.*

The leather of the couch stung when Marion sat up and peeled it away.

"I'll take you to work," JoSelle said over a glass of milk, "then I'll drive to my mothers."

Marion nodded. He could not think what to say. He did not mean to hurt her. He knew that sounded lame even in his head, but he truly had not. The frustration with life just seemed to have focused on her last night. What could he say?

He looked at her right hip.

"OK."

They drove to work. The sun was up, but clouds were forming. "It'll storm," he said.

JoSelle did not answer.

The window vibrated against his head. Marion closed his eyes and imagined the road to his office. There was a gas station at this corner and a deli on that one. Soon they stopped.

"I'll be back late tomorrow or Sunday," JoSelle breathed toward the dashboard.

Marion nodded and opened the door. The air was chilly and damp. "Drive safe." *I'm sorry I hurt you, but you should've trusted me.*

JoSelle merged with the traffic and drove off without a word. Crowds of people entered the office building, and Marion was pulled along. The opening maw of the glass and steel building took in all that entered. The dull gray structure rose toward the sky, and it filled more and more of his view as he drifted toward it.

Inside he followed the current of bodies toward the elevators, but in the foyer he saw a familiar shape. It moved. Marion crossed the current of people.

"Marion!"

"Arjun. Where have you been?" The other man looked different. He was wearing light slacks and polo shirt, not the customary gray nameless suit for the nameless employees.

"I feared you were in the accident with me, but I couldn't find you." Marion sighed. He was not sure if he should shake hands with or hug the other man. "It stressed me out."

"I didn't go with you." Arjun smiled and waggled his head. "I'm glad you are well, too, my friend, but you should have let me drive you home."

"I know." Marion turned toward the human tide. "Let's get to work. Larry wants an update."

Arjun folded his arms. "No. I'm done."

Marion looked back, unsure if he heard the other man right.

"I just came to say good-bye to you, my friend." He smiled and showed his white teeth.

Marion stared. He had been doing this job for years and could tell when someone was about to break, but Arjun had none of the signs.

They walked out of the towering building against the lowering human tide. Marion steered them toward the nearby coffee shop.

"I don't like the pressure anymore, and I don't like the new boss, Larry."

"I know, but are you sure?" Marion held the door open and several people rushed out.

"I'm moving."

Marion placed the order. "What?"

"My wife and I have been talking about it for some time."

"You can't be serious." Where could he be going?

"We've even saved a little money."

"Just wait." Marion turned around after paying, but Arjun was gone. The shop was full of morning workers getting gassed up for the day, but there was no sign of his friend.

"Arjun?" Marion called, but he knew it was pointless. The other man was gone, never to return. Marion walked to his office. Why had he not seen this coming? Everything seemed to be going sideways lately. He really needed to see someone about his sleep problems and headaches.

In the office, Alice looked at him then over at the clock. She frowned but quickly mixed a pout and a smile when she saw the extra cup.

"Is that for me?" She smiled and blinked a few times.

"Ah," he looked from one hand to the other. "Sure. I was going to give it to Arjun, but he's quit."

Alice stood and grasped the warm paper cup. "I didn't know he quit." She sat, popped the top, and gently blew on the steaming liquid. "I guess he couldn't take the pressure."

Larry walked briskly up. "Who told you?" He squinted at Marion. "I've only just received an email this morning."

"I met him out front, and he told me."

All that day a storm gathered outside the office windows and by afternoon large drops of rain spattered the floor-to-ceiling windows.

When Marion merged with the exiting tide outside, the smell of dust and rain filled his lungs. Large drops slapped the pavement and people's heads. He hurried to the bus stop and pressed beneath its inadequate shelter, waiting for the musty and humidified bus ride home.

The evening sky was black when he reached his apartment. *Flash. Boom. Whump.* Lightening split the sky.

The hall lights flashed when he reached his door, and
Marion flinched. Once inside, he peeled off his jacket and wet
shirt and tossed them onto the stacked washer-dryer in the
bathroom. He toweled himself off and ate his microwaved
meal of fried rice while he watched the news. Asian food was
good, but JoSelle did not like it, so he only got to eat it when
she was not around. Marion was glad she was not there.

No, he wasn't actually glad. Conflicting emotions
wrestled in his brain for dominance until he rang the match
bell and threw them both out.

Quiet.

He wanted quiet inside and out.

After the news, Marion lay in bed and looked at the
lightning flashing through the open curtains. The light left afterglow lines in his vision contrasting with the dark ridge of
the skyline. His eyes roamed from the window, and he
watched the flashes of light and shadow play across the tex-
tured walls and ceiling, imagining shapes and faces in the patterns. Tired his eyes closed.

The front door lock clicked, and the door swung open
then closed. Footfalls came up the hall, but he just lay there,
breathing.

Was he awake or was he asleep?

His heart raced, but he tried to control the pace of his
breathing. Was it JoSelle? She said she was going to her
mother's for the weekend. He wished he was facing the door,
but from this position he only saw the wall and out the window. Rain splattered the windows and ran down the glass,
creating ever-changing rivers. A flash of white filled the
room.

The color slowly faded to a light blue then to a dark blue and shapes started to form.

The bed room door moved. Marion blinked rapidly to get his vision to focus. He felt someone's presence in the room. He smelled perfume.

"Marion?"

He recognized JoSelle's voice. What was she doing here? She was supposed to be at her mother's house.

"Marion, are you awake?"

He rolled over.

Wall.

Ceiling.

He saw the rain-soaked form of his wife upside down.

They looked at each other.

Marion watched the water run off her and drip up to the floor and smiled to himself.

- - -

*You need to go back to your simple life.*

*You need to take control.*

Marion rubbed his forehead. "You should have stayed away. I'm still not feeling well. Maybe I'll go to a doctor on Monday." *I hate that smell. It might be why I get so many headaches.*

"I bought you some wax fragrances." She held up a brown bag.

*Why did you spend money on more stinky fragrances when you just found out I might be out of a job shortly?*

"They're supposed to relax you."

He just stared.

"You can try them later."

"Mmm." *Why would he want to stink up the apartment on purpose?*

She smiled. "I'll start you a bath," she turned around, "and get you a sleeping pill so you can rest." She looked back and slowly blinked. "Maybe I'll join you."

- - -

*You know it's time to take action.*

*It's time to get rid of him.*

*He's holding you back, and even he knows it.*

Marion heard water run through the pipes, and the bath began to fill. The echo changed as the tub filled. He removed his clothes and got in the tub. The water was hot, almost too hot, but his muscles relaxed as he lowered himself in.

"Ahh." A slow, long breath escaped his lips.

He settled on the bottom as the water continued to rise.

JoSelle pushed the door open. She had a glass in one hand and something cupped in the other. "How's that?"

"Mmm. Nice."

"Here." She reached out with both hands.

Marion took the glass and smelled the alcohol, but did not take the pill. "Isn't that a bad combination?" He sipped the drink.

"Just take a half if you're worried." She snapped the pill in two and held one half out. She placed the wrapper on the counter.

He took the half dose and put in on the back of his tongue. He always hated the taste of those things. He downed the drink and rested his head on the back of the cold hard tub.

The water was nice. He might even take a short nap. He closed his eyes and heard the front door open and close.

"Hello?" he called.

No one replied.

"JoSelle?"

No sound.

Marion blinked slowly. Had she gone back out? Was she getting her clothes out of the car?

He rested.

On the counter were some wrappers and no pills, not even a half of one. He tried to lean forward but could not move. He found it hard to concentrate. He wanted to get out of the tub, but was tired, so tired. The wrappers under the counter matched those on it. How many pills had he taken? Was it one or two? No, he took a half; he would be fine; he relaxed—he was so sleepy—just take a quick nap. No, he wanted to do something, but what? It did not matter he would do it later, whatever it was.

He shifted his weight and slid down. Something tickled his nose then his throat. He coughed, and coughed.

- - -

*You are in charge of your life now, JoSelle.*

## UNDER THE SKIN

Edward Matthews

*tap tap tap tap tap tap tap tap tap*

I catch myself. I'm doing it again. In graduate school I would tap my foot during every therapy session. It would go a hundred miles an hour without me even knowing it was happening. My patients found it distracting. My supervisors found it annoying. I was simply embarrassed to have a habit that was outside of my conscious awareness, much less control.

So, I forced myself to stop. I would focus on my foot for entire sessions, willing it to not move. There were times when I missed much of what my patients had said because of the concentration it took not to allow my foot to move. But in the end, I won. I broke that habit and it stayed gone for years, but now this new one has emerged. The therapy room can be so quiet sometimes. Just two people sitting together with nothing but tension and expectation between them. The silences are natural in therapy and for a time I was a master at them. I could sit pensively, looking compassionately and expectantly at the person across from me until the silence was broken by their next confession or complaint.

Now this. It's no longer my foot. That, at least, remains under my control. But my damned pen. My pen starts tapping on the arm of my chair or on my knee or the pad of paper in front of me. Its kinetic flurry making it a blur as it tap, tap, taps against whatever surface it pleases. It doesn't happen all the time, but it seems to happen when the patient in front of me is terribly interesting or terribly unnerving. And Brian is both.

I stop the pen from tapping and redirect my attention, staring at him. He looks younger than his twenty-eight years. And he hides his growing insanity well.

*Delusional Parasitosis.* I had not thought of that term in a long time, probably not since school. I had never actually seen a case of it. But then he walked through my door. He told me that he didn't need to be there. He said he wasn't "crazy." He said that the bugs were real, but no one believed him. His mother, a therapist herself, convinced him to see me. He said he was humoring her.

He is a good patient. He comes every week. He pays his bill, or more likely his worried mother pays it. He's active and seems to listen to what I have to say. You would not know how tortured he is just looking at him. But he is tortured.

"They came out of my body last night, Doc." He says this almost casually, but I see the worry in his eyes.

"Out of your body?"

"Yeah. They must have. I woke up around two in the morning with something crawling on me. I could feel them all over me, on my arms and neck and face. There must have been a hundred of them, a thousand of them, and they were fast. Not like when I see them moving under my skin. Then they look like an earthworm or a caterpillar, but not this time. I kind of freaked out when I felt them all over me and knocked everything off my nightstand trying to get the light on. But by the time I got it on they had gone back in."

"Back in? Back into your body."

"Yeah, they weren't there anymore. They weren't on me. But look, you can see the holes where they went back in. Look. On my skin."

He thrusts his arm at my face. I oblige him with a look, knowing what I will find. And indeed, my hunch is confirmed.

"I don't see anything, Brian."

This is almost a ritual for us now, him showing me his evidence and me not seeing a thing. He looks sad every time. Or maybe frustrated or maybe he's disappointed with me. Maybe he thinks a better therapist would be able to detect the evidence. To help him. He withdraws his arm.

"I know you don't believe me. No one does. They were crawling on my body. I felt them. Legs scurrying over my chest, over my face." His voice rises. "They were crawling on my arm, on my lips. Do you think I could imagine that? Do you think my mind would just make that up? Then they went back in. They came out and went back into my body. That's where they are. That's where they always are."

Brian has told me all about the bugs, the parasites, the worms. He has the story of seeing the tiny snaking figure of a worm pass in front of his retina as it swam across his eye. He's told me about the bulging forms traversing beneath the surface of his forearm like carnivorous caterpillars. He told me about the mites and their thousand scribbled pin pricks of itchy pain on his stomach. There did not seem to be rhyme or reason behind the infestations he was imagining for his body. It was as if an encyclopedia of different organisms had taken residence in him. To hear his descriptions, his body would have to be full of them like a scarecrow stuffed with bugs, human in appearance, but writhing and crawling on the inside. However, despite the multitude of creatures he described and their various insult on his physical being, each came without an ounce of physical evidence that I could ever see. Only he could see the evidence. He described in vivid detail the red trail on the forearm. The inflamed minefield of red pustules on his stomach. The entry and exit marks from last night. But each time, I saw nothing.

I reach down and take my coffee cup in my hand. The picture of the whales and stylized "Gloucester" written across the bottom remind me of a more relaxed time. But, I also do this at times when I want to stall. I have no idea what to say to Brian at this moment. It is no use to challenge the delusion directly. Having to defend his belief to me would only reinforce it, make him hold it that more tightly. I hold the warm cup in my hand, comforted by the feel and the memory it evokes, and slowly bring it to my lips. Brian mirrors my movement, picking up his cup and bringing it to his mouth. Whether he does this unconsciously or as a subtle mockery I cannot tell. We both sip at our drinks, looking each other in the eye, and both set them down again on the small table between us.

"Are you taking your medications?" I know what I am doing. I'm feeling powerless to help him. So, I turn to the drugs. Maybe the miracle drugs of psychiatry could do something where my "talking cure" is failing him.

Brian looks sheepishly down at his now empty hands. "No," he says. "They make me feel weird. And I told you, I'm not crazy. I don't need crazy person drugs."

The session ends, and Brian leaves my office without much further progress. This is how they seemed to go, and after each I find myself frustrated with my therapeutic impotence. He is not getting better. In fact, his symptoms have been progressing. When he first came to me, maybe three or four months ago, he spoke of the bugs in an almost abstract manner. He said he knew, despite a half dozen negative medical tests, that he had some kind of parasite, but was no more specific than that. Then came the itchiness and odd stinging sensations. Then the descriptions of the worm-trails and raised bumps. Now he believes that they are burrowing out of him and traversing his body while he sleeps.

I reach again for the comfort of the warm cup of coffee as I close my eyes and trace my memory of Brian's history and the spiral of his delusions. Again, I cradle the cup in my hands and feel its warmth. I sip, considering my next step with Brian. How do I give him relief?

*tap tap tap tap tap tap tap tap tap*

My contemplation is broken by the sound. But my pen is on the table. The cup is in my hand. My foot. My damned foot. This case has gotten to me. I left this habit behind more than two decades ago, but here it is again. Is it that I can't help him? Is my ego bruised by being stuck? Maybe. And he knows it. He comes back week after week to "humor" his mother. But I'm the joke. He doesn't want to stop believing. He wants his bugs. He loves his bugs. And he just comes back to get his mother off his back and to watch me squirm.

The cup is cooling, losing its soothing warmth. I set it down.

*Clink*

My cup hits something before it reaches the table. I look to the table and see two whales swimming playfully above the swirly lines of the word "Gloucester." My mind tries to reconcile seeing my cup on the table while having my cup in my hand. My brain feels frozen for a moment until my eyes make their way to my hand. In my hand is Brian's cup. I must have picked it up by accident.

"Damnit!" I yell, breaking the silence of the room. I quickly trace what I know of Brian's medical history. No IV drug use. No reason I know of to worry about hepatitis.

*But what about the bugs?*

No. I shove the thought away. Foolishness. That's a delusion. There are no bugs.

Despite this, as I pour the coffee into the sink I find myself looking more closely at it than I should. What are the little white specs? Just little lumps of creamer. That's all. That's all they could be. The coffee swirls and is gone.

That night I wake up covered in sweat. I cannot remember what I was dreaming, but I know that I was. I feel uneasy. The blanket on top of me is damp and clings to my skin and to my even wetter pajamas, cocooning me uncomfortably. I get up and change, trying to recapture some of the images from my dream. I feel chilled even though it is a warm summer night. I wonder, as I drift back into an uneasy sleep, whether I might be sick.

I usually begin our sessions with a vague, open ended question. I find that this allows whatever is important to the patient to come more quickly to the surface. This one, however, I open with a rather pointed question.

"Do you have any communicable diseases?"

I had looked through the information I had gathered during our first session. I generally take an excellent history, including medical. He did not reveal anything at that time.

"What? Why?" he asks. Did I catch a smirk? Is he looking at me just a bit sideways?

"Please just answer. It's very important."

"No. I'm pretty healthy. I mean, other than the bugs. I'm in pretty good shape."

"The bugs. How did you get them? You've told me all about them, but you've never told me how you got them."

"I don't know how I got them. They just appeared. I just started to notice what they were doing to me."

"But when you first noticed. Was it after some event? A trip? Something that stood out to you?"

"No. Not that I can remember. Maybe it was something I ate or drank or something. Maybe they were in something. I don't know."

*Something you ate or drank. Are you toying with me? Do you know? Did you do something to me?*

That night I take a bath. The warmth is soothing. I turn off the lights and light a couple of candles. I can relax in the dimmed light. I sit considering my past week. The coffee. The fevered nights. And I feel a very strange sensation on my right arm. It feels like a slight pressure. Like a brief throb. I look and see a small movement on my forearm. I stare in the dim, flickering of the candle. I don't feel anything there now. I cannot see movement. There is a lump trailing up my forearm. I trace the index finger of my right hand over it. A vein. It's only a vein.

I towel off and go to bed, laughing to myself at the power the mind has. I have been so caught up in this case that I have internalized it, taken Brian's thoughts as my own. I drift to sleep with a grin. Yes, the mind is powerful, and it is a trickster.

But I awaken the next morning with a peculiar sensation. There is a burning itch on my forearm. I trace it again with the index finger of my left hand. It is a line, straight up the arm toward the hand, but it is not on the vein. There is indeed a vein there, but the itch is running parallel, about a half inch to the side of the vein. I scratch at the line, but that only makes the burning sensation worse. And I think I may see the dim outline of the offending track, like a very thin misshapen trail ascending my arm, slightly sunken or disfigured. I stare, but I cannot be sure.

Brian comes, as usual, on time for our next session. He repeats the ritual, telling me about the latest activities of the bugs that reside in him. This time they appear to have invaded his inner ear and auditory canal. He describes in detail the deafening chittering and clacking he heard from inside of his head, the sensation of spindly legs moving frantically inside of his ear. He invited me to take a look, but having no tools to get a good look inside of his ear I had an easy path to decline the invitation. But this time he also describes his rather concerning reactions.

He says that he was going nearly mad with the sounds of the bugs, beetle-like he guessed from the clicking sounds they were making, and was screaming to try to drown out the sound. He said that he could barely hear his own shouts over the din, but he had to stop the sounds. And he had to stop the movement, the pin-prick legs scuttling about inside of his head. He stood with the intention of finding a Q-tip or a pencil or chopstick or anything he could use to quiet and still the creatures. He says that as he shot up from the chair he fell to the ground with a wave of dizziness, attributing this to the beetles being crowded into his inner ear and messing up the works in there. He fell and vomited and said that he stayed on the floor for a good half-hour, screaming, vomiting, crying.

"I'm worried, Brian. Your reactions appear to be getting worse. If this keeps up, if it keeps getting worse, what will happen to us?"

Brian looks up, startled. "What do you mean?"

"I mean just that. I'm worried about what will happen to you."

"That's not what you said Doc. You said us."

I laugh. "No Brian. I know you feel alone. I know you would like for someone to understand you and what you're going through. The mind is tricky. But I am worried about you."

The rest of the session was disjointed. It was what one of my colleagues calls "near misses," where every attempt to connect and every interpretation feels like it is just off the mark. Brian left looking afraid and downcast.

Two nights later I'm in my study engrossed in a book, the kind of detective fluff I savor to take my mind off the real-world pain I find myself steeped in every day at work. I pause and look up from my book. There is a soft rustle, but I can't tell where it is coming from. The sound continues and grows louder, louder. It sounds like someone crushing dried leaves against my ear. No. Not against it, but in it. The sound grows louder still, the fluttering and crackling filling my head. I drop the book and bring my hands to my ears, vainly trying to block out the sound that is coming from inside my own head. I think I'm screaming, but I can't tell. And I can feel them. I'm sure I can feel them. Legs and wings and soft bulging bodies inside my ears, deep inside, writhing, flapping their dusty wings, beating against my eardrum and all the tender parts in there. I find it hard to tell how long it has lasted, but as quickly as it started, it is done. The creatures are still or have retreated to wherever they may go. The only sound is a soft sobbing which I realize is coming from me. My face is wet with tears. My head aches from screaming. I am alone and on the floor of my study.

Brian enters the next session looking harried and anxious. He is about to speak, but I interrupt him. I tell him about the coffee cup. I feel my anger rising and point at him accusingly.

"You've infected me! You left your cup there on purpose because I didn't believe you. You did this to me on purpose."

"No. No. I wouldn't do that. Certainly not to you. You've tried to help me," Brian says startled.

"Then how did it get there?" I nearly yell. "How did the cup get by me, so close?"

"I don't know," he says. "and I…I don't think it works that way anyway" Brian stammered. "I don't think you could get it from my drink."

"You're lying! You said you thought you got it from a drink or from food. You want to prove it to me. Well, you've proved it. And they're growing faster in me, Brian. I don't know how you did it, but they're bigger and faster in me. It took you months to reach this point, but I'm here now. How do I get rid of them?" My face feels hot. I find my hands clenched. Brian looks frightened.

TAP, TAP, TAP, TAP, TAP, TAP, TAP, TAP, TAP

I realize I'm banging my knuckles on my chair with such force that they are an angry red. I feel nothing. I must regain my composure. I must get control.

Brian is staring at me, wide eyed. "Doc, I don't know what's happening with you but…"

He reaches his hand toward me, trying to console me. I recoil from him. I don't need his hollow gestures. I am in control. I am not the one who needs help here.

Brian pulls his hand back, I'm sure sensing that he has crossed a boundary. Seeing his deference, his fear, I feel my anger subsiding.

Brian stands and excuses himself, saying he has to go.

"Same time next week," I call after him feebly, trying to grasp at the professional role that was blotted out in my anger.

But next week never comes. A few days later I get a voicemail from Brian. He sounds frantic. I can hear his ragged breathing, his quick, high pitched voice. I can feel the distress.

"It's getting worse," he nearly shrieks. "This is what I wanted to tell you the other day, in our session. I wanted to tell you that they're doing something. They're biting or eating or something. I can feel them. I can feel them eating me from the inside. I have to get them out Doc. I have to get them out!" Then the line went dead. He must have hung up. What did he mean that he had to get them out?

I call Brian's phone, but it goes directly to voicemail. I leave a brief message asking him to call me back. I then call his mother. No answer there either. So, I phone the police, requesting a welfare check. I tell them that I am a therapist and I have reason to believe that one of my patients is going to harm himself. The conversation is brief and I am assured that an officer is on his way to check. Usually in these situations I receive a call back within a half hour, either from an officer or from my patient. Tonight, I wait. An hour goes by, then two, and I am about to pick up the phone to call the police to see if I can get any information when the phone rings. It is an officer.

He tells me that Brian is dead. I have dealt with police many times in my career. This is the first time I have heard an officer's voice shake like his does.

"I've never seen anything like this in over 20 years as a cop." He tells me that Brian appears to have cut himself deeply in numerous places, his stomach, legs, arms, head, face. And that he appears to have been trying to tear those wounds open when he died, likely from blood loss. They found him with his hands frozen in the process of pulling open the large wound on his stomach. The officer goes into garish detail, seemingly having to describe the scene he has witnessed, to get it out. He vomits the details of the carnage thought the phone and I bathe in it. I am awash in the horror and my own inability to prevent it. I saw it and I did not believe him. I watched as it escalated, as they became more active and aggressive, and I did not believe him. I stood by as they colonized and infested him. And I accused him when he tried to tell me what they were doing.

That night I sit in my study listening to the sounds of the legs and wings and bodies of my guests rubbing against each other. It is the sound of wind through dried leaves, crumpling paper, chittering and chirping, fluttering and scraping, and tapping, and tapping, and tapping. I feel the writhing and pulsing ball in my stomach and I know that they are on the move. They will snake through my arms and legs, traverse the soft bulbs of my eyes, invade my ears and nose and mouth. They will claim my organs, feasting on my soft liver, boring into my stomach, bursting through my bowels. They will take all of me and leave a hollow husk to dry on my study floor.

But I will not let them. Brian is dead. He saw it coming and could do nothing to stop it. In the end he was foolish. He was brutish. But I'm smarter. I'm educated and trained. I'm no surgeon, but I know enough of anatomy to do the job correctly. So, I take the knife in my hand and place it to my stomach. I will cut it open and they will all spill out, their hiding places will be revealed and denied them. I will stop them before they move again through my body. They will spill to the floor and I will crush them, stepping and stomping and laughing. I will crush them and burn them and kill them all. They will pay for how they have made me feel. They will pay for my fear and screaming and crying. And they will pay for you, Brian. I will kill them all for you.

## PORTRAITS

Charles R. Bernard

The old pickup rolls to a stop, shadows dappling the hood. The engine ticks irregularly as it cools, a quiet sound, peaceful in the shade and the pine-scented breeze. It's mid-morning. Even in summer, the woods in Lambs Canyon are cool come evening. Nighttime's damp, chilly grip hasn't fully relaxed yet, despite the cloudless day it's shaping up to be.

Piotr regards the woods for a few moments, letting the radio play softly. It's an old truck with an AM/FM that works (poorly), no CD player or other accessories. Piotr doesn't mind. He likes the radio. He enjoys the advertisements in particular, full of bright sounds and silly voices. The idea of these lively signals peeling off of the Earth and into the endless black of space, like fireflies or prayers, is sometimes a comfort to him.

Presently he removes the keys from the ignition and stashes them behind the sun visor. He lifts his eyes to the rearview mirror. In his reflection, a fleshy disk is pressed close to his face—a jarring landscape of exposed bone and rolling supernumerary eyes, blood-slick lips whispering thoughts of uproar and annihilation into his ear. A face. He concentrates, closes his eyes. When he opens them again, all he sees in the mirror are his own eyes, clear and pale grey like lake ice. They haven't figured out that they're wasting their time with me, he thinks.

The cab of the truck is impoverished, the upholstery beginning to unravel with age and the carpet rotted out down to the metal. The truck is empty save for Piotr and his backpack. The backpack is as old as the truck, but has been immaculately cared for. It is carefully packed and as neat as a pin.

He rolls his windows all the way up and leaves an envelope on the driver's seat. It bears one word—*Marta*—in exquisite handwriting.

Piotr's knees have seen better days. They have seen a great many days, in fact. They complain viciously, but they carry him up the trailhead and deep into the shade of the trees. He stops every half mile or so and drinks deeply—first gulps of water from a large canteen, then quick pulls from a flask. These nips from the flask pour hellfire on his heartburn, but mute the grievances of his joints. The liquor in the flask is *bäsk*, flavored with wormwood. It makes him think of Signe and her books, and then of Indonesia. Piotr grimaces as he drinks and thinks, bitter taste. Grim reminder.

He crosses a bridge over a rocky creek. The woods are cool, steeped in shade and permeated by the whisper-song of the water and the smell of wet stone. There's the scent of green things, too, which is welcome. Right now, down in the khaki dust of the valley where Piotr lives, everything is beaten flat and baked gold by the summer sun. Up here, it's cool pines and the rush of the breeze through their needles.

It's a long hike. Birdsong fills the air and echoes off of rocks resting in broken piles at the bottom of the mountain's slope. Geology is what he tells people brought him to this corner of the American West, back in the cold war stagnation of the mid-70s. The truth is a little more complicated than the mountains.

Hours into his hike, he splits from the trail, taking a rough path that threads deeper into the forest. It's barely more than a game trail, and the going is rough. He stops frequently to drink water even though he's not all that thirsty. He needs to be hydrated, Piotr knows. At his age, his blood doesn't flow as easily as it once did.

He arrives in the late afternoon. When he picks his way around the base of a large hill, there's a clearing on the other side, twenty feet wide at its center. The clearing is dominated by two massive stone figures. Although their true height is difficult to judge since the base of each is buried, he estimates perhaps eight feet apiece. They are both decorated with paint so ancient that their age, like their size, is hard to ascertain.

One is a grinning frog with bulging eyes that point crookedly in opposite directions. The frog has large flat teeth that have always made Piotr feel slightly ill to view. The other statue is a rabbit with a similarly manic smile, this one revealing a pair of big buck teeth that look like they could rip a man in bloody halves. When he'd first rounded the hill and found this spot, navigating to it with a compass and the map Signe had drawn him, the statues had startled him. Signe hadn't known they'd be there. She'd mapped the ley lines and indicated clearly to him where he'd find what they were looking for, but by then—1975—she'd been too sick to make the trip herself.

He thinks of her now as he feels the pain in his joints even beneath the pleasant buzz of the liquor, and regards the clearing's leering, black-eyed tenants. She hadn't been surprised back then, when the camera failed to capture anything in the clearing but blurs and shadows. "Spatiotemporal displacement," she'd said. Signe, with her books, ever intellectualizing, ever rationalizing. Piotr was the product of a brutal childhood that had unfolded against the backdrops of Catholicism and Communism. He was more comfortable with less refined characterizations. The statues, with their haw-haw grins and ancient paint, were *other.* They were from *somewhere else.*

This place that Piotr has made the work of his autumn years, this *trou de loup* (as first she, and now he, calls it) is one of many displaced places, places where those like Piotr and Signe can do their work. This is the only one that contains artifacts like the statues—solid structures that do not flit, mercurial, from place to place, the way the books of portraiture do.

He ignores the hungry stares of the stone frog and the rabbit, and makes camp while it's still light. The fire he makes is small and neat, and its smoke rises straight into the blue void. The wind that kept Piotr company all day doesn't reach this place.

Piotr brought a garden spade. Its surface is corroded and oxidized with use. As the last light of the day drains from the sky, he kneels in the clearing's center (sending daggers shooting through his joints) and begins to dig. It doesn't take long. The spade strikes metal with a muffled knock, and Piotr scrapes and pries until, finally, he pulls a flat metal box from the soil. He sets it to one side and lurches to his feet with a small grunt of effort. He brushes the dirt from his knees and then stands, finishing the bäsk in long, unhurried swallows.

The trees stand watch, their tops drenched first in gold, then in dark pink-purple. It's hard to tell what direction the light comes from but he can track the sun's retreat by the sky's colors. Soon the trees are garbed in deep blue shadow, cool and beautiful against a night sky sprinkled with stars as fine as powdered sugar, mixed and remixed from what would normally be familiar constellations. The same light show plays out against the stone of the animal statues, and as night falls, the firelight capers over their faces. "I see you, you spooky *dzwiki*," he chides them. His voice sounds strange in the quiet of the clearing.

"To name something is to have power over it," Signe once told him. That had been in Chapeltown in 1975, before the first of the riots. "A name is a shape, and when something has a shape, it is finite."

How right she had been, and how right she still was. Indonesia, he remembers, and Belfast. Hong Kong. In 1968, so many that we thought the whole world might tip over. And now the 21st century is in flames.

Piotr sets the empty flask aside and runs his hands over the box. Its surface is as cool and as damp as the soil in which it was interred. He pops its latches with his thumbs and opens it. Inside is a book. It's large, bound in old black leather worn as soft as felt. Its pages are made of rich, cream-colored paper stock, just beginning to yellow around the edges with age. He sets it aside. There are a few swallows of water left in the canteen, and he finishes them. He collects his folding knife and a small silver stylus from his bag and settles into his frayed camp chair with the book.

A bookmark—a piece of twine—marks Piotr's place about four-fifths through, but Piotr takes his time. He flips past pages, skimming them and stopping here and there. The book is an old friend. "*Bóg*," Piotr mutters, pausing on a page. He makes the sign of the cross, suddenly aware of the en-croaching chill of the night, his papery skin alive with goose-flesh.

Some of the book's pages contain writing—a great deal of it, all of it a muddy brown-red in color, and all of it written in Piotr's beautifully compact cursive penmanship. His hand is eminently legible, but a reader would be hard-pressed to decipher its meaning. Some of the writing is in Polish, some in German, some in Russian. A few words here and there are scratched out in neat English; "retrograde," "eminence," "rend," "chuckle."

The page he has stopped on does not contain writing. It's an illustration, also his handiwork and in the same brown-red ink. A portrait of a monster.

Piotr was always an able illustrator, if one lacking in imagination. In his college years, geology gave him an outlet for his talent. The subject matter was concrete, complex, and sometimes fantastical—layers of whirling, brightly-colored rock, and geodes like goblin treasure. When he met Signe, she'd encouraged him to practice more, to branch out, even to take a few classes on pen-and-ink illustration. It had paid off.

The portrait takes up a full page. It's rendered in lines and crosshatches so dense and precise that the effect is like a woodcut. It depicts a humanoid figure from its abdomen to the crown of its head. Its long, bony arms are wrapped around its narrow chest in self-embrace. It is clad in tattered formal-wear, ripped in places and stained down the front. Above the buttoned collar and its neatly tied tie, it has the wild-eyed head of a dog, its fur matted, its long tongue and winding through nasty-looking teeth. In the lower right corner of the illustration are a brief string of numbers and six neat words in block capitals: *LA LINGUA CHE LECCA LA FERITA.* "*The Tongue that Licks the Wound.*" An image, a name, a mish-mash language of description that would make sense to few other living people, but doesn't have to. Giving something shape makes it finite.

Indonesia. Belfast. Hong Kong. And so many more. He marvels, flipping through the pages. How many were in Signe's book, he wonders, by the time she died? How many monsters could she claim as hers by then? Monsters…Signe had called them "odiovores," eaters of hate. Monsters or odiovores, she had sketched *so many* of them. He can hear her chide him so clearly that it's as though her ghost has come to visit him. "Are we keeping score, Piotrek? Are we sure that our priorities are in order?" He smiles, and in that moment her absence, longstanding as it has been, feels like too much to bear.

He lingers over another one of the intricate drawings, this one labeled *DER GESCHMACK DER ZERSTÖRUNG,* *"the Taste of Ruination."* Its face, such as it is, consists of innumerable disjointed and interlocking jaws, busy with a complicated geometry of long yellow teeth. A pair of lidless human eyes, rimmed in inflamed flesh. They burn with lunatic hate. Which one was this he wonders? He's fought too many battles to keep all of them straight. The nature of the war—scattered across continents and decades—doesn't help. He skims back through the pages preceding the illustration, reading the mash of languages, numbers, and symbols. Ah, it had perseverated the last time in Roostock, Germany, in 1992.

Der Geschmack der Zerstörung had been a big one. These entities breach into human reality, he often thinks, like whales surfacing. Some manifest as particularly virulent cases of individual madness—the kind that work inside of a person like a hand forced into an undersized glove until the seams give out and the end inevitably comes, but more than a rip here it is awash in blood and mindless brutality. Most are much larger and so subtle, so crafty, that their effects are widespread and hardly perceptible, at first. Feeding on hate, they were the astral bodies of social violence; riot, pogrom, purge, and strife.

Piotr flips back to the illustration and runs his thumb slowly over the page, feeling the grooves in the paper left by tip of the stylus. He does this cautiously, as though the picture might bite him. It has an irrepressible malevolent energy, as though the image itself is alive. Perhaps it is. He's not sure what happens to the odiovores once they become trapped by the ritual. The thought that the subjects of his portraits might still live, festering and brooding in their unfathomable malice, is one that has kept him awake more than once.

He tells himself again not to worry. If they are alive in there, what of it? Only he can access his book. Anyone other than he who dug into the clearing's center would find nothing (provided they could even travel there, which would be an impressive feat on their part). Piotr, on the other hand, need only find one of the world's many hidden *trous de loup*, not even necessarily the same one where he had last buried his book, and dig. One day—a day that creeps close—he will die, just as Signe did, and then his book will become locked away, just as Signe's was. What principle is in operation here, what rules govern the operation of these things? He doesn't know. He knows so much less than she did, his mentor, his great love. He has her notes, reams of them, but not her mind. And, unlike her, he has no successor, nobody to whom he can entrust this calling.

He and Signe had both been surprised when their only child, Marta, had not inherited their gifts. Signe had located Piotr in the first place the same way that her old mentor had found her—the books. Piotr has been at this for more than a half-century now, and no name has appeared in his book. The few others like himself and Signe that they'd encountered and kept in contact with over the years had been skittish about fellowship, and over time had all died or vanished. He can't be the last, he reasons. Surely not.

Shaking off his reverie, he glances up at the statues again. They stare back at him with nihilistic cheer. The night beyond the red, dancing circle of firelight is impenetrable. It is time for him to begin.

In the Middle Ages, a *trou de loup* (or "wolf hole") was a simple trap; a partially-concealed pit with slick sides and a sharp, poisoned stake fixed with its point facing up at the bottom. A nasty surprise for any invader who fell into it. Piotr supposes that he is, in this sense, the sharpened stick that waits for the unwary. He sets up a TV tray (a recent and very useful addition to his camping gear) and opens to the first blank page in his book. He runs his fingertips over the untouched paper briefly. It whispers against his skin, smooth, heavy, and cool. He clears his mind until it is as still and as cold as a frozen lake, and then, hidden, lethal, he begins to bait the trap.

The song that he pours into his mind is one of several melodies that Signe taught him. There are more, notated carefully like a fisherman's lures, in her journals. It's a simple, jaunty, catchy waltz, the kind that you might hear crackle out of a carousel or an ice cream truck. Piotr brings it to life as it would sound produced by a calliope, the whistle so loud that he can almost feel it vibrate his skull. He pushes the song hard with his mind, sending it out into the night, into the darkness, into the temporal nullity where the odiovores make their home.

It doesn't take long. There are legions of them out

there, gardeners of madness, tending to the cultivars of sadism and death that their kind had such an affinity for. "A long time ago," Signe had told him very early on, "we wondered if they *cause* strife, or are just drawn to it. Experience and experimentation have taught us that they are the cause. Imprison one of them, and there's no telling how many lives you've saved. We can't perceive them properly as they are, my love."

"Hyperobject" is Piotr's word, not hers. Signe was gone by the time he'd happened upon the concept in an article about climate change. It fit comfortably with what the odiovores were and how they operated. He'd memorized the definition: "Hyperobjects are massively distributed in time and space to the extent that their totality cannot be realized in any particular local manifestation." The nonlocality makes it difficult to establish their shape, or velocity, or intent.

Especially intent.

The sound is so soft at first that Piotr has to strain to hear it. He focuses on the brainless, whistling tune his mind broadcasts into the black beyond the ring of firelight. He is a deep sea fisherman, line cast into the void. Then—here we go—the sound from the night grows loud and resolves itself. It's a sharp, incessant hissing like a gas leak. Something stirs at the edge of the writhing firelight, weaving in and out of the shadows, blurred by vibrating convulsions. It slows, solidifies in the murk, and a figure steps slowly into view.

It's huge—seven and a half feet tall, perhaps, with broad, bony shoulders and lean-muscled limbs. It's dressed in a loose-fitting shirt and pants made of thin, colorless material. Its skin is a beautiful tawny color. From its upper lip to the deep widow's peak of its long, straight blonde hair, it is lovely and androgynous. The lower half of its face is a shredded ruin as though its lower jaw had been pulled off in an act of extravagant violence. From the red, meaty shreds and dangling, liver-colored tissues of its upper jaw, jutted teeth, each at least two inches long and dagger-pointed. Its eyes are a rich, mellow brown. It stops and stares fixedly into space, transfixed by Piotr's song but oblivious to his presence.

Piotr unfolds and locks the blade of his knife, readies his stylus, and cuts carefully into his forearm.

Since Signe initiated him into these mysteries, Piotr has favored long sleeves, no matter the weather. Easier to make excuses for that than for a half-century's worth of scars left by precisely executed, neatly spaced cuts. This is the least of the sacrifices that he has made over the years. There are probably ways around the cuts—although he must use blood for the rite, and it must be his—but he's a creature of habit, and this was the way that he was taught. Because he cannot access his book to consider his career whenever he likes, the scars also have become a way of keeping track. Of keeping score.

He dips the stylus into the blood that bubbles and pools, and then begins.

"Keep your mind clear," Signe had instructed him, his first time. "Relax your grip on the 'now.' Follow their footprints, look at their fingerprints—the bloody trail they leave that gives us their shape. That, ultimately, gives us their undoing. What you're looking for is there, in the darkness. You have the gift. You can find it."

The odiovore that stands before Piotr, entranced and ensnared, has left a long, bloody trail that Piotr finds quite easily. The gift can only be described as an amalgam of other senses, and even that leaves something to be desired—but Piotr would compare the sensation of uncoupling himself and following the creature's tracks to climbing a long rope made of greased silk up and up into the taste of blood and the sound of trumpets.

The words Piotr jots down in his trance would convey none of this to the uninitiated. Perhaps they would think of what he writes as free-form poetry. That's not a bad metaphor, poetry, Piotr thinks. The ritual is highly intuitive, after all, more art than science, despite Signe's attempts to impose structure onto it. There are strings of numbers mixed into the words, and these occur to Piotr with no synesthetic context. Are they coordinates? Measurements? Something encoded even more deeply than the words? Signe had speculated and tinkered in her journals, but in the end, she was forced to accept them as another mystery that would, for her, remain forever unsolved.

There now, Piotr thinks as the words taper off. It's hard for him to keep track of time while he is in this liminal place, in this liminal state, and he's not sure how long it has been in the "between." He has written several pages. He has had to cut himself a few times to keep the blood flowing while he got everything down. Now, through some strange osmosis, he has a picture of the odiovore in his mind—not just the fleshy material avatar that stands before him, but of its manifestations throughout the past and into the future. The madness it has brought. The human grief and human hate.

Merciful God protect me Piotr prays reflexively. St. Petersburg, January of 1905, men gunned down under a frozen sky. New York City, outside Madison Square Garden, in February of 1939. Fists and sticks meet flesh. Teeth crack, screams are swallowed painfully. On and on, iterating backward and forward into flickering infinity. It's stronger than the average specimen. He can feel it with his mind. It's like a vast, four-dimensional eel, one long rope of incorporeal muscle.

He blinks, concentrates. For the final step, he needs to focus on the incarnation before him, the giant with half a face. It stands in place, shifting from time to time, hypnotized by the song in Piotr's mind.

He begins the sketch. The cuts on his arm burn. The bäsk liquor has kept the pain wrapped in wet wool, but muffled as it is, it's still there. He finishes the outline in quick, smooth strokes, a portrait of the creature from the chest up. He dips the stylus, scratches the page, dips again. Crosshatched shadows creep out on the paper. Piotr gets the mild-mannered eyes, the fanged and dripping meatscape of the ruined jaw.

He and Signe had called each ritual site a *trou de loup*, but that had always been half a joke and half a lie. The name implied equal footing between humankind and adversary, if not a defensive advantage on the part of Piotr and his ilk. But the truth is far less heroic. As far as he has ever been able to determine, the odiovores are not aware of any conscious human effort to resist them, even at moments of truth such as the one that Piotr is currently engaged in. We are, Piotr thought, viruses. Killer bacteria. Well, there may be no glamor in it, but this ugly świnia is about to catch a fatal case of H. sapiens Piotr.

As Piotr dabs out the final details of the portrait in his blood, the giant with the cloven jaw seems to sense that something is wrong. It tries to turn away, back toward the darkness beyond the firelight, or, Piotr supposes, back toward whatever it perceives there. It can't. Its limbs spasm but can't move. Its neck tenses, but it cannot look away.

Alarm blossoms in its eyes, and Piotr's smile becomes

a grin. He can feel its name now, can palpate the words with his mind. The creature has realized its peril too late. Now it's just the odiovore and Piotr, alone on this island of ritual ground, separated from Earth, separated from time. *Outside* of time. And because of that, Piotr supposes, it didn't see this coming.

He adds a string of digits to the bottom of the portrait. Signe was very interested in what these numbers might signify, Piotr less so. But he likes to imagine that they are like electrified bars on a cage. He dabs blood a few more times, and adds its name in block letters. *STEAM RISING FROM RED BONES.* When he finishes the final letter, a sound fills the air; a single loud, violent rasp, like the rending of some titanic sheet of fabric.

When Piotr looks up from the page, Steam Rising from Red Bones has vanished. It exists—he hesitates to say "lives"—only in his book now, soon to be reburied in the cold, damp ground.

Will the book ever emerge again? Or is he, too, soon to be interred? I'm so tired, he thinks, tired of pain. Tired of devils and their sick eternity-games Marta wants nothing to do with me. The woman I loved is gone.

The cuts on his arm itch and burn in a muted way that is almost pleasurable. Piotr levels an exhausted look at the jolly, grinning faces of the great stone frog and rabbit. They are slowly receding into darkness as his tidy little fire dies down.

"It's a damned age of madness. Why fight the inevitable?" he asks the statues. He doesn't want to lie to himself or tiptoe around the thought. Maybe better to end it right here, right now. He turns the knife in his hand speculatively.

The words strike him with force that feels electric, alive. It's unlike anything he's ever experienced while trapping the odiovores. Knowledge that is crystal clear and *on the move*, racing through him and burning with the compulsion to be free. His thoughts cannot deter the revelation. It is far too insistent.

Almost without noticing he's doing it, he makes another tiny incision on his arm and dips his stylus into the blood. On a fresh page, he writes a few lines. The relief is tremendous, and once the lines are out of him and on the page, he has no idea what he has written until he steadies himself, rubs his eyes, and reads the page.

It's a detailed description of a person. A young woman in Ghana, specifically, named Wafaa. She's 22 years old.

Astonishment and exhaustion are all he can feel. Is this God's work I'm doing? he wonders. Signe didn't think so. The best she ever did was "someone living outside time as we know it, just like the odiovores do." Maybe another species, maybe a different us. So much we don't understand, but also so much to pass on, to teach a woman that I've never met, whom I may not like, who may not want this burden placed on her. I can't even tell her, in good conscience, that I know us to be working on behalf of God and not some interdimensional pest control company.

He listens to the silence, and thinks.

Finally, he copies down Wafaa's information on a piece of paper in his wallet, carefully closes the book and places it back in its box. By the time he reburies it, Piotr is very exhausted indeed. He anticipates sleeping well, as he always does after a successful trap in this strange, timeless place, and, he anticipates, he will have the same dream he al-

ways does here, and only ever here. A vast purple sea, scintil-
lating, in which he will float as though in the womb. On every
visit, the dream fills him with deep peace and aching melancholy.

I will call Marta, he thinks as he lays down, and I will
apologize, and I will listen. And then, after I have told my
daughter that I love her, I will find this Wafaa. He stares up at
the roof of his tent, and breathes the comfortable, musty smell
of the canvas. She will choose. I will tell her everything, and I
will let her choose.

Piotr sleeps and outside his tent, the stone faces of the
rabbit and the frog grin endlessly into the night. The sky
teams with stars, shifting and fitting no recognizable configu-
ration for long. The soil slumbers, cool and damp and secret.
And, somewhere in the dark, creatures of infinite aspect taste
and test the weight of human suffering and madness, each one
a recurring stab wound, an echoing scream, but each, too, a
portrait waiting to be captured.

# ROADKILL

### Betti Avari

"Aren't you hungry?" she asks from the passenger seat. She pops a fry in her mouth, then licks the salt off her finger seductively.

I grin wickedly and shift into fifth gear. "Maybe."

The last thing I want is French fries, but she can never know what I hunger for. I crave a different main course.

"Are you?" I ask meaningfully.

She catches my drift and nods as she bites her lip. I turn off the highway, onto a narrowing street that leads through a rural neighborhood. It's dotted with aging farm-houses that grow farther apart the closer I get to the mountain.

We wind into the forest as the road begins to climb and when I downshift, I catch the bounce of her breasts in my peripheral vision. I begin to salivate.

Hunger and desire are, for me, inextricably linked.

She reaches across the cab, her arm beneath mine. Her slender hand comes to rest on my thigh, and my hunger grows. Her eyes search my face for approval, but I don't meet her gaze. Instead, I shift my hips slightly. She's caressing, exploring, kneading. I groan. My eyelids flutter slightly, until I see a sudden movement out my driver's side window. It's a flash and nothing more, then--

Smash!

The tires screech as I bring the car to a stop.

"What the hell was that?" Her voice is shrill.

I put the car in neutral and set the brake. "A deer."

"Did you kill it?"

My stomach growls. "I sure hope so." Silence fills the cab. "I mean...I don't want it suffering out there."

"What if it isn't dead?" She turns to peer out the back windshield, and her breasts brush my bicep.

My grip tightens on the stick shift. "Should we check?"

"And if it's still alive?" She's trembling slightly, probably in shock.

I almost mention that I have a knife in my left pocket to finish the job if necessary, but I don't want to scare her. I shrug. "I need to inspect the damage anyway."

I reach for my flashlight in the glove box, and she grabs my arm. "No, don't go out there. It's too dark." She's got a nice, firm grip.

"Don't worry about a thing," I chuckle. "I'll be right back."

I step outside, take a deep breath, and lick my lips. The smell of death is in the air.

We're around the bend from Lookout Point, and behind us, I see a twitching figure just off the shoulder. Perfect. The broken headlight hangs by a single wire, an inch off the ground, but I'm flying high.

I hold my flashlight steady to keep the circle of light focused on the road; if I shine it directly on the deer, it'll freak out the pretty girl trembling in the passenger seat. She's watching me, so I take my time and approach the deer cautiously.

There's frantic movement in her eyes, fear and confusion, but there's also lots of blood. No way it will survive a compound fracture and a broken neck. It's only a matter of time. I wish I could speed things up, put the beast out of its misery. My hand is twitching, anxious to reach for my pocket knife, but I don't think the girl would appreciate the gesture. She's scared enough already.

I give the poor animal one last glance before I turn away. It'll be dead soon enough. And then...I wipe the smile off my face before I climb back in, and I'm glad I do; concern is tainting that pretty pout of hers.

"It's dead. But the car's going to make it."

She's quiet.

"Are you okay?"

She nods.

I recognize this behavior. She's doing the typical girl, suffer-in-silence thing. I know a good cure for that. The hunger is stronger than the desire right now, and I don't want to play these games. Still, I wrap my hand around the back of her neck, rest my forehead against hers, and sigh, "I should take you home." I kiss her forehead and pull away to put the car in gear.

"No, wait." She puts her hand over mine on the stick. "Maybe...Maybe I'm okay."

"What do you mean?"

"I mean," her fingers slowly caress and thread through mine. "I was scared, but why let a dead deer ruin a perfect night?" she purrs.

"Maybe," I sigh, turning my face toward hers, "it's making this night unforgettable." My tactics work. Our lips are soft, moist and willing, and fit together nicely. I pull away a few inches and smile. "We should probably move out of the road."

A minute later, we stop at the edge of Lookout Point and I kill the engine. Our intertwining bodies quickly fog up the windows, and when she climbs back into the passenger seat, gasping for breath, my thoughts turn to food. My desire is satisfied, but my hunger is now at a painful level. After a minute or two of a cuddly cool-down, I pull my shirt on and tell her I have to go to the bathroom.

The contrasting cold air clears my head. I quickly shut my door and jog down the hill. My heart is pounding with excitement as I hurry to the place where we crashed. I scan the side of the road. The moon is rising above the trees, so I shouldn't need a flashlight to find the deer again.

Momentary panic constricts my airway. Where is it? It couldn't have wandered off with a compound fracture!

Ah! From behind a thicket of grass, a protruding hoof glistens. The deer is still lying beside the road, its body warm and steamy, like the cab of my car.

I look back toward the car. The girl will be waiting for me to get back to her, so I can't wait for the deer to cool the way I'd like. I would hide it deeper in the woods and come back later, but we're miles from town, and gas isn't cheap.

Beginning at the bottom of the chest cavity, I get to work, cutting the hide in quick downward slices. Fresh blood erupts in rhythmic beats. A pulse? The deer's eyes are dilated, but there it is, a faint pulse at its neck.

Until now, my harvests have been long dead.

Instinctively, I thrust my knife into the chest cavity. A hollow thud echoes in my ears and a visible sigh escapes the mangled carcass beneath me. It was suffering. I wonder if they all take so long to die.

It's weird to think that both of us were alive in the same dark forest, at the same time--pleasure and pain just three hundred yards apart. The stark contrast is unnerving. I was in the throes of passion while this animal was lying broken and afraid in the dark night, in the worst pain of its existence.

It's a good thing I came back to finally end its torment.

If only I could borrow the truck from the Coyote Refuge I interned with this summer, I could stash the carcass in a vacant field closer to campus. I could make sure its life didn't go to waste.

That internship is where it all began—the bottom rung, always picking up roadkill to feed the coyotes.

Those lucky dogs.

It wasn't my dream job to pick up bloated and maggoty coons, skunks, and deer all day—all I felt was disgust. At first, I almost quit the internship, but that would put me off course for graduation. On a whim, I stopped by the psychology department to see if the professor had any ideas for overcoming the nausea. He asked me a lot of questions about my fears, my goals, my relationships, then asked if I'd be willing to undergo hypnosis.

I agreed.

Overnight, my depression disappeared, my relationships grew more passionate. And, most interestingly, my prior revulsion toward the carrion I harvested off roadsides completely vanished.

Then I began to take interest in the stages of decay, found myself fascinated as the coyotes shredded the carcasses with ravenous excitement, and felt hunger for the very meals they shared.

I've never taken pity on the other harvests, because they were already dead.

This one is different, but my hunger is nevertheless overwhelming.

I grip the knife tightly and slit the membrane holding the innards together. I step aside as they spill to the ground. Scented steam rises into the night sky, and I take a nice deep breath. I can't fit the deer in my trunk, but if I could!

Sure, it's gross, but I can't bring myself to tell the psych professor any of this, or he might reverse whatever hypnotic spell I'm under. And, if he does, I'll lose all that I have: a ravenous sex life with a growing reputation, and an appreciation for the strongest flavor in existence.

I kneel beside the deer as excitement surges through my chest. I love my life. Where to begin? The leathery texture of the thick black nose is always a nice choice, but tonight, I decide to start on the organs. They're still warm, still fresh—which means their texture isn't as tender as last week's raccoon, or the cat on the highway before that. Maggots make the best tenderizers, and give the meat more flavor, but beggars can't be choosers.

I slip a cut of hot, slippery meat between my lips. It's chewy and tastes like iron.

I take another bite. Is this the spleen? The liver? Whatever it is, it's worth saving some for later. I stick what is left in my jacket pocket.

"Hello?" Her voice echoes down the hillside, distant, but unmistakable. "Are you down there?"

She can't find me here.

I wipe my hands on the grass and run through the woods up the steep side of the hill, then double back down the road. Her cellphone flashlight moves erratically in all directions, guiding me right to her.

"Hey!" I jog down the hill to meet her at the bend. "Did you miss me?"

She turns. "Oh, I thought you went down the hill this way. It's so dark up here." She sidles up beside me, then takes a step back with a scowl on her face.

"What is it?" I ask.

"Uh," she pauses. "You smell."

All I smell is the deer, and I salivate. This hunger is raw and urgent, and I haven't had enough. She didn't need an excuse for smelling like French fries, but I need an excuse for smelling like my dinner?

I swallow back my saliva. "Oh, sorry." I wrack my brain and come up with only one possible excuse for smelling the way I do. "I told you I had to go to the bathroom. I just needed a little, uh, privacy."

She stares at me for a hot second. "You mean...? Eew."

I shrug. "There's a reason I didn't invite you to join me."

She glares at me for a moment, then turns back up the road toward the car. The magic is over, and that's fine with me. "Okay...Let's get you home."

I look down the hill as I walk around the back of the car. I want just one more taste.

I turn the key. The engine sputters but doesn't turn over. The deer must have damaged something inside after all.

I drum my fingertips against the steering wheel; my nail beds are warm and sticky. I bite at one of them to suck on the moisture, and groan. With my car broken down, it might be a long time before another roadkill harvest, but if I leave the girl here while I go for help, I can grab another bite or two on the way to cell service.

"You stay here where it's warm. I'll go for help."

"We could walk together," she suggests. "There's safety in numbers. We should have cell service when we clear the trees."

I don't have a chance to disagree. She climbs out of the car and flips her cellphone flashlight on.

We wander back the way we've come, and every step closer, my hunger deepens. Intensifies. I can smell it in the air, feel it with my senses. It's so close. Just behind that bunch of grass up ahead, it waits for me. With every heartbeat, my hunger demands to be felt, until I can think of nothing else.

"You're quiet," she murmurs.

I don't respond. I don't have the capacity for thought right now.

She gasps, "Wait! I know what's wrong with you. You never ate. Are you sure you're not hungry?"

That is the wrong question to ask...

I don't care that she's watching, that her cellphone flashlight is cutting through the night as I bolt for the deer and lunge for the guts that are protruding from the hasty gash I made earlier.

Now she's screaming, begging me to stop.

I don't care that she's running toward town—she's wearing ridiculous shoes; I'll catch up to her in a few minutes.

I must, she's left me no choice.

She probably captured me on video, and I can't leave any evidence. But for now, I dig my hands in again and again, and whatever I can grasp is drawn to my mouth in a frenzy.

Then a new idea comes to mind.

I run after her. She's screaming and crying so loud that she can't hear my footsteps, and I catch her by the shoulders before she realizes I'm behind her.

"Shh! Don't be scared! It's fine. It's food."

She's on her knees now, here on the dirt road in the dark night, begging me through sobs to stop.

I kneel beside her, run my sticky hands through her hair and pull her to my chest. "Shh. It's okay."

I must help her understand, so I pull the best piece from my pocket. A peace offering.

"Here," I offer. "Just try it."

Her eyes are wide. She bites her lip.

"Please, try it! It's like jerky!"

Her phone's light is shining in my face. I reach for it, and she recoils with a terrified sob. My hands are covered in blood, which might explain her reaction. I slide my palm down my jeans.

What am I supposed to do now? She can't go to the police. They'll lock me up.

It isn't fair. This secret is the key to my survival. If they lock me up, I don't know how long I can go without eating this again.

I'll go mad.

She can't ever tell.

I grab her face, turn her to me so she can watch. Then I take a bite and chew it, swallow it down, to show her that it's fine. She gags, and her sobs intensify. No, she won't try it. She doesn't believe me. She's terrified. Her body is stiff in my arms, like rigor mortis. Like roadkill.

Maybe she doesn't understand. Maybe she never will.

What then? I have to keep trying. And trying again. If it's the last thing I do.

She knows too much.

She has to try.

Or else.

"C'mon!" I beg. "Aren't you hungry?"

# A LIGHT FROM THE RIVER

Mike Nelson

Pete pulled Jenny close and whispered in her ear. "Let's ditch this dance, it's boring."

"It's homecoming," she said, pushing him away. "That's the only reason I bought this dress and I plan to get more than two dances out of it. Besides, I think we're moving too fast."

"You didn't complain last Friday night," he said with a soft smile. "Besides, we're being careful."

"It's not about that. I, just…"

"I know, you want to date other guys. So, what's stopping you?"

She hesitated. "You," she said with a sly grin.

The slow song they'd been dancing to ended and the DJ announced a short break.

"Okay then," she said, taking his hand. "My friends have all seen us here. They'll vouch for me if my mother asks. So where are you taking me this time?"

"I know a few places."

She leaned close so nobody around them would hear her reply. "I'll bet you do," she whispered sarcastically. "And if you remember right, last time we almost got caught with our proverbial pants down. I don't ever want to do that again."

Thoughts of the river crossed his mind as they walked arm-in-arm to his car. He'd spent time along the levee. It was far enough out of town he knew nobody would bother them— but he'd only been there once after dark, and he swore he'd never go back. All the while he was sitting there in the inky blackness that night, waiting for the catfish to bite, he swore there was somebody watching him. That had been months ago though, and now he was desperate. He had to have Jenny home by midnight, so he didn't have a lot of time to drive around looking for the perfect place to park.

"Where *are* we going?" Jenny asked as the town fell away behind them, the road narrowed, and tall weeds and grass began to flank both sides of the road.

"I know a place by the river," he said.

"Oh, that sounds fun," she said with a soft laugh. "It's a hot night. Maybe we can go skinny dipping. I've never been."

Pete didn't particularly like the idea of swimming in the river. The water was ice cold and the banks were steep and muddy. But he didn't want to discourage her. He loved the *idea* of swimming nude with Jenny, even if it didn't seem too practical. Thoughts of his ill-fated fishing trip raised the hairs on his neck again, but the *other* thoughts that now flitted through his mind pushed those darker thoughts to the side.

Eventually the blacktop road turned to gravel and Pete had to slow down on the dusty, wash boarded road.

"How far *is* it to the river?" Jenny asked anxiously.

"It's only a little over three miles from town."

"I've never been out here before. Are you sure you know where you're going?"

"It's a straight shot, for Pete's sake," he grumbled. "It's not like we're going to get lost."

"What if we get stuck or something?"

"I'll turn around if it gets muddy. Trust me," he said stiffly. "I've been there before. It's no big deal."

She touched the back of his neck with her delicate finger tips. "Don't get grumpy," she said. "I'm sure we'll be fine. It's just seems so…isolated."

"I thought you wanted to be alone."

"I do," she said hesitantly. "But, well, I'm sure you've seen enough horror movies to know that a place like that is where the bad guy jumps out of the woods with an axe, or something."

Pete laughed, but behind his laugh, lay the same strange foreboding he'd felt that night on the river.

Spooked by his own thoughts, he decided he didn't want to go to the river and he began looking for a side road, or a wide spot in the road where he could turn around. Before he found a place though, the road turned abruptly to the left, paralleling the levee. They had arrived. Now he was committed. The river lay only a few hundred feet ahead of them.

"Oh look!" she exclaimed, as he hesitantly drove up on the levee and stopped. "The full moon is just coming up. I love the way the light reflects on the water. It's actually rather romantic. We won't even need a flashlight to find our way to the river."

"Stay put for a minute," he said as he opened his driver's-side door. "I think there's an old two-track road that will take us closer to the water."

A soft, humid breeze, carrying with it the heavy scents of river mud and decaying vegetation, rippled through the brush as Pete slid out of the car. He shivered, but it wasn't because he was cold. He was excited, but terrified at the same time.

His memory served him well. Just ahead of them, the headlights illuminated a vague set of wheel tracks meandering down off the levee. He hesitated, trying to convince himself to stay. What would she do if he chickened out now?

He reluctantly got back behind the wheel and eased the car down the steep hillside towards the river.

"Are you sure we're on a road?" Jenny asked anxiously. "I can't see a thing."

"Trust me," he said. "I know where I'm going."

"That's the second time tonight you asked me to trust you. Maybe I shouldn't."

Jenny gasped when she felt the front end of the car dip sharply towards the water where the levee met the river's high-water mark.

Not wanting to get stuck in the mud on the riverbank, he stopped, backed up, and maneuvered his old car through a multi-point turn in the clutching brush until his headlights shone back up the two-track behind them.

Throughout the entire turn-around, Jenny sat on the edge of her seat, gasping with fright each time he shifted gears and changed directions.

When he finally stopped, and turned off the ignition

she breathed a deep sigh of relief and settled back into her seat. He flipped off the headlights and darkness smothered them. Then out of the blackness, came that all-to-familiar feeling of dread. Goosebumps stood out on his arms. A tightness pressed in on his chest. He wondered if Jenny was feeling the same thing. If she was, she was probably thinking it had something to do with the un-nerving turn-around he'd just made on the steep riverbank. He knew If he asked, she'd probably freak out and want to leave, and he wasn't ready to do that—just yet.

They sat in eerie silence for a few long seconds while their eyes adjusted to the pale moonlight.

"Let's go check out the river." Jenny said, her voice dripping with tension.

The dome light flashed on and she was out of the car before Pete could protest. He hurriedly fumbled a small flashlight out of the jockey box. Thoughts of swimming nude with Jenny excited him. Running across a snake in the dark didn't.

"Hang on," he called out, just loud enough to be heard over the fluttering leaves. I've got a flashlight." He stopped before he said anything about snakes.

Using the flashlight, they picked their way through the tall grass and weeds until they stood on the bare, muddy riverbank.

She hesitated for a few seconds as she looked out across the river, but then she looked up at him and drew a deep breath. "This is so naughty," she giggled as she unzipped her dress. "Be a gentleman and turn off your light."

He turned off the flashlight and followed her lead. A few moments later all their clothes lay draped across the bushes behind them, and they stood naked in the silvery moonlight.

"The moon is brighter than I thought it'd be," she laughed nervously. "Don't stare."

She took his hand and held on tightly as they made their way down the steep, muddy riverbank to the water's edge.

Thoughts of skinny dipping in the old river may have seemed exciting enough, but the ankle-deep mud and the vicious swarms of mosquitos that attacked them—in spite of the breeze—soon brought them back to reality.

"I can't do this!" she shrieked, as she swatted at the pests. "I'm going to have bug bites in places where the sun never shines."

They turned around and struggled back up the river bank through the sticky mud.

"Let's get dressed in the car," she said anxiously as she plucked her clothes off the bushes. "We're going to be eaten alive,"

Once inside the car, Pete turned on the dome light and they spent the next few moments smashing all the mosquitos they could find—and then they noticed each other, and he turned off the light.

- - -

A while later, a brief flash of light, coming through the back window, briefly lit up the car's worn interior.

"Pete!" Jenny hissed anxiously. "Somebody's out there with a flashlight."

Pete sat bolt upright in the seat and glanced in the rearview mirror.

"That's not a flashlight!" he said as he spun around to look out the back window. "It's too big. It looks like a spot-light, and it's on the river. The way it's bouncing, it's proba-bly just somebody in an airboat."

"Let's get out of here!" she squealed.

"We're naked! If it's an airboat, it can't come up here on the levee."

"I don't like this," she cried, her voice bordering on hysteria. "Let's go. We can stop on the way back to town and get dressed."

Uttering a frustrated sigh, Pete twisted the ignition key, the motor roared to life, and moments later they were slowly rocking along the rough two-track on their way back to the main road.

Jenny turned around in her seat to look behind them. "It's following us!" she shrieked.

"That's impossible!" Pete yelled as her panic filled up his own senses. "Just seconds ago, it was on the river."

"I'm telling you, it's right behind us!"

Pete turned his eyes away from the twisting two-track just long enough to glance in the rear view. She was right! The blinding light was nearly on his bumper. Even though the light had clearly come from across the river, now it was swinging slightly from side to side, as if someone was holding it in their hand and running along behind them. Panic over-took him and instead of following the two-track, he turned the car straight towards the main road and stomped the gas petal to the floor. The car bounced wildly over hazards that the vague two-track had steered them safely around before.

Suddenly a dark figure rose up out of the bushes in

front of them.

Pete slammed on the brakes.

"What are you doing?" She screamed.

"There's a man!"

"Hit him!" she shrieked.

Pete jammed the foot feed to the floor again. The car lurched forward and then slammed into some unseen object hidden by the brush. The jarring impact killed the engine, and the headlights went out.

Before he could grab the ignition key to restart the engine, someone yanked his driver-side door open and rough hands dragged him out of the car. Penny's frantic screams filled the night air. The light behind them was gone, and the dome light was dead, but he could tell by her screams that someone had her as well. He fought with all the strength his adrenaline-laced muscles could muster, but in spite of that, he couldn't break free. Then someone pulled a rough bag over his head and drew a chord tightly around his neck to hold it in place.

Over the sounds of his own curses, Jenny's blood curdling, effort-filled screams continued to split the night air.

"Who are you?" he bellowed. "What do you want?"

Nobody answered.

Then someone yanked his arms behind him and bound them tightly together.

Jenny had quit screaming, but she hadn't quit fighting. He could hear the sounds of her frantic struggle nearby. Then those sounds began moving away. They were taking her somewhere.

Before he could say another word, they began half dragging him after her. The rough, tangled brush tore at his bare legs and feet as he tried to fight. Blind panic swept over him.

"What do you want?" He screamed at the top of his lungs.

No one answered. His captor's hands felt like ice on his bare arms. In spite of the fight he'd put up, they weren't even breathing heavily. Who were they? Were they even human? He remembered the cold eerie feeling that night on the river, and now he felt the same palpable dread all around him—amplified ten-fold. He wanted to scream again, but knew it wouldn't do any good. His captors, whoever they were, evidently already had a destination in mind, and screaming wouldn't deter them.

Long brutal minutes passed as they dragged him along. Fighting was futile so he stumbled along with them to avoid being dragged. He longed for a pair of Levi's. The skin on his legs was being torn to shreds.

Then he could smell wood smoke. He wanted to cry out, but fear paralyzed his throat. They must have a camp. Whatever they planned to do with them was near at hand. Memories of other abduction stories he'd heard on the news, or read about in the papers, raced through his mind. Nearly every time the man was bludgeoned to death or killed in some heinous manner, while they had their way with the woman. At least *his* agony would be short lived. Terror struck his heart when he realized what they obviously had in store for her.

Soon he could hear the sharp crackling of a roaring fire. Then the brush that had been clutching at his legs was gone and he could feel firm earth beneath his bare feet. He fought them again, but the hands shoved him brutally backwards against the rough bark of a tree, where one of them held him while the other lashed his upper torso tightly against the tree trunk.

He tried to call out to Jenny, but no sounds came from his mouth.

"Pete!" Jenny screamed from nearby. Her plea was muffled. They'd evidently pulled a bag over her head as well. "Where are you? What do they want?"

Again, he tried to answer, but couldn't.

"Talk to me, Pete. I'm scared!" she cried frantically.

He wanted to shout out to her, to tell her she wasn't alone, but he was mute. Was it fear that had slammed his throat shut, or some unseen power? They'd put bags over their heads. Why would they do that if they weren't going to let them go. In his mind, he was convinced that once they'd had their fun—whatever that entailed—they'd let them go. That small fact gave him some hope.

He swallowed hard, cleared his throat, and tried again and again to simply scream her name. Pain ripped through his throat. The harder he tried, the more intense the pain became until consciousness nearly fled, and he stopped trying.

Then he could hear the muffled thuds of more logs being hurled into the fire, and in a few short minutes, the flames roared even higher and the heat nearly seared his naked skin. Through the small holes in the bag's coarse weave, he could see the leaping orange flames of an enormous fire.

As the crackling flames intensified the unmistakable sounds of stomping feet pounded the packed earth around the fire, creating a distinct, eerie rhythm. The dancers' shadows randomly blocked his view of the fire. Then a strong chorus of unintelligible chants—almost song-like—rose up and flowed all around him on the smoky air. There had to be dozens of voices. In a way they sounded human. In other ways they didn't.

Jenny screamed, only this time her voice wasn't muffled by the bag.

"Pete, I can see them!" she raged. "They're horrible!"

The small comfort he'd taken only moments earlier by thinking about the bag, fled when he realized they weren't going to let them go! He struggled frantically to free himself, but he was bound so tightly to the tree, that all he could move was his head.

"Leave me alone!" she screamed again—louder this time—"don't touch me!"

The dark rumble of chanting voices, intertwined by Jenny's increasingly frantic screams, droned on. It seemed like it would never end. Then the tempo and the volume of the unearthly song increased, drowning out Jenny's shrieks altogether, until it reached an unbelievable crescendo that even drowned out the sounds of the crackling fire.

Then…silence.

Jenny screamed again, but this time her screams were not the screams of fear, they were screams of unquenchable pain - not unlike a wild rabbit, caught in a predator's jaws.

Then as suddenly as the chants stopped, her screams caught in her throat and ceased.

A frenzied unintelligible roar of approval arose from the unseen crowd, and the chanting began again. Moments later he could smell burning hair.

His blinding fear, the chanting, Jenny's screams, the unmistakable stench of burning hair, and finally the deluge of guilt over what he had done, crushed his mind. As the last few shreds of consciousness drifted away, all he could hear was chanting and crackling flames.

- - -

Sometime later Pete slowly became aware of sensations and sounds around him. They seemed familiar, but he couldn't quite focus. Then through the grogginess that still restrained his mind, he remembered the cold, rough hands and lashed out, trying to fight off whoever held him.

There was nobody there.

Then he realized that he was fully dressed and seated behind his car's steering wheel. The sack, and the chords binding his wrists were gone. The car's motor was running.

Hoping it had all been a horrible nightmare, he spun his head to look over at Jenny's side of the car. She was gone.

Through his foggy mind, he found the clock on the dashboard. It was nearly three AM! His headlights shone on a graveled road ahead of him, but there was nothing unique about what he saw. He searched the horizon. What appeared to be the town's lights twinkled in the darkness far off to his right. He vaguely knew where he was now. But he was a long way from the river—where he'd last seen Jenny.

Suddenly the sharp ping from his cell phone split the night.

He found his phone on the floor, drew it to him, and pressed the answer button.

"Pete?" his dad's voice rang out.

He tried to respond, but words refused to come.

"Pete," his father pleaded. "Can you hear me? Where are you! It's after three in the morning! We've been trying to call you since twelve-thirty!"

He tried to answer. He needed to say something. But when he forced his throat to respond, all that came out of his mouth was a mournful wail. He wanted to tell his dad where he was, that they'd gone to the river, that something had happened, and that Jenny was gone—but his thoughts refused to flow through his mouth.

"I can hear you!" his father exclaimed, panic stressing his voice. "Don't hang up! We'll track your phone."

Horrible, vivid memories flooded Pete's brain. He remembered the chanting crescendo, Jenny's screams of agony, and the stench of burning hair. The raw thoughts robbed him of conscious thought. Uncontrollable sobs racked his body. He could still vaguely hear his father's voice, but he couldn't tell where it was coming from—and he couldn't answer.

- - -

When Pete awoke, he was lying on his back in a sterile white room. His wrists and ankles were bound. An IV was taped to his right arm, and a pair of rubbery tubes wrapped around his face holding an oxygen apparatus against his nose. A small cluster of electronic monitors hung on a stand near the foot of his bed. Several wires attached to his chest and neck led to an electronic console of sorts, sitting on a metal stand beneath the screens. A man dressed in white scrubs sat on a chair at his bedside, carefully watching his every movement.

"Hello Pete," the man said softly. "How do you feel?"

He tried to speak—he wanted to speak—he struggled to do so, but no words came.

The man slid forward in his chair, looked into Pete's eyes and asked his question again.

"Where am I?" Pete's mind responded. He could feel his lips moving, but no sounds came from his mouth.

The man noticed his response.

"That's good," he said softly. "At least you're hearing me now. I'm going to tell you a few things and watch your monitors. Then, depending on your response, I'll know where we can go from here. First let me tell you that you're in the psychiatric ward in the hospital."

The man glanced at the monitors and jotted something on a pad of paper as Pete briefly struggled against his restraints; then he looked back at Pete and continued.

"It's Thursday. You've been with us for nearly two weeks. You've had a mental collapse of some sort. We have to assume it was from the trauma you lived through when you murdered your girlfriend."

Pete struggled violently to free his hands and feet. He tried to scream out. "*I didn't do it!*" Although he couldn't describe who had, or what they'd actually done to her, he knew he hadn't killed her!

Tears flooded Pete's eyes as he thrashed his head back and forth on the hard pillow. Deep uncontrollable sobs racked his chest.

The man quickly picked up a syringe lying on a small table at the foot of his bed and inserted the needle into a tube feeding his IV. Pete felt a warm sensation rush up his arm, and then—nothingness.

- - -

A nightmare rumbled through his brain in slow motion. They were crashing through the brush in his car. The light was nearly on them. Then he saw the man—perhaps for the first time—illuminated by his car's headlights, and by the bright light that had followed them from the river. His head and body were completely hidden behind a hooded black robe, but his face was bare. Dark, piercing eyes peered at him from between the folds of his hood. He held out his left arm towards them as if to stop the lunging car with some unseen power. A half smile curled his pale lips. His countenance extruded pure evil.

- - -

A voice entered his mind. "Pete," a male voice was speaking. "Pete, can you hear me?"

He concentrated on the voice and slowly he became aware of his body again. He was still lying on his back with both wrists and ankles restrained to the bed.

"We've given you some medication to help you wake up," the man continued. "Try to focus. Can you understand what I'm saying?"

Pete couldn't open his eyes, but somehow, he found enough control of himself this time to nod his head.

"I'm doctor Carlson," the voice continued. "Can you open your eyes?"

Pete searched for, and finally found his eyes among a rush of sensory information that was flooding his brain; and when he opened them, he found himself in the same sterile room, but this time the lights were low, and there were others in the room besides the doctor.

"Hello, Pete," the doctor's now-familiar voice said again. "The last time we spoke you were in pretty bad shape.

You seem to be a little better now. It's been a month. You should be stable enough to answer a few questions. We've moved you to a new facility. Can you talk?"

Pete tried his voice. A crackling sound came from his throat, but he couldn't make words. When he opened his mouth wider, his chapped lips split in a couple of places. He could taste blood. His thick dry tongue stuck to the roof of his mouth.

"Officer Jackson, from the sheriff's department would like to talk to you," Carlson said, moving away.

A new man abruptly filled his vision. This man appeared in Pete's drug-addled mind to be at least ten feet tall. He wore the brimmed hat and the dark brown uniform of the sheriff's department, and an enormous gold badge, appearing to be the size of a dinner plate, stood out on his chest.

"Pete," the man said as he sat on a stool by Pete's bedside. "I need to ask you some questions. Do you remember what happened after the homecoming dance?"

Pete's breath caught in his throat as he remembered the fire and Jenny's frenzied screams.

"You had blood on your hands and clothes. Jenny's clothes were in the back seat. There was river mud on your floor mats, and brush and dirt jammed into the undercarriage of your car. That sent us out to the levee. We found where you'd driven down to the river. We used dogs to follow your scent to a campsite. We found her charred bones buried in the ashes of your bonfire. There was a skull. The dental records matched Jenny's."

He paused to let what he had said sink in.

"We found a bloody knife stuck in a tree," he said at

last. "It had your bloody finger prints on it. We'd like to know where you got it. We've never seen anything like it."

Pete yanked violently against his restraints. The officer said nothing while he struggled.

"Did you actually think you could get rid of her body that way?" he asked after Pete quit thrashing around. "I'll admit you built a hell of a fire, but not even a gas crematorium can burn up all the bones."

In spite of being conscious, the horrific vision suddenly appeared in Pete's mind. He could see the campfire and hear the incoherent chanting. Then Jenny's unearthly screams and the stench of burning hair pushed him back into unconsciousness.

- - -

They brought him back out a few days later and kept him on a regimen of little pink pills, bed rest, and daily visits from the psychiatrist.

Through it all, they kept him chained to his bed. An orderly visited regularly to change his diapers but he saw no one else.

The horrific vision tormented what little sleep came to him. Now though, when the incoherent chanting began, it always brought him fully awake. He couldn't live through the ending again.

- - -

They moved him to another new room on a sunny spring morning. He could dress and feed himself, and although he was no longer restrained, the door and the wire-reinforced windows in his stark white room were always kept locked.

His parents visited him from time to time. His mom cried a lot when they came. He wanted to tell them his side of the story—the story that was locked up inside his brain—but he couldn't. All he could do was stare blankly at them and listen while they talked.

He was lying awake one night, wanting to sleep but afraid to do so—because that's when the nightmares came—when a familiar but terrible dread crept over him. He knew someone was watching him. He slid quietly out of his bed and crawled to his window. He didn't want to look out, but he couldn't turn away. When he peered through the glass a tall figure dressed in a long, hooded robe was standing just outside his window. The perimeter lights partially illuminated his face. Piercing black eyes stared through the window at him. Scenes from the river flashed through his mind and a mournful, primal wail began somewhere deep inside him—finally breaking free—piercing the night.

# VOICES

Jeffrey W. Kramer

The unfortunate case of Paul Bond, not his real name of course, will not leave my memory. I have treated many disturbed people over the years, indeed I have made it my life's work. But there are limits to our science. The specter haunting him would not be exorcised, the shadow darkening the life of this troubled man would not be lifted. He suffered a torment so deep it destroyed him. In the end, I did what I could.

I remember well the day I first met him. It was a stifling afternoon in late August when he walked up the steps to the ground-floor office of my old Victorian home in The Avenues. I could see him through the front window, standing in the shade of the old Maple trees, his face flushed with the heat. He hesitated before knocking softly on the door.

"I'm here to see Dr. Alex Keller," he said. "I have an appointment."

"I am she," I said. "You must be Paul Bond."

"You're a woman," he said with surprise as I stood aside to let him in. "I wasn't expecting that."

He wasn't the first person to make that mistake. The name was my father's idea. His friends thought he wanted a boy. "No," my mother insisted, "he just wants her to be treated like one." It doesn't always work out that way, so I like to take advantage of the name when I can.

I motioned him to a winged armchair on one side of the old stone fireplace and I took the other. He looked around the room, craning his neck at the high ceiling, studying its plaster ornaments, and looking uncomfortably at the antique furniture my grandmother had given me. He was a coarse-featured man in his forties with a heavy dark beard and broad shoulders. He wore old blue jeans and a plain button-down shirt, now soaked with patches of sweat.

"I never been to a shrink before," he began, "but I got to do something. It's gettin' so I can't sleep. And strange things is startin' to happen."

His eyes were dark and sunken, but not so deep I couldn't see the blaze of fear in them.

"What things?" I asked him.

"I see things," he said. "And I hear things."

"Tell me when this all began," I said to him. "And you need to tell me everything."

As he told me his story, he leaned toward me, as if someone might otherwise overhear him. His rough hands were folded together tightly. He explained, how years earlier he had met a woman—I'll call her Sally—at a whiskey bar on Salt Lake City's Main Street. She was sitting alone. He took the stool next to her and after a while they began to talk. That night he went home with her and they had sex. He told me this shyly. It was plain he wasn't comfortable talking about such things with a woman.

I did what I could to put his mind at ease. He began to tell me more of their story, haltingly at first, and with his eyes fixed on the rug at our feet. They were wild in their sex together—rough, and much as I take pride in being a professional, my face must have betrayed me. "It was her idea," he insisted. Although I had my doubts, I did not say so.

The two met again the following night and soon they were seeing one another regularly. She worked as a waitress in one of the upscale chain restaurants downtown and made good money. "The convention business," Paul explained, his voice a little angry. "Those guys are here without their wives, and they can't ever resist a pretty girl."

He pulled out his phone and showed me a picture. A woman stood posing in a field of wildflowers on a high hillside overlooking the Salt Lake Valley, blond hair gleaming in the sunlight. Her eyes were hidden behind dark sunglasses and her lips were colored a deep red. She wore a yellow tee shirt stretched tightly across ample breasts.

"She was a nice-looking woman," he said, his pride evident as I handed him back the phone.

"Was?" I asked.

He shifted in his chair and studied the rug again before answering.

"I was getting to that part," he said. "It's kinda' hard to tell."

Now, I'm trained not to judge people. It's not the way to help them. My training tells me what to say, but it doesn't cut off how I feel. What he told me that afternoon hollowed me out a little. Even now, I don't like to think about everything he told me that day. But this, more or less, is how our conversation went.

"We was getting it on that night," he said. "You know, like usual."

"I'm not sure I do know," I said. "Why don't you tell me?"

"Well I already said she liked it rough. So I was riding her hard, kind of slamming into her, and she starts screaming at me, calling me names. So I slap her a few times, and she don't stop."

"You say she liked it that way?"

"Sure. It was part of the routine, you know?"

"Go on."

"So's I put my hand over her mouth, but she bites it, and now I start screaming." I watched his face closely as he relived the moment. His mouth was twisted in a grimace and his eyes narrowed. "Then I grabbed her around the throat like this." He held up his large hands, curled like two giant vices. "And I start squeezing." He was panting now and his face was flushed.

I gripped my chair, my knuckles going white, just as his must have done that terrible night.

"She starts pounding on me, bucking like a bronco. And I'm like going crazy, crazy hard, you know?"

"What happened?" I said, my voice suddenly hoarse, "Tell me you let her go."

He shook his head slowly, his eyes burning with the memory. "So's then I explode, you know, and it's off the charts. I'm sweatin' and breathin' like I just run up two flights of stairs." He was looking straight ahead, his eyes ablaze. "Then I rolls over, and she don't move. 'Sally,' I says, 'Sally, come on.' But she don't respond." He pounded the arm of his chair. "Goddammit!" he shouted. "She didn't goddamn move."

He started to shake then, slowly at first, until his whole body heaved. He covered his face with his hands, sniffling and drawing in short, violent breaths.

"Did you kill her?"

"She was dead, I know that. I read later in the papers maybe it was her heart gave out."

"What do you think?"

"Mostly I try not to think about it."

"Were you questioned?"

"No. I guess she had plenty of men visitors. The cops didn't seem too interested."

"Why are you telling me about this now?"

"She's come back."

My notes at this point show my diagnosis was "schizophrenia" and I suspected the cause. The next step was to learn more about my patient's delusions and hallucinations. I knew I had to be careful, at least in the beginning, not to question whether they were real. I needed to earn his confidence.

"How do you know this?" I asked.

"She visits me at night."

"A dream, perhaps?"

"No, she's right there in the room. Just staring at me with big angry eyes. She don't ever <u>say</u> nothin'."

"You said you hear things too?"

"Screams. I hear her screaming sometimes, awful just like that night. Maybe when I'm walking down the street, or maybe just watchin' TV. It jerks my head around. But I don't see her then. It's like she's hiding somewhere."

He was leaning forward in his chair with his elbows on his knees, holding his head in both hands. I could see he was suffering, but I was thinking of Sally.

I gave him a prescription for an antipsychotic medication and I told him he must come to see me again. He told me he would do so.

For the next several months he came to see me regularly. Sally's visits, he said, were becoming more frequent. He would tell me about them in vivid detail. They were taking a dreadful toll on him. He was a big-boned man, but he began wasting away before me. His clothes hung loosely from his frame, like faded rags on a scarecrow. I insisted that he keep seeing me and I doubled the dose of his medication.

Fall gave way to winter. The big maple trees clung to their last withering leaves, their barren limbs etched against increasingly somber skies. Paul continued to see me faithfully. I can still see him dragging his feet slowly up my front steps, big shoulders hunched forward, his head bowed in the bleak November light.

One especially cold day we sat in our chairs in front of the hearth, where I had lit a small fire to battle the fierce chill. He held out his hands to warm them, then looked up at me with dark empty eyes. His cheeks were sunken and his grizzled face had lost all color. The room was aglow with radiant heat but I could see him shivering.

"She won't leave me be," he said, his voice weak. "Not ever now."

"Go on."

"When I go to the bar, I see her sitting there, watching

me. Or I see her face in a crowd. I can hear her moaning. And sometimes, I'll be sittin' on the couch, I hear her talking to me. I turn up the TV and I can still hear her talking to me."

"What does she say?"

"'Why Paul?' That's all she ever says. Just 'Why Paul?'"

"Do you answer her?"

"Oh God, yes. I've said 'I'm sorry' a thousand times. I told her I didn't mean it. It doesn't matter. She just stares at me, shaking her head. Then at night, I can hear her crying. Or I wake up because I can feel her poundin' on me."

"She's real to you, isn't she, Paul?"

"It's no dream. I can tell you that." He hung his head down, took in a deep breath and let it out slowly. "It ain't no fuckin' dream."

"Have you been taking your medication, Paul?"

"Just like you said. But things is gettin' worse, not better."

"You need to give it time," I told him. "With time, the medication will do its work."

The truth was that his condition had become much worse. But I didn't want to tell him that. I wanted him to keep seeing me, to believe in the treatment. That's also when I gave him a second medication.

Other patients filled my days but Paul was never far from my mind. I was looking through his file one day when a new idea came to me. It was unconventional but I thought it could be useful. I had become familiar with Paul's routines. We talked often about his life and he described the places he would go and where he would see Sally. Perhaps if I saw those places for myself, I might gain some insights. Maybe I would see some of the visual triggers that brought on his episodes with Sally.

So, one day in early December, with wisps of snow swirling under a shadowy and threatening sky, I turned up the collar on my coat and headed out to see Paul's world. I drove past his apartment and cruised the streets he often walked. Then I stopped at the whiskey bar on Main Street where he had first met Sally, and it was there he often returned. Indeed, I had suggested to him that he do so.

It was early evening. A warm glow radiated from the bar into the dusky street like a welcoming beacon. Inside, soft yellow light bathed the dark woods and gleaming brass. The sweetness of beer and aged whiskeys mingled in the air. I could see why Paul liked to come here. I headed for an empty table in the corner, ordered a glass of white wine, and sat watching the work-day crowd gather.

It wasn't long before Paul came in. He moved furtively toward an empty stool at the bar, glancing once over his shoulder. When he was settled, he raised a cautious finger toward the bartender. The young man nodded and brought him a squat glass filled with ice. He filled the glass nearly to the rim with a deep amber whiskey. Paul took a long pull from his drink and set it down carefully. Then, suddenly, he snapped his head around. I could see him staring at the woman seated alone at the end of the bar. His lips were moving, as though he were speaking to her, but his words were lost to me in the din of the crowded room.

I hurried over to him, touching him lightly on the shoulder. He flinched and spun around, peering at me with wild unseeing eyes. I rested my hand on his back and could feel him shaking.

"Paul, it's me, Dr. Keller."

"Oh, oh, yes," he said. Then he gripped my arm. "Do you see her?"

"That's Sally, isn't it?" I said to him, following his eyes toward the woman at the end of the bar. She had blonde hair, but it fell across her face, obscuring it as she looked down at the screen of her cell phone. The bartender set a pint of beer down in front of her.

He nodded his head. "Did you hear her?"

"No, Paul. What did she say?"

"Paaauuulll," he said, drawing out his name in a low voice that sounded like a moan. "Paaauuulll." He shook his head and took another long pull from his whiskey. "Like she's in some kind of pain."

"You poor man," I said to him.

He poured down the last of his whiskey and signaled the bartender for another.

"Did you take your medications today?" I asked. "How are you feeling?"

"Tired, real tired. It's like I can't sleep anymore. And I get so jittery." He looked anxiously toward the bartender. "The whiskey calms me down some, I guess." The man poured another drink and slid it over to him. Paul drank half of it before setting the glass back down.

A movement at the end of the bar again pulled his attention. The woman was on her feet. Paul stared at her as she gathered her purse and walked toward us, still looking down at her phone. It was hard to see her face, but I caught a glimpse of bright red lipstick.

"Sally," Paul called. His voice was strained and urgent. "Sally!"

The woman seemed not to hear him. She passed by us quickly, close enough for the scent of her perfume to wash over us.

"Did you smell that?" he said, gripping my arm again, harder than before. "That's Sally! That's her perfume!"

"Yes, it is, isn't it?" I said. He had told me about it often.

He hopped off his stool to follow her as she disappeared through the door. I had to gently restrain him.

"Paul," I said, "you can't follow her. She's not from this world."

"But she's real. You saw her."

"She's real to you Paul," I said, easing him back to his seat. "But you can't ever have her again."

When I left him that day he was plainly in great distress. I knew the danger to him would only increase with the holidays, when loneliness and despair tend to worsen the dysphoria of the mentally afflicted. You may think I should have prescribed in-patient treatment. Instead, I made him promise he would come to see me again.

The day of our next scheduled appointment was fiercely cold, with a brisk north wind rattling the windows and scouring the icy streets. There were colorful holiday lights strung on the light poles and decorating the nearby homes, but they struggled against the gloom of that dreary winter day. My parlor was quiet but for the ticking of an old-fashion clock. I waited for him before the fire. I waited, but he never came.

Christmas passed and then the New Year's holiday, yet I heard nothing from him. My phone messages and texts to him went unanswered. I began to think I might never hear from him again, when the phone rang one day in late January. I was surprised to hear his voice.

"Dr. Keller," he began slowly, "I know I was supposed to see you over the holidays. I wonder if I can come see you now. I think it's important."

"Of course," I told him. We made an appointment for that same afternoon.

When he arrived at my door I scarcely recognized him. His face was hidden by a thick beard that had spread like a wild bush down his neck and up toward his blackened, listless eyes. His clothes were disheveled and the odor of his unwashed body enveloped us. He was but a thin and frail reminder of the man I had first seen six months before. I held his elbow to steady him as I guided him to his usual armchair by the fireplace.

"Paul," I said. "You poor man. Tell me what's happened to you."

"That medicine you gave me ain't workin' so well. I still can't sleep much, not without some whisky to help me, anyway. And Sally, she won't never let me alone now. And now I see her laughin' at me."

"What's she laughing at, Paul?"

My question only increased his agitation. He shifted in his chair, looked away, then opened his mouth to speak, but the words caught in his throat. He swallowed and tried again.

"I can't do it no more," he said, looking at me with

pleading eyes. "You know, the sex thing. It ain't workin'."

"Do you mean sexual dysfunction, Paul?"

He dropped his head and nodded almost imperceptibly.

"That's to be expected, Paul. You need to keep taking your medications."

"I do, mostly. But some days I feel better when I don't."

"That's an illusion, Paul. You need to keep taking them. You know I've told you that."

He nodded and remained silent.

"What else is Sally saying to you, Paul? Is there anything more?"

He started rubbing his hands back and forth along his thighs, staring at the floor.

"Paul," I said to him, "you need to look at me."

He raised his head slowly, as though it were a great weight.

"'Paul' she says to me, 'Paul you ain't got no right to keep on livin'. You ain't got no right.'"

"What do you think, Paul?"

"I...I don't..." He squeezed his eyes shut and his lips began to quiver. His body started to shake, gently at first and then more violently. He cried softly.

"Paul," I said, "you did a terrible thing, didn't you?"

His head moved slowly up and down, but he would not look at me.

"You need to come to terms with it, Paul. You know that, don't you?"

He was sobbing now, no longer trying to hide it.

"Answer me, Paul. You need to make things right, don't you?"

"I didn't mean her no harm," he said between sobs. "Sally, she knows I was soft on her. Why don't she leave me alone?"

He hunched over in his chair, clutching his head, his shoulders trembling. I watched silently. After a while, I helped him to his feet. He was still shaking as he pulled his coat tightly around him before stepping out my door. I watched him stumble out into the harsh and unforgiving winter night.

February brought a cold spell but the snow was unrelenting. I didn't go out much, not wishing to stray far from the warmth of my fire. I would often sit in the flickering light, feeling the heat on my face and watching the snow fall. I saw other clients in the weeks following Paul's last visit, but I did not see him.

When the news came, it did not take me by surprise. The report in the *Tribune* was brief. A male aged 43 was killed when he stepped in front of a moving Trax car on Main Street. He was knocked to the rails and dismembered when the train passed over him. The police identified him as Paul Bond of Salt Lake City. He had a note in his pocket linking him to the death years before of one Sally Tucker, a local waitress. She was found dead in her apartment from what previously was believed to be natural causes.

As I write this, the first buds are showing on the maple trees and tulips in bright shades of red and yellow are waiving gently to me outside my window. They remind me of Sally, with her lips shining and her hair glistening so many years ago on that beautiful spring hillside. She didn't deserve to die. Should Paul have lived? There are limits to our science, limits to what we know, of course, but these are not the only limits. We have choices to make when we see the evil in men's souls. And when the voices speak to us, we must listen.

## GHOST CAVE

C.H. Lindsay

Billy hid his Goldwing behind a clump of scrub oak, grabbed the rope, and hiked up the box canyon until he found the large dead pine tree and metal hatch that marked the entrance to Ghost Cave. He dropped his pack and pulled out the lock picks he'd taken from his dad's toolkit. His friends weren't going to stop him this time. He'd show them he wasn't afraid. Twice before he suggested coming to the cave and twice the others decided to go somewhere safer. But now, there was money on the line. And his reputation.

He tested one pick after another until he found one the right size for the padlock. All the while he heard Ashney beg him to ignore the neighborhood bullies, to stay with her. Maricón, they'd called him. Cobarde. Tonto. Not even the memory of Ashney's nails digging into his arm or her skin paling to milk chocolate would stop him tonight.

The tool caught in the keyhole and he swore. "Careful," he warned himself. His dad would take a belt to him if he broke it. He took a deep breath, let it out slowly, and tried again, listening as he gently moved the pick until he heard the click of the lock. There. "Easy peasy." Once the padlock was off, the chain quickly followed. "If they didn't want anyone to get in, they should have made it more difficult."

He put the picks, lock, and chain in the small pocket of his backpack, then opened the hatch. The stench of mud, limestone, and something sickly sweet assaulted him. He always forgot how bad caves smelled, but he would get used to it soon enough.

He tied the rope to the dead pine tree, tested it to be sure it would hold, then put on his climbing gear. He checked his harness to make sure the carabiners were hooked up properly and dropped the rope into the hole.

His jeans and flannel shirt would be enough protection tonight. From everything he'd read about the cave, it was a moderately difficult climb, then a fifteen-foot drop to the cave floor.

He only had to stay long enough to take a few photos, pocket some rock samples, and climb back topside. Nothing he hadn't done a dozen times before. Never alone, but he knew he could do it. Besides, once he won the bet, they'd stop calling him a coward.

He strapped on his helmet, checked that the light worked, and clipped onto the rope. "On belay," he said— more out of habit than anything. He listened to make sure no one was coming to stop him. Then he sat on the edge of the hole, slipped on his gloves, tightened the rope around his waist, and climbed down to the first ledge.

Billy felt his body relax now that he was finally on his way. Getting into the cave itself was usually the hardest part of the descent. Now he just had to keep his cool and take it one step at a time.

He quickly got into a routine: climb down to the rope, drop the coil down the next opening, crawl or climb to where it landed, then adjust the rope and do it again.

Billy wondered how long he'd been in the cave. He paused to check his progress against the map. Not far enough. He needed to pick up his pace or he wouldn't get home in time. His folks would probably ground him for a month. Would they call the police, or assume he was getting into trouble again? Ashney would worry if he didn't show up at school tomorrow.

Or would she? Had she smiled at Luis when Billy took the bet? It looked like she was standing awfully close to him at the party. He shook his head and then thought better of it as it made him a little dizzy. No. He had to be imagining things. She didn't like Luis. Or so she'd told him. "It's the air," he said. "It reeks down here." Saying it out loud helped him get his thoughts straight. Of course Ashney wasn't interested in Luis, it was just his worry about getting stuck in the cave messing with him.

He moved a little faster, still careful about his footing. The rope caught against a rough outcropping of limestone and he gave it a sharp jerk, thinking of Luis. The rope came free, taking a chunk of rock with it. He listened as it crashed down the tunnel, but it didn't go far enough for him to tell how close he was to the main cavern.

He settled into a routine that kept his concentration on his descent until the passage dropped several feet. Billy checked how far it went and grinned. His first real challenge. He pulled the rope tightly around his waist and leaned back to half-walk, half-slide down to the next ledge.

He was almost to the bottom when he found a small opening into a long, low-ceilinged cavern. The light from his headlamp glittered off gypsum flowers and crystalline soda straws. It looked like the inside of a geode. Billy balanced against the far wall so he could pull off one glove and take some pictures. He wouldn't send them just yet. Not until he was out of the cave. Or he'd wait until he was home, then send the pictures. He wanted to see the surprise on their faces when they found out he'd really done it. And then he'd use the fifty bucks to take Ashney to dinner. Or buy her a tattoo. A nice rose on her ankle with his name on it so that Luis would know she was his.

He slipped his phone into his belt pouch, put his glove on, and continued his descent. By now, the scents of the cave were barely noticeable. Even the odd, sweet smell seemed more illusion than reality. Too bad he couldn't find what caused it and take some back with him. It reminded him of when his friends gave him weed. The thought made him chuckle.

As he climbed further down, he became aware of the sound of something scuttling around. Occasionally he'd hear gravel falling. Had to be his imagination. Too long in the absolute blackness around him. He shone his headlamp around, just in case, but he saw nothing. "See? Just my imagination." He hurried a little faster, just in case.

The passage narrowed and he had to crawl on his hands and knees. There was a short, high-pitched whistle up ahead. It was almost the pitch of a teakettle. It startled him and he hit his head on a rock.

He wasn't going to think about the noise. He had to get down, get that stupid picture, and then get out of here. Going up would take longer than coming down and he had to be home before his folks woke up.

He almost missed another sudden drop in the passage. It was only the rope he pushed ahead of him falling that alerted him. It also reminded him that he had to slow down and pay attention.

He heard another noise. It wasn't a whistle this time, or scurrying. It was laughter. Luis, mocking him. "You don't have the cajones. Maricón. In fact, I doubt you have any cajones at all." And then they all laughed. All except Ashney. "I'll show you," Billy hissed. He heard more laughter that turned into the sound of rocks falling.

He checked the map, pleased to see that he was almost there. He turned sideways to get past an outcropping of limestone. And got stuck. He swore in a dozen languages. It made him feel better.

He tried to pull back and make another go of it. And failed. He was truly stuck. Billy twisted and pulled until he had one arm free of his backpack. That allowed him to inch forward, but his pack stayed behind. When he was finally around the rock, he grabbed for the pack. It slipped out of his hands and fell between two rocks. He swore again.

Another teakettle whistled, just out of sight. He shone his headlamp on the rocks to see if he could locate the origin. It had to be from a steam vent, but as far as he knew, there'd been no geothermal activity in the area in at least 300 years.

Something out of the corner of his eye moved. He turned to see a pale, ghostlike image floating in the air for a moment before fading away. It reminded him of Ashney and how she'd paled when he said he was going to Ghost Cave. She believed in ghosts. But there were no such things as ghosts. It was just steam from whatever made the whistle. "So much for trying to scare me," he taunted the darkness.

He twisted around another rock. It gave way and he fell several feet, hitting his head against an outcropping before he got the rope under control. "Stupid, stupid, stupid." It was mistakes like that that got people hurt. Fortunately, his helmet took the brunt of the damage.

Continuing down the passage, Billy saw his backpack in the mud. So, maybe not so stupid. If he hadn't slipped, he would have missed it. He pulled out a granola bar and then slipped the backpack onto his shoulders.

Several rocks clattered onto the ground ahead of him. Out of the corner of his eye, he thought he saw something large and white scurry away. He turned to have a better look, but there was nothing. It had to be steam. That would explain everything, even the sweet odor. "Go away, steamy ghosts," he mocked. His words didn't sound as confident as they should have. He blamed Ashney.

He went down another drop and through a low-ceilinged turn. From what he remembered of the map, he should see the top of the cavern any moment now. The passage opened up and he straightened, brushing against a large spider web. Billy jerked back, and lost his balance. Only by hanging tightly to the rope did he keep from falling, but he still managed to hit his shoulder on a rock. It was the stupid spider's fault. He hated spiders- - -especially ghostly white cave spiders that glowed in his headlamp.

He looked for the spider, but there didn't seem to be one around. He brushed off the web and hurried down another bend, slipping again on the mud and almost losing his grip on the rope. Cave spiders were supposed to be tiny. This one had to be enormous. He had no desire to run into it.

His head throbbed from pain and stress. Somewhere nearby he heard hissing. Or was that just the sound of the silence ringing in his ears? Maybe coming alone wasn't such a good idea.

He negotiated another outcropping of rock and saw the spider. It was as large as a watermelon and ghostly white.

It lunged at him.

Billy threw himself to the side and raised a forearm defensively. The creature grabbed onto it and held on. He screamed and flung the spider against a rock, pulled the rope around him and hurried away. The spider was nowhere to be seen.

Not much later, he came to the end of his rope. He had one shorter one in his backpack and pulled it out. Hopefully it would be enough to finish his journey. He looked around for the spider, but there was no sign of it.

He came to a steep incline and tied the rope to a stalactite and dropped it down a steep incline and began his descent. A small cascade of falling rocks made him look up. The spider was now above him. Its eyes glowed malevolent green in the light from his headlamp as it watched Billy. He cried out and practically slid to the bottom. He picked up the rope and almost ran down the narrow passage and took cover behind a bend.

The tunnel turned again, and there it was. The opening to the giant cavern. He braced himself so he could shine the headlamp down the hole. The light went ten feet into nothing. "Finally." He dropped the remainder of the rope and listened as it hit bottom. He scooted to the edge so he could free climb down.

He turned onto his belly and wiggled backwards until his feet were dangling over the edge. Another high-pitched noise made his ears hurt. He turned his headlamp back down the tunnel and saw the giant spider staring at him. And then he saw dozens of tiny white ones swarm around it and all head towards him.

His scream was almost as high-pitched as the spider's as he threw himself backwards over the ledge

But he didn't get off cleanly. His foot tangled in the knots and he lost his grip. Only his foot kept him from falling.

He regained control of the rope and held himself steady as he maneuvered his foot to free it. But not before the spiders swarmed down his pants leg and began to bite.

Billy screamed and kicked to get them off him, but he only managed to pull his foot free of his shoe.

The rope slipped through his fingers and around his waist. Stalactites and gypsum formations flashed past his headlamp as he fell, landing on his backpack and tumbling down the muddy incline to stop hard against a pile of cave rubble.

Billy tried to move, but his whole body hurt and he couldn't take a deep breath. He heard another squeal. Spiders. He turned his head just enough to see hundreds of them coming at him. The giant white spider dropped onto the ground beside his face. "Tonto," it hissed.

The tiny spiders swarmed over Billy. "Tonto, tonto, tonto," they echoed and bit him. He cried out, but it only allowed the spiders to crawl into his mouth, down his throat, and into his lungs. He wanted to scream, but he couldn't take a breath. He was going to be sick. He was going to die.

The giant spider leaned closer. "Cobarde," it hissed, its fangs dripping venom. As it leaned in to bite him, all faded into a sweet-smelling mist. Ashney was right, he should never have come to Ghost Cave.

# BLANK CHECK

Michael Darling

Killing demons is risky business and a hunter gets just one chance to do it right. One lousy chance to send the thing back to brimstone before a whole lot of death and destruction. Miss that first shot and there would be murders and funerals and apologies and, even worse, a stack of paperwork *en route* to a suspended license.

Realistically, Mark Slocombe was here for the bounty.

He lay prone on the grass in a circle of salt, binoculars trained on the empty building across the park and on the other side of the street. The building was surrounded by a chain link fence with signs proclaiming "Danger" and "Keep Out." If he spotted anything suspicious, however, he'd ignore those signs quicker than diarrhea ignores a sphincter.

Daddy needs a new alimony payment.

3:21 am and something moved. The shadow eased from one pool of darkness to another and Slocombe spotted it after four hours spent lying on the grass, the cold ground sending cold fingers up through his black jeans and his black flannel shirt until his elbows and knees and every part of him in between were damp and shivering. Every scrap of his clothing was natural. No polyester or nylon or anything that would have been a decent barrier to the elements. Manmade materials would have given him away. Made him easier to spot, even behind the protective ring of salt. Demon hunting the old way. The only way. The way that had worked for centuries. This was how his father had hunted and his father's father. It was how he would teach his son to hunt.

He watched the figure in the cloak melt through the gap between the rusted door and the crumbling brick.

This was it.

With as little motion as possible, Slocombe reached for more salt, stiff muscles protesting. He poured a circle in front of him, just inside the circumference of the bigger circle he'd been hunkering in all night. The new circle was only slightly larger than a silver dollar and a silver dollar—real silver—was precisely what he put inside the new circle. On top of the dollar, he put a black feather from a crow and on top of the feather, a yellowing sliver of bone. When he was satisfied with the placement of the objects, he reached out with a cramped arm and with his finger, he pushed a small portion of the salt aside, breaking the larger circle by a fraction of an inch.

More waiting.

Please. Not four hours more.

If necessary, he would wait until dawn. Once the rays of the morning sun painted the tips of the mountains pink, the likelihood of a spell being successful dropped to zero, give or take a decimal point. If the shadowy figure he'd seen entering the building were there for some other kind of activity, it wasn't Slocombe's problem. On the other hand, if they were there for necromancy or summoning, he'd know and somehow find the will to get up from his cushy vacation on the grass to take care of business.

The coin/feather/bone in its shelter of salt sat between him and the abandoned building. The opening he'd created in the larger circle of salt would allow a tiny spyhole through, but there was still a salt barrier between himself and the site. Like using a periscope to track ships on the surface of the ocean, this arrangement allowed him to track magical emanations coming from the building ahead.

It was possible for him to be caught, but it would take a prodigious expert in magic to find him. Or—it had to be said—it would take a demon.

An hour passed.

Then another.

Then the bone twitched. The coin flared red. The feather caught fire.

Time to go.

Slocombe felt his pulse throb in his ears long before any running brought his heart rate up. The excitement always came from the inside when he stretched his aching muscles, stiff from too much time in a fixed, frozen marathon of waiting. He poured more salt over the feather to cover the acrid smell and to hide the magic. Then he scattered everything over the dirt with his shoes. All the while, his blood pressure rose and by the time he trotted across the park with his bag of tools, he was panting like an overweight bulldog.

He reached the gate in the chain link fence and stopped. Something was not right. The gate hadn't been chained shut and the door leading into the building stood ajar. Having one barrier to access standing open would be someone's negligence. Having two felt more like an invitation.

I should get out of here. Right now.

Slocombe had detected magic. Rather, the coin/feather/bone detector had. The problem with magic was differentiation. It was like electricity. The power came in basically one flavor but could be adapted for use in a myriad of ways. The only way Slocombe would know what it had been used for would be to go inside and find out. With the gate and the door standing open, he was smelling a setup.

As he'd told his former business partner, if it looks too good to be true, run away. His former business partner had also been his wife. She'd been very good at running away.

Screw it.

Slocombe backed off. He took a last look and was about to turn when he caught a glimpse of a round face under a thatch of blond hair.

Oscar?

The boy had peered at him and then vanished into the shadows.

This was *really* not right. Oscar, his son, was supposed to be with Slocombe's mom. There was only one way he could be here near a summoning site.

Fanny had brought him.

Fanny. Fanny Teller. The name he wrote on checks month after month. The checks with the alimony and child support. The checks he hoped he wouldn't have to pay much longer. Shouldn't have to pay much longer because ex-wives in an asylum don't collect alimony.

He'd better go in.

Slocombe squeezed through the fence and sidled up to the door that should have been shut but wasn't. He glanced through the gap. There wasn't a lot of hallway but it was illuminated with reflected moonlight tinged with the sickly, jaundiced stain of lights from the neighboring parking lot. He held a piece of carved smoky quartz in one hand to help hide him from searching eyes. Then he took a deep breath and walked through the door.

The ground floor was clear. Not a surprise. Spells usually worked better belowground. Working his way down the dark stairs, pausing halfway to let his eyes adjust, he wondered where Oscar had gone. If it even had been Oscar.

There were other spells. Changeling spells. Glamours.

He paused again at the bottom of the stairs. The space was dim but there were no footprints in the dust, no trace of activity except maybe from rats or cockroaches hoping not to starve.

Up then.

The light improved as Slocombe climbed the stairs. The building had five floors plus the basement. The first floor up from ground level was abandoned and the second floor was as well. The third floor, however, flickered with candlelight. Cautiously, he took the final few stairs. The third floor made sense. It was the architectural center of the building when separated from the foundation. Slocombe could do an entire doctoral dissertation on psychic resonance, trans-planar refraction, and cross-dimensional oscillation, why materials and structure affected conjuration of spirits and demons.

There was little chance of getting a Ph.D. for that, even if he wrote the thesis.

He tried to get a feel for the floor, sense who was here besides himself. Especially Oscar (if it was Oscar) and Fanny and anyone else.

Or anything.

The summoning circle he found had been used. The chalk lines were still intact but the candles were spent. The room had been draped in dark plastic to block the light but was otherwise empty. Slocombe scanned the concrete, looking for footprints—claw marks—but everything around the circle had been swept clean before the summoning had begun and there were no clues to be had. Not visible clues anyway.

Turning his attention to the symbols, he read the hastily-scrawled pedestals and descenders. He decided the summoning had been a minor one. The target had been a lesser imp, nothing more. And the name of the—what was the summoner's name?

"You just missed it." The voice that floated out of the shadows was soft and silky but nonetheless made every tiny hair on the back of Slocombe's neck rise. Her voice had been the first thing that had attracted him to her, years ago, floating lightly from the opposite side of the cocktail party, catching his ear with its Londoner lilt.

"Fanny." He locked eyes with her. Blue, bright, tinged with madness. "What have you done?"

"Make no mistake, love. I'm nowhere near done." Fanny stepped toward him as if to meet him. He stepped toward her. "Where is Oscar?"

The sting of the needle in Slocombe's calf muscle was like an electric shock. Heat spread instantly from his calf into his thigh, climbing higher even as he knees buckled and he fell forward.

"Don't move a muscle, my love." Fanny was strong enough to flip Slocombe over on his back. He was powerless to resist.

"Stop," Slocombe mumbled. Events unfolded in slow

motion.

Fanny settled herself on top of him, straddling him with a wiggle, teasing.

"Get off."

She pouted. "You didn't used to mind. Once upon a time." She leaned over and kissed him hard on the mouth. "Remember what you said once?"

"Get off." In an odd, detached way, Slocombe's mind treated him to a list of things the tranquilizer was doing to his body. The paralysis was nearly complete but his autonomic systems were unaffected. Heartbeat, which was elevated. Respiration, which was fast. And he could use his eyes and voice. "Fanny. Where's Oscar?"

"It was about kisses."

Slocombe remembered. He'd felt poetic as he and Fanny prepared for their wedding. He'd drifted into philosophy. "Terminus versus impetus." His consonants were slurred and he felt fuzzy from the inside out.

"That's right." Fanny clapped her hands. "You said some kisses are an impetus to love. Other kisses are an end. A terminus." She kissed him again. As she broke, she put a wide piece of duct tape across his mouth. "Guess which one this is."

Slocombe rolled his eyes as Fanny dismounted.

I have to get out of here.

I should have stayed out in the first place.

But Oscar had been here. Inside the building.

"This is all your fault, you know." Fanny whispered in his ear. "I tried to keep Oscar away from you. Used my alimony. Paid people to ruin your reputation. Hide incriminating things in your house. Somehow the police never found what I wanted them to find."

"I found them all first." Slocombe tried to say it but could only grunt.

The photos. The stolen property. He'd found everything and gotten rid of it before it had become a problem because his house was guarded by measures seen and not seen and Fanny wasn't adept enough to circumvent them. She was barely able to put together an adequate summoning.

Overhead, in the shadows, something moved. It took only a moment to recognize the shape of an imp.

Why was the imp still here? What had Fanny needed the imp for?

The imp scuttled across the ceiling like a lizard crossbred with a crab, improbably upside-down. He had some chalk. And he was making marks with it. On the ceiling.

The imp needed to die. To be banished back to its domain. But a hunter gets just one chance. Unless he gets none.

"You should be proud too." Fanny was rambling on, lost in her own little sociopathic stream of consciousness. The fine line between quirky and crazy had been hard to spot, especially within the demon hunting community, which was rife with the unhinged-adjacent. Slocombe was one of the few who'd figured it out and he'd gotten Fanny institutionalized but not well enough.

She hadn't killed anyone? Had she? To get out? Didn't really matter, he decided. He couldn't feel his arms or legs anymore but he could feel the black hole of dread in the pit of his stomach. It told him he was about to be her victim.

She ran on, "I'm using everything you taught me to defeat you once and for all. So…we need to go. Oscar come say good-bye to daddy." Fanny bent down to whisper so loudly it was almost a shout. "It was important we kill you together. Kind of a mother-son bonding moment."

Oscar slid into Slocombe's field of view. His beautiful boy. Only now his son's eyes were a hot, glowing green.

"I gotta take the little guy home so we can get this imp out of him. But don't worry. I remember how. You taught me. And in an hour, it will be sunrise. Then the men will blow up this building and you'll be dead. And don't think I didn't remember to ward this floor. After I'm gone, nobody will be able to see you or hear you."

Oscar—or his body—waved goodbye. "Let's go, Oscar."

Slocombe listened as their footsteps receded. Fanny's silky voice wondering out loud if they should go for coffee and hot chocolate on the way home and whether imps could taste hot chocolate if the host was drinking it.

Then it was quiet.

Slocombe blinked back tears. Above him, the second imp worked with the chalk. Slocombe recognized the patterns, although they weren't complete.

The imp dropped to the floor and pulled the tape off Slocombe's mouth with a perfunctory *skritch* sound.

"You'll be interested to know," the imp said, "her ward went up successfully."

Slocombe's voice was strained. "Thanks."

"Her Latin is truly terrible. She conjugated a plural in the original incantation which is why I'm here along with the imp that took over your son. Her summoning invited us both. I thought it looked like fun."

"What are you doing up there? On the ceiling?" Whatever it was, it wasn't good.

The imp jumped straight up, landing with all fours on the ceiling.

"Well," the imp began conversationally. "I saw the circle she had done to summon us. And I caught on to the fact that she would bring someone here for a killing. And I also caught on to the fact that this building is coming down and you'll be squished flat between the floor and the ceiling. Her word. 'Squished.'"

Slocombe understood. "Don't do this. Please."

"Oh. I can't stop myself. I really want to see this." The imp's shrug was upside-down but effective. "You can't see the circle underneath you, but it still has the symbols intact. All I'm doing up here is changing a few details."

"Don't. Do. This."

The imp swept down, landing on Slocombe's chest in an instant. He barely felt it. The imp locked eyes with him. Bright. Tinged with madness. "I. Want. To."

Back up to the ceiling.

Slocombe's tears dried up, replaced by nausea. The imp was inscribing the name of a major demon. A nasty creature. Very large. Very wicked.

Slocombe saw the future play out in his mind. The circle he was on was like a blank check, the account numbers were all in place and there was a signature too. All that remained was to enter the recipient and the value. That's what the imp was doing above him. Filling in the blanks.

At sunrise, the building would implode. The two parts of the summoning circle would come together. His blood—squish—would fuel the summoning and one of the most vile of all demons would take over the body of his ex-partner and ex-wife.

The last thought Slocombe would have would be how his son was going to be raised by a demi-god from hell.

Wasn't that different though, when you think about it.

I should have killed her, he thought. I should have killed Fanny. I had one chance to do it right.

# FORAGING

Daniel Yocom

Adrian carefully placed another morel into his second bag, figuring he had at least a couple of pounds of the expensive mushrooms now. After placing the bag into his day pack he headed back towards the truck. Last year's forest fires had left dark scars across the landscape, but the mushrooms were plentiful. Devin and Dominique even said this was the best year they ever had foraging in the Uintas. And Devin was going to help Adrian sell the morels in Salt Lake City. The extra money would be good since his student loan hadn't come through yet.

Instead of taking the roundabout path he had taken down the mountainside earlier, he headed right up the slope to save time. The breeze pushed clouds and lifted off his hat. He snugged the slide up to his chin, adjusted the brim, and turned away from the wind to rub ash and dust from his eyes.

Off to the side, near a burnt trunk he noticed a dense patch of mushrooms.

They weren't morels. Adrian didn't recognize the grey squatty growths. He pulled out his borrowed copy of a mushroom identification book from his leg pocket and went through the pictures. He couldn't find them.

He sat on a rock and skimmed through the pages he'd

already flagged with the descriptions of mushrooms in the area. Nothing.

He may have discovered a new species. That would be something to help out his biology class.

He took out his phone and opened the camera.

He took pictures of the mushroom patch. There were two rows. Each was about two feet wide and five feet long, running almost parallel of each other, with about a foot between them. He took pictures of the tree and the other plants around, because Dr. Hawkes said there were connections at the last club meeting.

Adrian remembered more of the presentation and about gathering samples. He took out his Buck knife from its sheath and a fresh bag from his day pack. He didn't want to cross contaminate these with his morels. He cut a couple of the new ones as close to the ground as he could and placed them carefully in the bag. At the club meeting they had talked about putting caps on paper to see the spore pattern, so he collected another one that's cap hadn't opened yet, and placed it in the bag.

Picking up a third, Adrien turned it over to get a closer look at the gills of the cap. He turned to create a windshield with his body and he snapped the stem out from the middle of the rusty-brown gills and studied the cap flat in his palm.

He tapped the top of the mushroom a couple of times and adjusted his position. He brought his hands close so he could peek under the cap. He tilted it so one side barely lifted up. There was spore in his palm. It was a powdery black-grey dust that quickly blew away on the wind swirling around him.

Adrian decided to fill the bag with the new mushrooms instead of just taking the few he already had. He even dug one up with his knife so he could examine how it grew from the fibers in the soil. He didn't remember what the professor called that special filament, something like mice-helium.

He worked happily with the knowledge he had found something new when he noticed the light fading. He looked up as darker clouds caused the color of the mountainside to wash away like it was under milky moonlight. Even the mushrooms right in front of him no longer looked gray, but bone white.

Adrian needed to get back to the truck before a storm broke. They could be wild and dangerous in these high mountains.

He finished loading the bag and slid his thumb and finger along the top to seal it. He wiped the blade of his knife on his Levis and slipped it back into its sheath on his belt.

It was early afternoon but the light was dim. At least he wasn't driving. It was Devin's truck and he would know how to drive it on muddy roads. Devin knew the area well, he and Dominique had talked all the way up here how they had driven all over these logging and two-track backroads.

Adrian rubbed the dust off his face and licked his wind-blown lips.

The color faded more as though it were being carried away on the breeze. Adrian searched out a route up the hillside.

The gusts moaned as they cut through the dead and living pines, swaying aspens, and the occasional tuft of grass. The only other sounds Adrian heard were the crunching dirt under his boots and his own labored breathing from being so high up in the mountains. He had to stop to catch his breath, but not for long. The sky was a threatening slate grey. He pushed himself up the incline. His heart beat against his ribs and he could feel his pulse in his temples.

A level area made the hiking easier, but his heart continued to race. He slowed his pace and took deep breaths. At least the pounding in his head had settled down.

A groaning noise rose from the trees in front of Adrian. He paused and wondered, staring at the blackened grove. He didn't know what it was and he didn't see anything.

He wanted to sit and rest, see what the, noise had been, but the threat of a mountain storm pushed him on. Adrian didn't want to get caught out in the open, especially if there was lighting. There wasn't much left to burn in the area, just scorched ground and blowing ash. Still, he didn't want to get fried by a bolt.

He watched the ground to make sure of his footing with each step he took. The breeze blew with a steady low howl as the few branches left gave it voice.

Adrian jumped when he heard the call again.

Someone—no, *something*—walked towards him. It had the shape of a man but the skin color was wrong. It stumbled and swayed unevenly as it headed towards him. The creature raised a hand and let out another call—a grumbling, growling sound that raised goosebumps down Adrian's arms.

The wind shifted and kicked up a cloud of ash. After it passed over the creature the thing moved closer. Its skin was a sickly grey and strands of white hair blew up from a skull that held colorless eyes.

Zombies were made-up creatures from movies and television.

Adrian clenched his eyes shut then looked again.

Oh, God. It was real.

The creature stumbled forward with its arm stretched out. Adrian's breathing came in quick pants that were approaching the speed of his pounding heart.

He stepped backwards without looking away from the creature coming at him. His next step was on a rock that rolled out from under his foot. He fell to his hands and knees.

Quick as his life, he rose clenching the rock that had felled him and threw it at the monster.

The thing ducked with an agility zombies never had on TV. At least the rock made the creature pause. Adrian looked around for someplace safe he could run to. The burnt slope gave no cover and the zombie was between him and the truck.

No! The creature was coming from the direction of the truck. God, no—Devin and Dominique.

Adrian had to do something. He had to make sure Devin and his girlfriend were safe. He kept his eyes steeled to the creature in front of him as he felt for the handle of his knife. The thing seemed to understand the threat and stopped advancing. It moaned again and shook its hands.

There was no way Adrian was going to allow a brain-eating monster to get him or his friends.

He drew his blade and screaming ran at the monster. The fast action and sudden noise made the creature stumble back in retreat.

The Buck knife led the charge and sunk deep into the zombie's thigh. It screamed and black liquid spread down the thing's denim pants. Adrian pushed forward and felt the blade slide along bone and continue on until it ripped open a ravine of flesh. It finally caught on some fabric and flipped out of his hand.

The force of Adrian's attack, and the ripped muscle, left the creature on its back.

Adrian knew he hadn't done enough to stop a zombie. He had to decapitate it or destroy its brain.

The creature held its leg. It tried to stand. It was still coming after him.

Adrian picked up a cantaloupe-sized rock with both hands. He took a step back and then brought the rock down with adrenalin-precise accuracy on the back of the zombie's skull.

It flopped prone facing the sky.

To be sure, Adrian pounded with the rock. Black gore splattered his boots and the surrounding ground.

He dropped the stone where the zombie's head used to be.

Adrian hurried up the hill. He had to warn Devin and Dominique.

He was almost to the truck when a second zombie stood up on the far side of the vehicle. It was facing away from him. Adrian slid to a halt on the loose gravel as the creature scanned the area in front of it.

Adrian moved to the side to keep hidden by the cab of the old Ford.

What had it been doing? Where were Devin and Dominique?

No. They couldn't have...

Adrian had to know.

He moved forward as he watched the creature and kept hidden as much as possible. He was careful since the monster was downwind. He wouldn't smell the creature's rotting flesh, but the breeze might carry his scent and sounds towards the thing by the truck.

Adrian crouched lower the closer he got until he squatted next to the truck.

He reached for his knife and found the empty sheath. He looked back down the path. There was no way he would be able to get the weapon without being noticed by the zombie. He needed another option.

He couldn't just leave. Adrian didn't know for sure where he was. He could try to follow the two-track Devin had drove up on. No. He couldn't leave his friends. Even if those things had already killed them, he couldn't just leave them behind. He looked up with a silent prayer asking what to do.

The truck squeaked as the zombie bumped against it.

The Ford's tailgate was down from when they pulled stuff out of the bed earlier. Adrian duck-walked to the back of it. He peeked around the edge of the bed and saw the handle of a shovel.

He moved a little further not seeing the creature.

The truck squeaked again.

The wind lifted wisps of hair up over the far side of the truck. The zombie was there.

It was squatting down to eat his friends.

Adrian had to do something.

He stepped quietly around the back of the truck as far

as he could get towards the other side and still reach the shovel.

He paused, and took a steadying breath.

Adrian dragged the shovel up as he twisted in a spin around the far corner of the tailgate. The sound of metal scraping metal would alert the monster so he moved fast.

As the creature stood, Adrian spun to make a full swing of the spade. The look on the zombie's face was horrific and it screamed.

Adrian dropped his shoulder to adjust his swing. The flat of the blade caught the creature on the chin with his upward swipe. Its head snapped back into the truck and dented the cab behind the passenger door's window.

Adrian pulled the shovel back and cocked his elbow for another go. The monster slumped forward and fell on its face. Adrian took advantage of the situation. He shifted his grip and drove the spade down just above the thing's shoulders. He stomped down until the blade dug into the rocky soil beneath.

He pulled the shovel up and grabbed the door handle with his free hand. It was locked. He went to the driver's side and found that door also locked. There was no way into the truck without breaking a window until Devin returned. At least the zombies hadn't eaten them.

Adrian crawled into the bed of the truck grasping the shovel like a lifeline. He didn't know if the others had been attacked while they were out foraging mushrooms. He had to believe they were okay since the zombies had continued hunting.

He would wait there for his friends to return and they would all get out of there safe.

# ROSALIND

Anna Marasco

*Dear Rosalind,*

*I still think of you. Your raven black hair cascading past your shoulders in waves, contrasting your button up white blouse, like a murder of crows twisting against a cloudy sky. Your hair is a fitting color—sleek like dark souls carried by ravens. I passed you in the airport and you dropped your brochure.*

*"How clumsy of me," you said.*

*"Not at all." I lifted the brochure from the tile floor and handed it to you. Your acrylic nails scratched my hand. A simple scratch, red like your lips. It was the first time we touched. The ghost of your touch still stings my skin. I need it again. Your flesh against mine.*

*Until next time,*

*Seth*

Seth wrapped his fingers in the groove of the steering wheel. He'd considered buying a new car, but the Buick had been in his family for generations. It held his memories of girls he took home to mother. She rejected each one. No female was good enough for Mother. But, in their defense, he was never good enough for Mother, either. One day, he'd find *the one*. The one that would look past all the faults his mother magnified.

Car lights passed, scanning Seth's face. He stared, unflinching except for his constricting pupils. Memories spun in his mind of the airport—blurs of people speeding past, eyes to their phones, not even glancing at him. To them, he never existed. But Rosalind. She dropped her Tower of London brochure and breathed warmth on his face when they both reached for the folded pamphlet. Her eyes were like emeralds screwed into her sockets. Her stare cut his heart, an organ he thought he'd lost with the last girl. Just thinking of Rosalind puttered his heart like she restarted it.

"What's your name?"

"Rosalind."

"Seth." His name barely fell from his lips. Stuck in his seizing throat. Rosalind's image strangled him. Every thought escaped his mind except her.

*Rosalind,*

*Even your name is a song on my lips. I never want to stop saying it—Rosalind. I wonder what your skin smells like under the Sep-*

*tember sun? I bet it's sweet like
your name, like a rush of plume-
ria blossoms caught on the wind.
I wonder what your lips taste like
after Mexican food—are they
salty, or do they have a hint of
jalapeno? I'm sure they are both.
We are meant for each other, my
dear Rosalind. I feel you burn in
my heart even though you're not
here. Don't worry. One day,
we'll be together. Hopefully, it's
sooner rather than later.*

*Yours truly,*

*Seth*

Seth watched houselights flick on one room at a time from his parked car. The tall Tudor brick stretched up from a cracked cement foundation surrounded by dried grass and blooming red roses. Wood slat blinds cast slits of golden light to the street. The television flashed on and Rosalind slid onto the leather couch, under her powder blue microfiber blanket.

*My sweetest Rosalind,*

*Your blanket is luckier than I
ever could hope to be— wrapping you, warming you in a soft
cocoon. You sigh into it. I
synched our TVs so we can
watch the Kardashians together.
Well, almost together. You're in*

*your living room, blinds cracked
ever so slightly like I'm watching
you through static on a screen.
I'm in my car, tablet in one
hand. I'll let you guess what's in
the other hand. Don't worry, my
hands won't be lonely for long.*


*Love forever and always,*

*Seth*

- - -

Seth held the carving knife over the sink and drew it across his palm. Blood seeped into the stainless steel sink in a steady flow of scarlet. He wrapped his hand in a green plaid hand towel. He'd planned his cut. It would bleed enough, but not so much that he'd pass out before the hospital.

Seth sighed. Days like today reminded him of his mother. Her shrill cackle of a voice crept through his mind like a spider burrowing below his skin. "You can't even handle a knife," she'd tell him. "No wonder why no woman wants you. No woman wants a man who can't cook." It was two years ago, right before she died. She had to prop herself up on her oxygen cart, her frail body shook as she waddled to the cutting board. Her loose wrinkled skin hung on her bones like pale dried plums. She took the knife from Seth and cut the tomatoes herself. Her bony fingers trembled, sliding the knife in and out. Each tomato squished at the knife's dull blade. Seth hugged his mother from behind. Wrapping his arms around her, he took the knife back and plunged it into her sternum. She was his first.

Seth's blood soaked through his cotton rag. He

wrapped a thick white bath towel from the linen closet around it. The scent of fresh linen laundry soap mixed with iron blood bled through the Buick's cab.

Holy Trinity Hospital was a bright carcass across town, stretching above the boxed housing project homes. Uniform windows spanned the rectangular building like a balanced game of golden dominoes. Seth held his wrapped hand. Fluorescent lights hemorrhaged a sterile white as he shuffled into the emergency room. His blood stained the white towel in a splatter of scarlet tie-dye.

"Dr. Hammersmith will see you momentarily," Nurse Dennison said.

"Is there another doctor available?" He hugged his hand tighter to his chest. His pulse beat a steady rhythm through his palm.

"Dr. Crane is the only other doctor in the ER tonight. But she won't be available for another 45 minutes."

"It's all right. I'll wait for her."

Seth sat in the lobby. His stomach churned and nausea burned his esophagus in a tight reflux. He rested his head on the back of his chair and stared into the exposed tube lightbulbs hanging below ceiling tiles. How he wished he might escape into the crawl space and watch, undetected, as the doctors mended wounds.

"Strickland?" Nurse Dennison's voice was a nasal buzz in her chest and Seth flinched. "Strickland, Seth?"

Seth stood and shuffled to her. She led him to an exam room and he peeled his towels from his hand. Threads of flesh stuck to the cotton.

"Dr. Crane will be in shortly." Nurse Dennison didn't

look at him and exited the room with a quick turn.

Seth lay on the exam table. The door creaked open and the doctor clicked her boots on the linoleum floor. Seth sighed. His breath slid his lips to a smile and he closed his eyes.

"Mr. Strickland?" Her voice was a song against hums of fluorescent lights.

"Yes."

"You cut your hand?"

Her soft fingers found his wrist and she turned his hand over. Seth flinched.

"It's okay," she said. "Let's take a look." She rolled the leather-topped stool to Seth's bedside and he opened his eyes. Her raven hair fell just below her shoulders and her green eyes squinted behind designer glasses. "Tell me what you did here."

"I was—"

*No woman will want you if you can't cook for her,* his mother's voice whined in his head.

"I was cooking dinner and the knife slipped. I've never been good with knives."

"That's just fine. We will stitch this up and you'll be good as new." She threaded the needled and Seth held his breath. He watched her draw it through his skin. In and out, she pulled his flesh back together. Her careful stitching sewed the broken parts of his heart and he breathed again.

> *My dearest, dearest Rosalind,*
>
> *Your mind is brilliant, encyclo-pedias are based on it. I want to*

*kiss you. Perhaps sucking face will allow me to absorb the spark that feeds your synapses so that I might possess some intelligence, some skill that you do. I followed you home after the hospital and you got a flat tire along the way. I expected it, though. I impaled the tire with the screw you pulled from it.*

*Yours,*

*Seth*

"I don't understand how a screw can get stuck so deeply in my tire. These are brand new." Rosalind had pulled her black SUV to the side of the road.

"It's just rotten luck." Seth pumped the car jack's crank. He'd pulled his Buick off the road behind Rosalind, when her brake lights flashed. The Buick was invisible behind blinding headlights focused on the back of her car. She wouldn't recognize it when Seth parked on her street.

"I'm lucky you were here, otherwise, I'd be stranded forever."

"You helped me. It only makes sense for me to help you."

*Sweet Rosalind,*

*I keep your thread stitched in my hand. It's a gift from you and now a part of me, like you soon shall be. You left early for the hospital today and I watched you leave. The spare key is still in the hide-a-rock in the garden. I made a copy of it. You can never have too many spare keys. I stole your used syringe from the Vitamin B12 shots you've been giving yourself. I injected myself with it. Now I have you pumping through me with every beat of my heart. Every part of you will soon be every part of me. Your blood poisons me with your lust for life. Give me your memories. Feed me your soul. Maybe some day I will be as powerful as you.*

*Yours lovingly,*

*Seth*

Rosalind returned early from the hospital and Seth sat in his car, fingers tightened on the steering wheel. Rain drizzled the sidewalk and he watched her fumble her keys in the lock before swinging the front door open.

*Darling Rosalind,*

*I plugged your bathtub drain with my own thick hair. When you left for work this morning, I snuck back in and drank a cup of your used bathwater. Your essence is now my essence. The molecules and dead skin you*

*flushed from your body are now
my body. It's like you gave birth
to me.*


*See you soon, Mommy,*

*Seth*

Seth smiled, cracking his window slightly to listen. Garbage day was tomorrow. Rosalind stepped out the front door with two large bags stuffed with trash. She opened the garbage can and paused. Seth's smile spread wider, cracking to a snorting snicker. He stuffed it back, not wanting to close his eyes even for a second.

*My lovely Rosalind,*

*Your garbage is even perfect:
neatly organized between trash
and recyclables. Sometimes, I
rearrange them. When you
bring more garbage out, you
transfer the plastic bottles back
to the recycle bin, cursing to
yourself that you "could swear I
put them in the recycle bin" and
I laugh because you're so cute
when you lean into the garbage
can.*

*Old pizza and leftover box wine
stain your gray sweatshirt, the
Red Sox one. I forgave you for
that. I've always been a Yan-
kees fan. But love knows no
bounds. Garbage smears across*

*your body. You dirty girl. I beg*
*the clouds to make me the rain,*
*clinging your clothes to your*
*body. Your sweatshirt looks a*
*lot smaller wet, shrinking*
*against your chest, giving you*
*free breast implants. They look*
*so much bigger when wet.*

*Your dirty boy,*

*Seth*

- - -

"Do you want to grab dinner sometime?" Seth's re-flection in his bathroom mirror always looked more yellow.

"Would you like to grab coffee?"

If there was one helpful thing his mother taught him, it was that practice made perfect.

"Do you like watching the stars? I like watching the stars." With each recitation of each conversation starter, his voice steadied and became less shaky.

"Do you like cheese? I like cheese. Smoked gouda is my favorite. It's gouda. Get it?" He shook his head. "Stupid Seth. She's too smart for puns." He punched the mirror and his fist left a spider web ripple in the glass. His knuckles frac-tured cracks that trickled a mandala of blood across his hand. He wiped it down the thigh of his jeans.

*Rosalind,*

*I cut myself again today. It was*
*for you. It's always for you.*

*How do I ask you for a date,
when you strangle me from the
inside out, making me unable to
speak? You made a commitment
to save people. But every day
without you, I die. Your dark
hair falls in long strands like
plucked feathers from crows. I
want to cut it, close to your
scalp. A nick on your skin and
the air will taste like salt, like
the iron rotting on your head.
I'll lick the blade. You'll watch
my tongue and want it inside
you. Don't be embarrassed, I
want your tongue inside me,
too. Soon, our tongues will meet
and our saliva will taste like
your last meal.*

*Yours dearest,*

*Seth*

- - -

Seth breathed in his running exhaust, waiting halfway
down the block from Rosalind's house. Her windows were
dark. He tapped the steering wheel, a low rap like drizzling
rain on the windows.  It was unlike her to break routine.
Where was she?

Lights cut darkness in his mirror and her black SUV
passed his parked car. Seth released his held breath in a deep
sigh. She was safe. She pulled into the garage and the door

slid closed.

Seth crept his car, lights off, to the front curb. Lights flicked on one room at a time. The kitchen blinds were open, flashing golden light across the dried front lawn. Rosalind pulled a turkey from the oven and slid it to the stovetop. She held an electric knife over it, a smile stuck on her lips. Seth's mouth slithered to a smile. She always did that to him. She smiled and he couldn't help but mirror her.

> *Rosalind,*
>
> *You worried me. You came home late tonight. I thought you were dead in a ditch. But when I saw you pull your car into your garage, I breathed again. My heart resumed beating. You carve that* turkey *with your electric knife. It vibrates through your whole body. How would it feel if it were inside you? I bet you've already stuck the handle in there. I can feel your vibrating body pulse against mine.*
>
> *Sincerely,*
>
> *Seth*

Rosalind sliced the turkey and laughed, placing the cuts on gold-trimmed china. The man in the navy blue sweater wrapped his arms behind her. He was taller than Rosalind and shielded her from the peeping window. His arms hugged her tighter and he kissed her on the cheek.

Seth flexed the steering wheel as if he were strangling

a throat. His heart cut against his chest like a dagger had sheathed in his aorta.

"No." It started as a whisper, a croak in the back of his throat. "No." It grew louder. "No!" He threw open his car door. "NO!"

Seth flung open her front door and ran to the kitchen. "Rosalind, what are you doing?" The words that stayed lodged in his mind finally fell from his lips. "I love you!"

"What are you doing?" Her voice cracked and the man in the blue sweater tucked her behind him.

"Who the hell are you?" The man said. "Get out!"

"Not without Rosalind." Seth planted his feet, his hand resting on the counter near the plate with sliced turkey.

"Why are you here? You followed me? How dare you follow me!" Rosalind backed away, closer to the dining room.

"Why are you backing away?" Seth took a step towards the man but his eyes stayed on Rosalind.

"You stay there." The man held up his hand to Seth. "Ros, call the cops."

"My phone's in the car." She sighed.

"Yes." Seth said. "Call the cops. They can take this guy away and we can be together."

"I'm not going anywhere. You need to leave." The man swung at Seth and caught him against the cheekbone. Seth held onto the counter, his arm shaking to hold up his weight. He grabbed the electric knife and flipped on the switch. He spun and dug the knife into the man's neck. Blood exploded and the man's head flopped sideways against his shoulder. Seth kept the knife against the man, whose knit sweater unwound bloodied threads in the vibrating blade even after he fell to the ground. The electric knife stayed powered on, its power button jammed, and Seth left it on the body.

"No!" Rosalind screamed and dropped to her knees beside the man. "Arthur. Arthur!" She held a towel against his neck, stuffing it into the wound. Arthur groaned. Blood encircled his head, covering the black and white tiled floor.

"You're a doctor, Rosalind. You know he won't make it."

"Why did you do that?" She pulled another towel from the counter and pressed it against Arthur's neck.

"That's just another thing I love about you. You're more concerned about saving someone else than yourself."

Rosalind shifted her eyes to Seth's and stood to run.

"Wait," Seth grabbed her wrist. "Don't worry. I'd never do this to you. I have something special planned."

> *Dear Rosalind,*
>
> *This isn't how I wanted our love to begin. Your tears carve trails on your cheek, streaking pale lines in your makeup, cracking your porcelain. I had to do it. I had to do it for us. Protecting you is much harder than I thought it would be. I wonder what you'd feel like with my fingers inside you like a puppet. We have plenty of time to find out.*
>
> *The Only Person Who Will Ever*

*Love You Like You Deserve,*

*Seth*

- - -

Rosalind's SUV creaked as Seth locked the breaks on a gravel driveway. A house with a bent frame bled slivers of light from boarded up windows.

"I saved this for our wedding night. We'd fix it up together. Our children would have a large yard with a white picket fence. They'd have so much room since there are no neighbors for miles."

"Please, please." Rosalind whimpered, crying dry tears.

"I like your car. It's smooth on the gravel." Seth leaned into Rosalind, resting his forehead against her cheek. He inhaled. "Your tears smell like the ocean."

*My Sweetest Rosalind,*

*Tears drown your cheeks and light sparks your eyes as if they conduct electricity. The same electricity that ignites in my heart. You're even more beautiful when you cry. I want to touch you, to pull you into me. How might your skin feel on my body? A fresh suit sleek on my flesh as if we were born together, as if we were a single solid entity. Your warmth is my blood. I am but a carcass without you. Fill me with everything you are and I will fill you.*

*Yours forever,*

*Seth*

Seth led Rosalind into the house. Floorboards creaked under their weight. Rotting wood and damp mothballs burned the air.

"I know it's not much," Seth said. "But it is ours."

Rosalind pulled back, tugging her wrist in Seth's grasp. "Let me go!" She yanked herself free and ran from the house to her parked car.

"I locked it." Seth said, standing on the porch and jangling the car keys. "We are out in the middle of nowhere. But you can never be too safe."

Rosalind ran down the gravel driveway.

"Darling!" Seth called, running after her. "Darling, don't you want to come to bed?"


Rosalind ran faster. Seth pumped his legs harder. His thighs burned. He had to catch her with as little force as possible. He had to save his energy. He needed it for later.

Seth lunged and wrapped his arms around Rosalind's legs. She fell. Dirt scuffed her cheek.

"My darling, I am so sorry." Seth crawled on top of her and cupped her face. "I'm so sorry. I just want to take care of you."

"Please. Please don't kill me."

"That's not part of my plan yet."

"Are you going to rape me?"

"I would *never* rape you. I would never steal something so sacred from you. We only do what you're ready for."

Seth pulled Rosalind to her feet. She tugged and jerked, but never strong enough to escape again.

"You're going to love it here. The other girls didn't. But you're not like them. You're the one."

> *My wonderful Rosalind,*
>
> *I always imagined the first time we went to bed together, you'd wear a white see-through nightgown and you'd have grown your hair out a little more. A light curl of your dark hair caresses the bottom of your breasts. You'd hold your arms to me. I'd pick you up and carry you to our waterbed. In my mind, it was always a waterbed. It reminds me of the ocean, and of how your tears smell. But you ran away from me. And you wouldn't wear the nightgown. I didn't want to tie you down. I don't want to do anything you don't want to. But I have to keep you safe. I thought you were smart, but you no longer know how to be safe. It's up to me now. I will do anything to keep you safe. That's how much I love*

*you.*

*Yours always,*

*Seth*

He tightened the restraints on Rosalind's wrists and ankles. The leather exam table propped her up to a semi-reclined position so he could see her eyes. God, how he loved her eyes.

"I have to apologize," Seth said. "The basement lights don't do you justice." He tucked her hair behind her ears.

"What do you want from me? I can give you money. Any amount you want."

"I don't want money. I want you, Rosalind. I love you."

She closed her eyes and turned away.

"Look at me when I'm talking to you!" Seth wrapped his fingers around her face and pulled her eyes back to look in his. He squeezed tighter and her lips plumped a deeper red. Tendons popped in the back of his hand. Rosalind choked on her breath.

"I'm sorry." Seth released her jaw. "I just love you so much. Sometimes I can't control my love. You make me go crazy."

Light from the bulb swinging above Rosalind's head flashed across her face back and forth and back and forth. Seth caught it and watched the glow in her eyes.

"I can't help but wonder what your eyes have seen." He traced the lines creasing the borders of her eyelids with his index finger.

Rosalind glared, holding eye contact with him.

"You're not like the other girls." Seth polished his Damascus herring knife with the hem of his polyester shirt. "They always plead and never stop. They don't even look at me. But here you are—fascinated. You can't take your eyes off me."

"I'm disgusted." Rosalind growled. Her clenched jaw throbbed a pulse at her temples.

"Hey!" Seth held his hand to her throat and leaned his face to hers until their noses touched, leaving the knife on the table next to her head. "I've given up everything for you. And you're ungrateful. I should just—"

Seth released his hand and unbent his posture, straightening his shirt and smoothing his hair. He reached his hand into his pocket and pulled out a black velvet box.

"I was saving this." Seth turned the box in his fingers. "But maybe you don't deserve it."

Rosalind's eyes spread wide like Seth wanted to do to her legs.

"You're right." She said. "I don't deserve it. If you're going to kill me, please just do it. Please kill me quickly."

"No, no, no!" Seth cupped her cheek. "I don't want to kill you. I never wanted to kill you. I want to understand you so I can love you better."

He smiled a crooked-tooth smile. One canine hung over his bottom lip. He took the ring from the box. A black diamond reflected dim light like sparks in Rosalind's eyes. He placed it in the groove of her collarbone and took the knife resting by her head. He found her fingers and locked them in his. The Damascus blade swirled like marble against

Rosalind's clean flesh. He pressed the blade to the ring finger on her left hand until it snapped like he cut a baby carrot.

Rosalind cried out, kicking and thrashing. Her restraints held her like Seth's hands wanted to.

He slid the ring on her severed finger and held it in front of her face. "You deserve this ring more than anyone." He placed her finger, ring attached, in the groove of her neck. Her panting breath rocked it, up and down, like the finger tapped Morse code on her skin.

Seth smoothed curls that fell across her face. "Tell me you love me. Remind me that you were the one all along."

Sweat pricked drops on her skin and her hair fell back over her eyes.

"Oh, dear me. I did this all wrong." Seth smoothed back his own dark curls before scratching the scruff on his face. "I cut off your finger, I was supposed to start with your hair *then* your finger. I screwed up. Will you ever forgive me, my sweet Rosalind?"

She held her breath, a groan croaked from the back of her throat.

Seth held scissors to Rosalind's hair and cut her locks, a handful at a time. He piled it into a ponytail and held it below his nose, inhaling its scent.

"Your hair smells like the roses outside your front door."

A tear fell from the outside corner of her eye.

"Let's make sure I do the rest right." He placed a hand -written note next to Rosalind's freshly shaved head. A small knick in her scalp dribbled blood on the page. "One—tie down. Two—Hair. That's the part I screwed up. Silly me.

Three—ring. Okay, okay. We are onto four—digestive tract."

Rosalind's eyes widened. "No, no. Please, *please* don't."

"The other girls begged, too. Their pleas were annoying. I ripped out their tongues."

Rosalind closed her mouth and clamped her jaw, keeping her eyes glaring into Seth's. Yellow light rocking back and forth above her head reflected in Seth's round glasses.

He sharpened the knife on Rosalind's leather ankle restraint. He lifted her shirt. Her bare stomach pulsed her breath in short spurts.

"Please," she whimpered. "Please."

"I'm helping you. I'm helping us." Seth's voice was calm. His fingers slid a steady line with the knife, cutting into Rosalind's flesh from her sternum to below her belly button. Blood seeped in a continuous flow until scarlet covered her pale abdomen.

Seth's lips slithered to a smile and he peeled back her skin. "You're so beautiful, inside and out."

Rosalind breathed deep breaths as if trying to focus her thoughts away from the pain. Tears burned her eyes red, but she didn't take them away from Seth.

"You're different from those girls. You're stronger. You want to live." Seth dug his fingers into her intestines and gave a sharp pull.

Rosalind coughed a scream but stuffed it back.

"What? You don't want me to hear you scream?" Seth caressed his cheek with Rosalind's viscera; the sleek sheen glinted in the dim light of the basement. He danced with her intestines, spinning a circle around the table. He ran his fingers up and down like he stroked Rosalind's thin body against his own.

"Let me go." Rosalind choked.

"You're amazing. How are you even speaking?"

"If Arthur were—"

"What? Alive? If Arthur were alive he'd save you? Goddammit, Rosalind!" Seth dropped the intestines in a pile on Rosalind's open stomach and her scream cracked between his words. "You left me in pieces. So I did the same to you. But now I can't figure out how to put you back together. Is this what my broken heart looks like? Because, it sure as hell feels this way. I just wanted us to be together." He dropped to his knees, pressing his crying face in Rosalind's intestines. His tears salted her wounds and he wound his fingers on her smooth calf.

Rosalind's eyes rolled back and she convulsed—limbs flopping like the wriggle of intestines that fell from Seth's fingers.

"Stay with me, Sunshine." Seth cupped her head. "My light goes out when yours does."

Rosalind exhaled a long gasp and her body stopped moving.

"Thus with a kiss, I die." Seth grabbed the knife and crawled on the table beside her. He pressed his lips to hers and stabbed her chest. He reached his hand below her sternum and pulled on her heart. With his other hand, he stabbed his own chest and collapsed on top of her.

*My dear, sweet Rosalind,*

*You've always been the one. You*

*were the one waiting for my scal-
pel to dissect, for my fingers to
hold your heart as we both take
our last breaths. This is how
much I love you—I'm going to
cut out my own heart for you.
Isn't that enough? When will it
be enough, Rosalind?*

- - -

"What's your name?" Seth asked. The airport blurred around him. She was all that existed.

"Rosalind." Her lips parted a brief smile.

"Seth."

Rosalind rubbed her arms, goose pimples pricked her skin.

"They always keep the air conditioning way too high in Terminal Two," he said.

*Your nipples would agree,* he thought.

"May I walk you to your gate, Rosalind?"

"Thank you, but I'm meeting someone."

Seth watched her walk away. He pulled a pen and paper from his bag and sat on a black cushioned chair at Gate B12. He drew his pen across the page.

*Dear Rosalind,*

*This will be the first of many let-
ters I write you. If you only knew
what I have planned for us. Our
hearts shall beat as one in a
symphonic display of our love.*

*But, for now, I shall just quote*
*for you Romeo and Juliet:*


*"Love is a smoke raised with the*
*fume of sighs;*

*Being purged, a fire sparkling in*
*lovers' eyes."*

# THE LIGHT AT THE END OF THE ROAD

## Levi Robinson

The foul stench of death pressed in on her from all sides, seeming to take form as it clung to her skin in the hot July morning. The sound of hundreds of flies vibrated its way into her bones as she squatted down to get a better look at the poor animal, whose life had been ended by what had to have been one of the many semi-trucks that called these roads their home. Looking at the dark brown blood baked onto the asphalt, she guessed it had been simmering out here all day yesterday. She looked into the doe's eyes, and wondered if she was a mother—wondered if this creature had known what was happening to it, but guessing it was all over too quick to even matter.

Penny had been working for the Department of Public Works collecting roadkill in Cache County going on six years. It was a job most people didn't want, but she figured someone had to do it. And she didn't mind anyway. In fact, she had fallen in love with the job almost right away. She felt a weird sense of honor, almost a sense of humility being the one to deal with the remains of another creature. It gave her pride to know she was doing a service not only by making the roads safer but by offering some level of respect to the animals that happened across our path. To her, it felt like something close to equilibrium—close enough, anyway.

But she had to admit, today was not off to a good start.

Lately, she had found herself becoming more and more uncomfortable around the dead animals that were usually her only company. Something about the eyes, she thought. There was a time she could look into the eyes of the deceased creatures and see something like relief, but lately there had been a change. More and more, the eyes seemed to be wide and glassy with terror. As if at their death—they had seen some unimaginable horror waiting for them—just past the thin veil.

She took a step back and examined the scene once more as she began to slip into her protective overalls and gloves.

"Huh," she said to herself, cocking her head ever so slightly to one side while also slipping into her face mask. The blood pattern around the remains seemed to almost curve and spiral across the black top. Certainly an unusual pattern. And those eyes. Those god damn eyes wouldn't stop staring at her. Staring into her, as if begging for some sort of respite to its suffering.

Best to just get this over with and get out of here.

- - -

About a half hour later, Penny was finished loading the carcass into the work truck and was spraying the unusual blood pattern off with a pressure washer. She felt dirty all over, but knew that this was just all part of the job…a job she was beginning to have second thoughts about.

When she was younger, she worked for a seamstress fixing old dresses. She was pretty good at it, but had never been delicate enough with her big, manly hands. This work suited her more, even though some days weren't the greatest.

She would feel better once she got back to her one bedroom apartment and took a nice, hot shower. A prospect that seemed so far away with this much time left in the day.

After getting everything stowed away, she hopped back into the cab and set off down the highway. Plenty of more roadkill out there for her to collect

"Penny, come in? Over." A man's voice screeched over the air waves and into the CB radio that hung under the dash. With a half-smile, she reached down and picked up her end of the walkie.

"Good morning, Donald," she replied. "To what do I owe the pleasure?" Donald was a decent man, in her humble opinion. A thing that seemed to be in short supply these days, and she was glad it was him working dispatch today instead of someone else. Mostly just glad to hear another person's voice.

"You get that deer off eighty-nine dealt with? The old-timer that called it in, said it was a bloodbath."

"Nothing I can't take care off."

"Someone should give you a raise."

"Well, you be sure to put that in Terry's ear next time he decides to pay the station a visit."

He let out a sarcastic chuckle out over the radio. "Hopefully I'll be retired by then."

"You and me both. You got anything for me?"

"Does a bear shit in the woods? Just got a call from some young guy, saw a deer off over by Turner Grove campground. Said it was pretty messy."

"No problem. I'll check it out and give you a ring in a

bit."

"Sounds good. Over and out."

She hung the receiver back up in its cradle in front of the radio and traded it for the coffee in the cup holder.

- - --

After a long day of scraping dead animals off the road—three deer, two raccoons, and a cat—Penny finally got that hot shower she had been daydreaming about. She let out a sigh of relief as scalding water washed away the stink of decay that had been following her since that first deer this morning.

She couldn't stop thinking about that one. About the first one. It had put her in a weird mood that she couldn't shake ever since. She felt dirty and uneasy and worst of all she felt paranoid. Earlier, when she had been picking up one of the raccoons, she could swear someone was watching her. Observing her from the tree line.

For a second she was pretty sure she even saw a pair of eyes, glistening in the darkness.

Once she was scrubbed clean, she actually had begun to feel a little better. Her mind had started to fill with mundane thoughts, pushing down the dark ones somewhere into the back of her skull, where she no longer fixated on them.

Unfortunately, she barely slept at all that night. Once the lights went out, those intrusive thoughts of being watched had creeped their way from the back of her subconscious to the forefront of her mind. Once she did finally manage to slip into sleep, her dreams were plagued with the gruesome images of the dead, calling out to her.

After all these years, she was the only one who understood their suffering.

At one point during the night, she bolted upright and immediately flipped on the lamp and threw back the covers. With the light on, and her nightmare fading away, her heart started to beat slower. After a moment, she was able to lay back down and resume her restless slumber.

She was sure something had been licking her feet. And for just a split second, she was convinced a pair glossy eyes were staring gleefully at her from the end of the mattress.

But of course, it had all been a bad dream.

- - -

After a few days, she started to feel like things were almost getting back to normal for her. No strange blood patterns. No misinterpreted looks from dead animals. However, the nightmares hadn't let up as much as she had hoped, leaving her tired and disoriented throughout the work week.

"Penny, come on in, over," Don mumbled from somewhere under her dash. She was driving along a stretch of frontage road, looking for nothing in particular. Feeling dazed despite the 3 cups of coffee.

"Penny, you there?"

She looked down at the walkie hanging down near the floor with slight confusion. She was careful to keep her eyes on the road as she leaned down to grab it.

"Penny here," she almost muttered in return.

"Hey, where you at?"

She looked around the roadside briefly and the passing trees on either side. Turns out she was a little farther east than she thought she was. Must have been zoned out longer than expected.

"Uh…About six miles east of Willow pond. Headed east."

"Huh, you're a little ways out there, aren't you? Wanna flip around and head towards 74? Someone called in a couple bucks between…135 and 147."

"I'm on it," she said back without much enthusiasm, pulling onto the shoulder and flipping around.

"Thanks Pen…You feeling ok? You sound a little under the weather?" Don asked, sounding genuinely concerned.

"I'll be fine. Just haven't been sleeping too good lately."

"I hear that. That damn baby keeps me and Jen up all hours of the night. Anyway, gimme a call if you need anything."

"Sounds good. Over and out."

Knots had begun to form in her stomach as she hung up the receiver and headed west.

- - -

Penny came upon the scene just as the sun had started to set in the western sky, casting a deep red glow across the valley. At first she didn't understand what she was looking at. The animals had been so mutilated and destroyed that it was hard to tell where one ended and the other began. Blood, bone and flesh flooded the small, one lane road. It was if god himself had reached down and tried to erase his creatures from the earth.

Except the heads, both of which lay entangled together by their antlers, resting neatly at the end of the patch of gore.

Her truck had stopped about six feet from where the initial impact must have occurred. She stared dumbfounded, not sure of how to even register the sheer violence, let alone begin cleaning up the mess. Feeling like it belonged to someone else, her hand reached down and grabbed the walkie.

"Don, you there?"

For a minute there was only static and the sound of the idling vehicle.

"Don here. What's up, Penny? You catch a bad one?" Don sounded like he was eating something. Sitting at his desk, no doubt, eating those cheese crackers he so much enjoyed.

"I've never seen anything like this…The force it would have taken…It's incredible." She knew she sounded dumb, but didn't really care. She quit caring what people thought about her ages ago.

"Like, what we talking about here? Semi?" he asked, always sounding genuine.

"I'm not sure. Whatever the hell it was, it had to have been huge and moving like a bat out of hell." She felt a little better, hearing someone else's voice.

"Need me to get someone out there?"

She contemplated that for a moment. It was getting late and would probably be nice to have someone out here to help her with this disaster. The only other person who ran roadkill duty was Earl, and she didn't care for the man one bit.

"Nah, that's ok, Don. Just had to let you know I might be running a little later getting back tonight, that's all."

"You sure. I can get Earl on the horn if you need him?

Just say the word."

"No, no. That's fine. I can take care of it."

"Alright, well let me know if you change your mind."

"Will do. Over and out."

She placed the walkie back in its cradle and got out of the truck, before she lost her nerve. Better to just keep her head down and power through.

Just like any other day.

As she watched the water and blood flow like rivers into the ditch, she realized she had been kidding herself. Things hadn't gotten better. They hadn't gotten better at all. Her nerves felt just as exposed as the ones torn loose from the dead animals she was in the process of cleaning up now. Insides on the out. Vulnerable and destroyed.

After she had gotten most of the gore shoveled up and the blood washed away, she took a moment to examine the heads. Because, of course, she had been putting them off till last, afraid to look into their eyes. Afraid of what she would see.

It was nearly impossible to separate the two severed heads from one another. Their antlers were so intertwined into each other's flesh and bone that it would take some heavy tools to separate them properly. In the back of her mind, she wondered what the skulls would look like mounted on her wall.

The two skulls, fused together in a final, violent embrace.

She tried to look at them sideways, with her peripherals, as she leaned down to pick them up and place them in the black bag that would carry them to their final resting place. She tried, but the red western sun glistened off their dead eyes, making them seem to glow and draw her in.

She looked away and reached out with one gloved hand, ready to grab the mass and hide it away.

*Penny.*

Her body froze and her blood ran cold as every hair on her body stood up straight. Was she crazy, or had something just spoken her name? The words seemed to come from everywhere and nowhere, as if uttered by the very air itself.

Suddenly she was acutely aware of the heat swarming around her. Swallowing her up. She felt as if her skin was about to catch fire and had to resist the urge to scream.

When she heard the laugh, she was no longer able to hold back her shriek.

A dam broke and her fight or flight took over. She kicked at the heads and ran towards the truck. She hopped into the cab, started the truck up, and took off down the road in reverse.

As she backed up, she tried not to look. Try as she might, she couldn't help but stare in horror as the two decapitated deer heads laughed together, as if sharing in some sort of terrible inside joke.

- - -

Naturally, Penny had barely been sleeping at all. She couldn't get that inhuman laughter out of her mind. It kept her up at nights, and on more than one occasion, she was sure she heard her name. Voiced by some unholy abomination—something neither alive nor dead, something unborn—creeping its way from under her bed or behind her shower curtain. Tormenting her.

Yet, by some miracle, she kept on working. And no one seemed to really notice any change in her. Yes, of course, Don had mentioned the bags under her eyes on one morning after a long night of sleeplessness. But such things were easily explained away. She had always kept mostly to herself anyway, so from an outside perspective, not much had changed for Penny.

But everything had changed.

She was jumpy and on edge all week, finding ways to avoid or rush through her work. The animals she had disposed of, catching sideways glances at her. Whispering gossip and telling secrets to one another.

As she drove down a long stretch of highway 89 with dense forest shoved up against the roadside, she thought about last night. She could still feel the maggots crawling through her fingers.

She had woke up in a panic—something that had become all too menial as of late—only to find herself behind the wheel of her pick up. At first, she was confused. Who wouldn't be? The last she remembered, she was tossing and turning on the couch, trying to fall asleep to some late night infomercial. Then, mercifully, she must have dozed off for a while. When she came to—sitting in the dark, listening to the crickets chirping away near her car port—she became vaguely aware of her raw, bare feet, covered in dirt and scratches.

Before she had time to fixate on her feet, she felt something squirming in her hands. Something large and wet, emitting a dank odor. Fear had begun to rise in her chest from somewhere down deep, and threatened to grab hold.

From on top of the hill, a car swung onto the road, briefly filling the cab of the truck with warm orange light. It wasn't long, but she had time to see.

On her lap was the two deer heads, skewered together with the flesh eaten away enough to reveal almost all the teeth, pulled back in a ghastly grin. Maggots squirmed in her lap and across her hands.

The fear had graduated into full blown terror. All her nerves seemed to catch fire with panic so intense she wasn't even aware she was screaming. She flung the rotting mass onto the passenger seat and bolted out the door and into the safety of her apartment.

She was pretty sure that the skin around the antlers had started to rot into the shape of a spiral.

Eventually, after the safe light of dawn, she made her way back down to her truck.

Nothing.

No apparent sign of anything wrong. Even the dirt off her feet was gone (wiped clean, perhaps?).

So she went about her day. She knew it would probably be better to take a sick day, and she had definitely earned enough PTO to take as much as she needed. She couldn't decide what was worse: Sitting at home, stewing in her thoughts? Or scraping roadkill off the side of the highway? Even though the animals had been provoking her, it seemed worse when she was on her own. Nerves on end, just waiting for the dead creatures to find some way to torture her. Teasing her with questions. Questions that were almost certainly better left unanswered.

Why her? She asked herself. Why had the animals focused on her? She had been good to them, hadn't she? She supposed it was because she saw things no one else ever cared

to notice. Small details, here and there. She could read people.
Oh, yes. A small glance off to the side or the twitch at the corner of a mouth. She could always pick up on the small things.
The coincidences. There had always been so many coincidences. Things too perfect to have just happened by chance.
She wasn't sure if she believed in God or not, but she was
sure about fate. That there was something planned for all of
us. That maybe, there was some force behind the universe,
pulling on her strings, making her dance like a puppet on a
stage.

Giving in to the things that were happening to her, actually made her start to feel better, accepting her fate.

She contemplated this as she drove, looking for more
lifeless creatures, laying on the side of the road, just waiting
for her to save them.

As if summoned by the thought, she rounded a bend in
the road and glanced the familiar sight of roadkill up ahead.
She couldn't quite tell from this far away yet, but at least there
didn't seem to be an excessive amount of blood. A sign that
usually pointed to more strange encounters she had been having. But despite all this talk of accepting ones fate and coming
to terms with her situation, her stomach was doing back flips.

It didn't get any better by the time she pulled up to the
scene. In fact, the butterflies in her gut seemed to be doing
full on gymnastics.

There were no deer in the road, which in itself was not
unusual. Even though deer was the most common, she ran into all kinds of animals in her profession. Skunk, rabbits, dogs,
cats and any kind of varmint you can imagine, but rarely more
than one at a time.

Lined up in a straight row was a dog, two cats, six rabbits, a skunk, a fox and three squirrels. All laying with their heads down, crushed by a singular force. To her, it looked like they were praying.

She got out of her truck and stood staring dumbstruck at the would-be congregation. A few feet from the fourteen crushed skulls was a spiral, painted on the asphalt in what looked like grease.

She was trying to wrap her head around what she was seeing. Trying to take it all in. She couldn't help but think that this display had been presented for her—this theater.

Scared of the awesome forces that could do such a thing, she braved a closer look. On the critters faces that weren't totally destroyed, she saw bliss.

- - -

That night was another sleepless night. After seeing the animals (praying) laying in the road like that, she didn't know what to do, so she just left them. Left them and went home. Don had called from the office a couple times, but she just let the machine take it. He left a message saying they were worried and asking if she was ok. Penny thought someone might come over if she didn't answer, so she called them back. Told them she was ok, just had some stomach thing. Maybe food poisoning. Don wished her better and said he would talk to her soon. She smiled and sounded pleasant.

All the while she had been carving spirals into the kitchen table with a pocket knife. By the time she got off the phone she had made a half dozen. She almost didn't even realize she was doing it. She felt hypnotized, sucked in.

Later she tried to watch some TV, but couldn't focus. She kept seeing spirals everywhere and seeing strange things happening on the TV. She even saw a commercial for a diner that specialized in serving roadkill. Kind of like a gimmick. She knew about these places, of course. They were another good way to make sure the animal didn't die in vain. She had thought about trying it sometime, but could never bring herself to do it. She spent too much time with those creatures to do something like that to them.

Everything had started to feel unreal. Like the world around her was just some illusion, painted on the surface to hide the true dark nature of reality lurking underneath.

She was hearing whispers now. Voices of the beasts, fallen prey to the highway. Calling out to her to join them. Telling her she was the only person who could comprehend the truth. Baiting her with the secrets of life and death.

Everywhere she turned, she caught a glimpse of something out of the corner of her eye—a paw, darting quickly under the bed. A reflection of some horned thing in the mirror—but just for a split second.

She paced back and forth, back and forth. She knew she needed to do something.

- - -

She couldn't quite remember how she had gotten there, but sometime in the earlier hours of the morning Penny found herself standing on a long stretch of highway, surrounded by trees. Her feet were aching and even bleeding in a few parts. She was confused of course—confused about how she had somehow blacked out and walked here—but she also realized she was completely naked from head to toe, and covered in some sort of grease.

In the moonlight, she could make out the spiral on the ground, etched in the same fatty substance that covered her body.

Pins and needles danced across her skin, causing her to break out in goose flesh. Daggers of panic shot into her stomach, and she thought she might pass out again…Until she heard a whisper.

It was faint, but clearly from the tree line. She looked up and saw them.

Just inside the darkness were hundreds of dead animals, standing along the trees and watching her. Their eyes dead and their flesh falling off their bones. A light appeared from somewhere down the road, igniting small glares in all their eyes, and making its way closer to her.

The whispering grew louder, but she couldn't understand what they were saying. They were on all sides of her, watching and speaking in some unknown tongue. She felt as if they were speaking words of encouragement. To her they sounded excited.

She started to laugh as the light grew closer and closer, her audience joining in and laughing with her. Soon, she would be free from torment. Soon, she would have all the answers.

The trumpets blared and the light enveloped her.

The last thing she heard was her own mad glee.

# THE DARK PLACE

C.R. Langille

The clouds churned above Rosa, threatening to release another torrent of rain at any moment. The storm had come upon her without much warning. One moment it had been sunny and warm, the next, dark, gray, and thunder bellowing all around her.

Rosa picked up a rock from the ground. It was still wet from the recent rains and leeched what little warmth was left from her skin, but it was real. She was sure of it...well, mostly sure. She had lost her pills when crossing the river. At first things were fine, but as the days turned into weeks, things were getting fuzzier. Since getting separated from Mama, things were getting worse.

*They are coming, mija! Run! I'll lead them away!*

That was two days ago. Mama didn't show up at the big tree that looked like a skeleton. That had always been the plan since hitting the mountains. Meet at the skeleton tree. The man with the big beard and soft eyes marked it on their map. It was supposed to have supplies. It didn't have anything but a gym bag full of empty protein bar wrappers. Ever since the rain, it was getting colder and colder, and Rosa couldn't wait anymore.

Mama wasn't coming back; however, *they* were coming. The falling temperatures told her that much.

*They bring the cold with them, mija.*

She had to find somewhere to hide, and somewhere to get warm again. Otherwise, she'd freeze to death before *they* or anyone else ever found her.

She had spied the cabin from below, its green, metal roof catching a lone ray of sun. It was as if God himself had given her a sign. The hike up had her huffing and puffing for air, and the dirt road was slick with mud. Yet, she found it.

The cabin was two stories tall. The number two was carved into a sign near the door. Rosa bounced the rock in her hand before sending it through the cabin's window. The noise startled a nearby bird and it flew off with a caw.

The wilderness fell silent as the bird retreated to another part of the forest, a part that didn't involve rocks hitting windows. Rosa listened, trying not to breathe. Had *they* heard? She prayed they hadn't and unlatched the lock on the broken window and crawled into the cabin.

She found herself in a small kitchen and immediately opened up the fridge and cupboards. The fridge was empty and turned off, and the cupboards only held a handful of cooking implements and seasonings. Rosa's stomach growled, dejected.

She turned on the faucet to the sink and pipes rattled, yet surprisingly water began to pour. Rosa leaned over and drank up the water. It had a strange, metallic taste, but she was thirsty and didn't think much of it.

A branch snapped outside, louder than a gunshot. Rosa turned off the water and sunk down onto the floor.

They had heard her break the window, she knew it.

Rosa held her breath and closed her eyes, hoping they would move on.

*Be careful, mija, for if they get you, they'll take you away to a dark place. A place where you'll be lost. They'll take you away and you'll never be found again!*

Rosa didn't want them to take her away to a dark place. Her mother's words had scarred her from an early age and ever since her mother first uttered them, Rosa had looked behind her shoulder, always on the lookout for *them*.

*What are they, Mama?*

*Demons, mija. Demons. They bring the cold and darkness with them. As cold as ice.*

There was a creak from the boardwalk that was beside the house. Rosa stifled a scream and bit into her hand. Tears ran down her cheeks and her heart felt as if it would tear through her chest.

Rosa shivered and her breath formed small clouds of condensation in front of her face. Another sign they were close.

*They suck your will to live, draining you of everything decent until you're just a thing, no longer a person. You'll change when they take you, until one day, you're discarded, or even worse, mija—you turn into one of them.*

Rosa crawled toward the hallway. The hard floor sent waves of pain bouncing through her knees as she scuttled across the fake hardwood. Rosa scurried past the main entrance but stopped.

The door rattled as if something was trying to force its way in.

The wind outside picked up and thunder boomed in

the distance. Lightning flashed and sent shadows dancing all across the wall. Shadows that moved like people, but not. Shadows that encroached ever closer to Rosa.

She got up and ran up the stairs.

*Stupid.*

The wind howled and sent something crashing in the kitchen below.

The door shook along with the entire cabin. She was sure they would break in at any moment and come take her away to the dark place. Upstairs there was a hallway with a room on either end. In the middle of the hallway, facing the stairs, there was a tiny door, about a quarter of the size of a normal door. A small end-table was slid up against it and there was a handwritten sign that read: Do Not Open.

A window broke downstairs and Rosa let out a scream. She ran into one of the bedrooms. It was a simple lay-out with a bed with folded linen stacked on top of the mattress; a cheap, wooden nightstand; and a chair upholstered in an ugly floral print that smelled like it a retirement home. She closed the door behind her and slid the chair over to block the entrance. It was dumb but better than nothing.

Rosa pulled a blanket off the pile and crawled under the bed. She covered herself with the blanket and waited.

The wind screamed and the cabin shook. Thunder boomed across the mountaintops and the lightning created a light show throughout the room.

*They come like a storm, mija. Lights rolling like lightning across the sky. They make noise everywhere they go, because they don't care…by the time you hear them, it's already too late.*

They never came upstairs, or if they had, Rosa never knew. She woke up underneath the bed, wrapped in the blanket. Drool ran from the corner of her mouth and had pooled on the floor. She lifted her head and bumped it against the metal frame of the bed.

"Ay, Dios mio!" she said and slid out from under the frame. Her head throbbed and every muscle in her body protested as she stood.

Rosa tip-toed to the window and peeked out. The sun shined brightly across the valley below and the winds had died down to a slight breeze that tickled the aspen trees.

She listened as hard as she could, but the cabin was silent. Perhaps *they* couldn't find her, so they left? Rosa opened the door to the bedroom and winced when the hinges let out a long squeak.

As she walked past the small door as cool draft blew from underneath, lightly touching her exposed ankle. The sensation caused her skin to break out in goosebumps and she shivered. Rosa would have to remember to give that door a wide berth. There was something about it…she couldn't quite figure it out. Perhaps it was the way it was blocked off? Or maybe the note saying not to open it…something she didn't like. Or maybe it was because she knew that behind that door was a dark place.

*They will come to take you away to a dark place.*

Rosa hurried down the stairs and found the cause of the crash from earlier. A tree had fallen during the storm and broken the large window above the couch. Shards of glass littered the floor, catching the sunlight in a hundred different ways. It should have been a beautiful sight, instead, it only sent waves of pain through her head.

Her mouth was dry so Rosa walked over to the sink and turned it on. The pipes rattled again, but there was another noise, a knocking. She took a quick drink and then turned off the faucet, but the knocking continued. A few small raps, then quiet. It came again in rapid succession. Then it stopped.

Rosa walked toward the front door. She reached for the doorknob when the knocking happened again. She froze.

It hadn't come from the front door but from upstairs. Rosa climbed the stairs, her eyes locked on the small door that looked bigger than before, almost towering. However, when she stood in front of it, it only came up to her chest.

"H-hello?"

Only silence and the note: Do Not Open.

*When they take you to the dark place, mija, you can't see anymore. After a while, you lose count of how many days you've been in there. All you see is the others. The others they have taken. Others like you.*

The knocking happened again. Quick thuds against the wooden door. The knob shook with the knocks and Rosa fell backward and almost toppled back down the stairs.

*They* were here. *They* were coming for her.

Rosa scrambled to her feet and ran down the stairs.

"Mija, stop!"

It was Mama's voice, and it was coming from behind the tiny door.

"Mama?"

"Sí, it's me. Can you help me?"

Her mother's voice was soft, muffled. As if she were

further away. Rosa climbed the stairs until she found herself in front of the door again. There were noises from downstairs, but she couldn't focus on those. They faded into the background, almost like a buzzing. Voices too, but she didn't listen. Her ears were tuned to her mother's voice.

"Mama, how did you get in there?" Rosa asked.

"Open the door. It's so dark in here."

Rosa moved her hand toward the knob but hesitated. Do Not Open.

"I...I don't know. I'm scared, Mama."

The cool air caressed her skin from underneath the door, and the knocking happened again, more distant than before.

"I know you are, mija. I'm scared too. It's so dark. I can't see anything. You have to help!"

Tears rolled down Rosa's cheeks and blurred her vision. She reached out towards the door. From downstairs came a crash as something busted into the cabin. Footsteps pounded from below, but Rosa didn't care. Her mother was in trouble, and only she could help.

She grabbed the wooden table. It was heavy and hard to move across the floor but squealed as she forced it away from the door. Rosa turned the knob and cracked the door open, peering into the darkness.

There were a few small holes in the wall and sunlight tried to creep into the small room, but the shadows were able to keep the light at bay. Rosa couldn't see anything.

"Mama?"

Something moved in the corner, scratching against the

wood. Rosa turned toward it just as something small and white flew past her. She screamed and threw her arms up over her face as the *thing* hit her then fluttered away. Rosa tried to see what it was, but it had already flown downstairs before she could get a good glimpse. She hoped it was just a bird. It had to have been a bird.

Rosa got to her knees and started to dust herself off when something else moved into the small room. A slight creak of the floorboards followed by a crack that sounded like bones grinding together.

The voices in her head were getting louder. Something was coming up the stairs, but she didn't pay it any attention. Instead, her gaze was transfixed in the darkness and the two pinpoints of light that had just blinked at her. Eyes like those of a cat at night.

Rosa wanted to move. She wanted to run as far and as fast as she could, but she was frozen. Her legs refused to budge other than tremble in rhythm with her heart.

*"Mija, is that you?"*

The voice was death, littered with rot and decay— gravel against wet sand. There were more pops and cracks as the thing in the darkness moved. The eyes came closer.

*"Come…help me out of here."*

From the dark room, a hand emerged. It grasped the doorframe with gnarled fingers the color of birch bark and dirt. Bones ground against each other as the hand grasped the wood, crackling through the air. Long nails extended like talons and dug trenches into the wall.

Rosa took a step back, her legs finally able to move.

*"Don't go, mija. Come in here and HELP ME!"*

Rosa turned and ran down the stairs. The thing scrambled across the hardwood floor above her, its nails clacking as it came after her. Rosa turned the corner too fast and stumbled down the last flight. She got to her feet and wobbled towards the door.

*"Mija! Come join me and the others in the darkness! Don't go!"*

Rosa glanced back and instantly wished she hadn't. The thing stood on the landing and pointed at her. Its mouth was large, larger than any person's should be. Long limbs stretched towards the ground and it had twisted, greasy hair the color of burnt coal.

Rosa screamed and ran toward the door but ran into something solid. She fell back on her butt and scrambled back on her hands and feet. Standing before were six figures with solid black eyes draped in matching shrouds of ice.

*They* had found her.

# PALINOPSIA

Joni B. Haws

Thunder startled Mara awake, electric hands pulling her from dreams to the oppressive darkness in the room. The red numbers of the digital clock were bloody scratches on black canvas. Rain lashed the bedroom window as the dregs of sleep fell away. Another low rumble slunk through the house, reaching through the mattress and up her spine.

Mara had never grown out of her fear of thunderstorms, the way the unexpected bursts of light bleached every surface, the sound resonating through a person from everywhere and nowhere. It hadn't helped that as a child seeking comfort, her father would mock her, shaking her with a loud yell during the biggest thunderclaps instead of pulling her into the protective embrace she longed for.

"Suck it up, Scarecrow," he would say. "Who you gonna run to if there's a storm when you're all grown?"

Justin puffed evenly beside her, dead asleep.

With a groan, she remembered the grill which she had seen still left open as the party guests were leaving. It would be a birdbath by morning if she didn't go down and shut it. She pulled back the covers and stood. She was all grown.

The darkness in the house was thick enough to choke on, all ambient light encroached by the storm, but Mara could navigate it with her eyes closed. Eight steps to the door, five across the landing to the first step.

The kitchen tile was much chillier on her bare feet than it had been before. Mara could smell the dishes still waiting to be washed and said a silent prayer of thanks that her mother-in-law didn't have to know about them. "I've been surprised how much mess Justin is willing to live in," she could hear Danielle's voice say. She must have forgotten that Justin had hands too.

Thinking of Danielle ushered in the shame from earlier in the evening and she pushed the thought away.

The rain intensified against the patio door, a distant flash illuminating the open hood of the grill haloed in clouds of bruised purple. She slid the glass door open, angry tree branches lunging from above.

Out and in. Five seconds.

The moment her foot touched the wet concrete was like the detonation of a landmine. A crash of impossible, ultra-white light washed over the world, forcing her eyes closed. The boom of thunder, more than just deafening, vibrated through her bones, her teeth, her guts. The magnitude of the strike, simultaneous blinding light, and engulfing roar so powerful it sucked the wind from her lungs, could not have terrified her more had the ground disappeared beneath her.

Grill forgotten, she jumped back into the house, throat streaked with a scream.

She hurdled up the stairs to the bedroom, batting at the strange after-images that painted themselves on the darkness. Justin, to her disbelief, still puffed away, unmoved. With joints still buzzing, Mara leapt into bed. Sobs poured from her the moment she wrapped her arms around her husband's safe form, their earlier argument disregarded.

"What's wrong?" Justin asked, voice muzzy. Mara couldn't answer. She could not put her fear into words. It was more than just being startled, it was the feeling of being so very tiny, the possibility of being consumed by forces too big to comprehend.

And there the vision plaguing her now, the picture flitting about the room as she blinked to clear it. Mara had been blinded by the pure, wretched burst of light. Now, imprinted on the shadows, she saw the bright, hollow image of a person, arms stretched out as though basking in rainfall.

Her blood was electric, and though Justin pulled her close, rubbing her arms with his calloused fingertips and tucking an "I love you" into the recess of her neck, she couldn't calm. There had not been anyone else outside, she was sure, yet there was the image, a luminous figure on a photograph negative, seared onto the darkness. The man with the out-stretched hands.

- - -

That day, before the thunder and lightning arrived, another storm had been brewing. The argument couldn't have come at more inconvenient time.

Despite her extra-strength deodorant, the pits of Mara's top already bled with dark circles. She eyed the clock for the tenth time in two minutes, stabbing toothpicks into little smoked sausages and cubes of cheese. She took deep breaths to still her shaking hands while she lined the white serving tray. Vacuuming had led to the discovery of dust on the baseboards, and she had decided last minute to scrub her bathroom in addition to the guest bath, because some people were snoops.

Now, most of the hors d'oeuvres weren't prepped.

Justin sat, dressed in a blue polo and his best-fitting jeans, scrolling through files at the kitchen desk. His sandy hair, still damp, would air-dry into its signature wave, the result of a fortunate cowlick. His knee bounced while he hummed under his breath.

"Whatcha doin'?" Mara asked with faux nonchalance.

"I told Sadie I'd send her a couple of the new tracks to see what she thinks."

Mara's breath hitched, her jaw muscle flexing. Side-step, Mara, she thought. Now's not the time.

"Right now? The party starts in fifteen minutes and your parents are always early. Do you think maybe you could get the grill started?" She ran a careful wrist along her eyebrow, sweeping hair from her eyes.

"Just one minute."

"They'll be here in just one minute. Geez Justin, it's your dad's birthday, maybe you could lift a finger to help your wife instead of sending love songs to your girlfriend." The words popped out like paper snakes in a can.

Justin turned his head with an exasperated tilt. "Really? We've been through this. Sadie is my friend. She has always been just my friend."

"Do you make out with all your friends?" Why was she doing this?

"Mar, you cannot be mad at me for things I did before we even met. Yeah, I kissed her, but we never actually dated. If I had wanted to be with her, I would have tried to be with her, but I didn't. I chose you. And I've done nothing to betray that in the four years we've been married."

Mara flipped on the faucet, washing her hands like they held the plague. "So, what you're doing right now, that's not betraying me?"

The doorbell rang.

Justin gave her a pleading look. Could they just call a truce and get on with the evening, those eyes said. She glared back at him. She didn't want to call a truce. Her carefully chosen outfit, freshly touched up brows, and meticulously applied lashes were all just wrapping paper concealing an inferno of anxiety.

Justin answered the door with a jaunty "Hey," no hint in his voice that anything was amiss. Mara hoped he was preserving as many of the meticulous vacuum lines as possible, so his mother would notice.

Mara took another deep breath, rubbing her palms on her thighs. Shoulders back, smile on. Please, dear Lord, let no one look in the oven to find the dirty dishes she hadn't had time to wash. Mara heard distinctive back-clapping as Justin wished his dad a happy birthday. How easily he could turn on the charm.

Danielle stepped into the kitchen from the front room. Her gaze crept over the full strawberry clamshells and bulging grocery sacks. "Need any help, Mara?" she asked.

Mara was wise to this trick. Show no vulnerability. "No, I got it." She picked up the tray of sausages and cheese to take it to the table—And tripped on the high-heel wedges she'd slipped off while standing at the counter. She fell with a grunt, plastic tray tumbling to the tile along with its contents.

Danielle reached out an impotent hand while Mara's cheeks burned.

"I'm fine. No worries, I got it. It's fine," Mara said, ignoring the stinging in her ankle.

Danielle stooped to pick up a few token sausages, placing them on the tray. There, she'd helped.

"Well, at least it wasn't the food people actually wanted to eat," she said, patting Mara on the thigh.

Mara smiled up at her with all the warmth of November, then turned away and began gathering the mess, hiding her glistening eyes behind a curtain of chemically straightened hair and dutiful industry. The doorbell rang again.

It was going to be a long night.

- - -

Mara woke with a headache gnawing at her temples. She remembered feeling like she'd never fall back asleep after her middle-of-the-night scare, her fruitless efforts to squint away the image of the man with the outstretched arms.

Even now, with sharp slants of sunlight shooting through the blinds, she still saw the image in her eyelids. It was more indistinct now, the edges consolidated to display a crooked cross painting itself on the ceiling, the walls, the square of folded toilet paper.

She was so tired.

Mara didn't have to be to the salon until 11:00, but wanted to see Justin off and maybe get a workout in. She pulled on a pair of sweatpants and padded down the stairs.

Justin was on the phone.

"Yeah, I feel like it's missing something. Listen to it with headphones and tell me if you think I should add a stronger baseline."

Apparently, Sadie was the first thing on Justin's mind this morning. Mara wondered if Sadie was afraid of thunderstorms. Justin gave her a brief glance as she shuffled by, acknowledging her with a flick of his eyebrows.

"Oh, speaking of background vocals," he continued, "I've got a new call and response love song. Think you'd want to come in and lay down the female tracks on the demo?"

Mara bit her upper lip while retrieving a mug and the box of Bengal Spice tea bags. The ethereal figure bobbed along their surfaces. No matter how many times she told herself that two people singing a love song together did not mean they were in love, she could not fight a stab of jealousy. So what if she was being irrational? Justin knew how much it bugged her that he stayed close to Sadie, still asked her to collaborate. If he loved Mara, couldn't he just cut those ties? Mara pulled a fat apple from the fridge, reached for a knife from the block by the sink, and made a mental note to do the dishes.

Justin laughed, a hearty sound so big he had to throw his head back to let it out. "I forgot about that! Didn't we call her 'Spork and Mindy?'" Another gleeful squeal.

Mara had no idea what they were talking about. She wanted to take an axe to each of their private jokes, lobotomize all the things they had in common from their stupid little—Icy pain sliced through her finger. Mara sucked in a breath, looked down at her hands, and after a moment of dumb disbelief, began to scream.

In her right hand she held the knife. On her left, blood streamed, dripping in thick rivulets down her palm and forearm from the open wound where finger met hand, or rather,

where finger *should* have met hand. The finger itself lay inno-
cently on the cutting board, wedding ring still attached, the
princess cut stone glinting in the morning sun.

Mara dropped the knife and gripped her wrist, instinctively squeezing to slow the flow of blood. How could she
possibly have severed her finger without damaging those
around it? Her heartbeat became a timpani, booming in her
ears, pounding behind her eyes, and throbbing agony into the
gushing absence of her hand.

She stumbled backward, into Justin's arms, whimpering, "No, no, no," a litany strung together into a single word.

"What's wrong?" Justin asked, the concern a copper
note in his voice. "Mar, what's the matter?"

"My finger!" she moaned, thrusting her damaged hand
into the air. Blood tumbled over the ridges of her knuckles,
sliding to her elbow before dripping in viscous splats onto the
floor.

"Which finger?" He reached for her hand. "Did you
smash it?"

She shifted her gaze, and disbelief, from her hands to
her husband. "Smash it? I freaking cut it off!"

Justin straightened, peering into her eyes, searching
for signs of jest. Before she could protest, he had taken her
hand in his, "What are you talk—"

"No," she cried, trying to pull away, her remaining
four fingers rigid stalks.

No. Five rigid stalks. Justin pulled her left hand into
his own, studying each of her delicate, clean, non-severed fingers. The stone on her ring drooped heavily toward her pinky.

"Are you hurt?" Justin's eyes squinted nearly shut

when he was concerned.

She could only stare at her unblemished hand, pulling her fingers into a fist, then flexing them again. No pain. She glanced at the cutting board where she was sure she had seen her own amputated finger just moments before. The apple sat sliced neatly in half.

Her legs turned to water and she sank to the floor, bringing a reluctant Justin, still gripping her by the arm, down with her. She leaned against the cupboard, letting her head fall back.

"Mar? Hon?" Justin's voice seemed far away as she closed her eyes. The strange image still remained, a bright figure against black. Only now the shape had changed. One outstretched arm was drawn in, the crook of an elbow visible, hand a stumped fist, as though prepped for a fight. And though the shape was only an outline filled with light, Mara detected that the tilt of the head had changed, that if the thing had eyes they would be staring right at her. Right through her. Her headache boomed, and she forced her eyelids open.

- - -

Mara spent the next hour in a cycle of crying, deep breathing, and calling clients to postpone. She rescheduled all of her appointments, gulped down Excedrin, and climbed back in bed. Her mind crept along the events of the past 24 hours as if it were a minefield, careful not to put too much weight on the most terrifying moments. The finger, the light-ning strike, Danielle's smug burn the evening before. It was a good thing Danielle couldn't see her now. Her Justin deserved a wife as strong as he was, someone who could march step-for-step with him up the mountain of success.

Justin had marched himself right out the door and to

work fifteen minutes after her… what? Vision? Delusion? With a kiss on the cheek, and the sage directive to, "Take it easy," he had trundled off to the warehouse job he hated, but which paid for electricity a lot better than a series of beautiful chord progressions. Mara brought a hand to her waist. Maybe it was for the best they had no children. They were barely making ends meet as it was.

As if on cue, a text came through from Danielle, sent to both Justin and her.

"Just wanted to share the good news! Look at Karen's new grandbaby! Number four! Isn't he just a doll? Can't wait until I have pictures of my own grandbabies to share! Kisses, Mom."

Attached with the message was a photo of Justin's aunt Karen holding a swaddled bundle of powder-blue muslin, round, pink cheeks, and a cotton beanie.

The faint glow of the clenched-fisted man white-washed the photo, taunting her. Danielle's hints were getting heavy-handed. If she only knew.

Mara wanted to throw her phone at the wall but instead set it down gently on the bed. Lots of people had miscarriages, and two didn't necessarily make a pattern. She clung to her doctor's assurances that there was nothing wrong with her, that it was just a fluke, that they had every hope of carrying a baby full term.

Curling into a ball, Mara turned her face into the pillow and sobbed. It wasn't fair. Why did so many people end up with pregnancies they didn't want while her anxious womb remained empty? Her mind filled with her father's voice, snide and hard, "Girlie, you better figure out a way to fill out. A man wants a woman with enough tits and ass to soften his landing. We like women who look like they can pass down the family line. Turn yourself into a good sow and some guy will pick you up."

Mara pulled her shoulders up, physically shying from the words of a man who had been in the grave for over two years. "I'm not a sow," she said through clenched teeth, while at the same time wondering if he had been right. Maybe her straight hips and flat chest meant her body wasn't fertile soil for a baby to germinate.

The afterglow man pulsed brighter in her vision.

She ran her hands through her hair, rubbed her face. She needed a shower. Maybe that tea she never drank, and a Netflix binge. Mental health day.

Mara stood in front of the full-length mirror while she undressed. She had always been thin, but her appetite had dropped lately, making her hip bones jut even more, leaving space between her skin and the waistband of her underwear. Without a padded bra her breasts looked wistful, even the nipples a muted pink, as though trying not to bring attention to themselves. She had a figure New York runways would pay a load of dimes for, but in Layton, Utah, she was just a collection of sticks unfit for bearing children. She let her gaze crawl along every angle of her body, the shape of the afterglow man a laser tattoo tracing the line of her eyes.

She pulled the elastic from her dark tresses and shook them out, letting them fall in a heap over her shoulders.

A stinging cramp shot through her stomach, folding her at the waist. She straightened, looking in the mirror, and gasped. Where moments before smooth, taut skin lay, a cavernous hole festered from just below her ribcage to the slope of her traitorous hips, as though eaten away by ravenous mouths. The skin around the maw in her torso exposed bloody, ragged tears, bits of flesh hanging by sinew. Heaps of slick intestine lay along the pelvic floor, the stone knobs of her spine snaking upward backstage. Through one crenulated, golf-ball-sized hole, light pierced through her back. No stomach, no reproductive organs, just pus-like masses of writhing maggots feeding like bees busy in a hive.

Mara didn't scream. She gulped in breath after breath, hungry for oxygen, for reason. She felt sick to her absent stomach, reaching a ginger hand to her torso but unable to force contact.

Missing abdomen notwithstanding, she was going to puke. She flew to the toilet, bending just in time for the yellow bile to hit the water. Over and over she retched, long after there was nothing left to throw up. When the spasms eased, she pulled away from the toilet, trailing her fingers along the skin of her stomach, the pit of her navel. She looked down to see the same nude self she saw in the mirror every day. Stars tinged her vision while the afterglow man, bigger, as though he had taken a few steps closer, loomed. One hand rose in the foreground, reaching toward her, its eyes transformed into opaque smudges, like black fingerprints.

Mara huddled in the corner, the bathroom tile chilling her bare buttocks, and wailed, lubricating her terror with tears.

- - -

Two days later, Mara slipped in the back door of the salon, unable to escape over-dramatic Lexi, who hugged her shoulders and asked if she was okay. Mara folded her sunglasses and slipped them in her bag before hanging it on her hook in the break room.

"I'm fine." A complete lie, but everyone's favorite.

She endured identical greetings from the other stylists while she tied her apron around her back and went to prep her station. Her headache, a persistent thrum, had never gone away since Monday morning, and she'd been in a sort of willful trance since the tummy episode, never letting her thoughts touch anything beyond basic functionality. She had barely left bed, drowning her senses with several seasons of Friends, and the non-threatening platitudes of Leslie Knope. The afterglow man bobbed on the screen beside the jaunty characters, but she pretended it wasn't there.

Justin had washed all the dishes.

Her first client of the day was Connie, an old lady who came in once a week to get her curls set. Connie's red lipstick bled into the cracks of her wrinkled lips, and the tips of her fingers bent in unintended directions, but she was a cheerful woman with bright eyes and denture adhesive strong enough to outlast several hours of gossip.

She squeezed Mara's hand with the strength of a hummingbird before settling into the chair. Mara had to pump it way up to make Connie tall enough, knowing she would offend if she offered a booster.

"Are you feeling better, sweetheart?" Connie asked, this appointment being one of those rescheduled.

"Yes, much better now, thanks." Another lie. The pressure behind her eyes intensified, and she pressed her hands to her sides to still them. She wished she'd opted for flats today. The world felt off-balance.

Mara retrieved a comb and started smoothing out sections of the woman's ashy-blonde hair. Her roots were showing, but she could last one more week.

"Ready for a wash?" she asked.

Connie grinned like a skeleton. "Best part of my week!"

Mara helped Connie off the chair, then held out an arm for her to take as they walked to the wash bowls.

"Mara, honey, you are skin and bones. I don't know if you're holding me up or I'm holding you."

Mara forced a thin laugh and said nothing.

Connie took this as invitation. "Really, Mara, you need a sandwich. If your elbows poke out any farther people might think you're a dolled-up scarecrow."

Mara stiffened, the sound of her father's voice reverberating between her ears. "Hey there, Scarecrow, what're you gonna do about that hair? You're not going out like that, are you?"

Mara reached up and touched a curl lying on her shoulder, willing it not to misbehave. No, she wasn't a scarecrow. She had scared away those insults by now, hadn't she? She had forced her naturally bushy hair into sleek compliance, grown into her large teeth, trained her lanky elbows and knees to move with grace and agility. Justin told her she had a majestic beauty, the thing that had drawn him to her.

Sadie was squat, only coming up to Justin's shoulder, but her curves were conspicuous, balanced, and perky. It was a safe bet no one had ever called her "Scarecrow."

The shampoo bowls were in a separate room blocked off from natural light and lit up with soft, low-watt bulbs. Mirrors covered the walls both in front of and behind the sinks, visually doubling the bunches of silk flowers lining the floors and shelves. The smell of lavender permeated the small room from an oil infuser. It was an easy way to trick clients into feeling they were getting a spa experience.

The afterglow man shone like a flashlight on all Mara surveyed. She ignored him. It.

After settling Connie's neck in the ceramic crook, Mara began massaging her thin scalp beneath a flow a warm water. Connie closed her eyes, smiling faintly.

"People might think you're a dolled-up scarecrow," Connie's voice chimed, on a loop in Mara's mind. "A dolled-up scarecrow. A dolled-up scarecrow."

The voice morphed into that of her father, accompanied with his signature slow-head-shake. "You look like a god-damned scarecrow. Your blind dates won't know whether to take you to the movie or strap you to a cross in the berry patch."

Mara blinked, willing the voice from her mind, and a tear spilled onto each cheek. Her father was dead. Dead in the ground.

"Could you rub a little softer, please," Connie asked, voice strained.

"Oh, I'm sorry," Mara said, looking up.

She caught her reflection in the dim light and froze. She could not stop herself from turning toward it.

Mara's hair, normally dyed to a silky chestnut, stood out in knotted, grey clumps, some areas of her scalp completely bare save for weeping, red sores. The skin pulled so tightly around her gaunt face that the skin beneath her eyes pulled grotesquely away from the sockets, horrible goggles of tortured, angry flesh. Her nose, tip shriveled away, exposed the dark triangle of her sinus cavities. She tried to scream, but could not, as her lips were stitched closed in a ragged seam of bloody twine.

Beside her in the mirror the afterglow man stood, taller than her trembling frame, radiating a sickening light, his eyes now endless, dark pits. He had no mouth, yet Mara knew he smiled. Her client forgotten, Mara stared at the reflection, unable to blink. The luminescent hands of the figure rose, its mannerisms familiar, the curve of the arm, the angle of the wrist, closing first one finger, then the rest, around Mara's straining neck.

- - -

Connie propped herself up on the armrests, watched as her hairdresser, whose high cheek bones always made her long for younger days, stood fixated on her reflection. She registered the terror on Mara's face just before the girl lost consciousness and dropped in a heap of denim, floral cotton, and stiletto heels.

- - -

Justin heard Sadie approach and looked up, rubbing his eyes in a way that he hoped didn't look like swiping at tears, and stood to greet her.

"I hope you don't mind my dropping by," she said, leaning in to wrap one arm around his back. "When you said Mara was in the hospital, I got worried, but I don't want to intrude."

Justin gestured to a mustard-colored chair identical to his own. The harsh, fluorescent lights of the lobby gave them a sickly cast.

"It's okay. It's good to see a friendly face. I, um, haven't said anything to my family about it yet. Her mom is flying out, and some friends from church stopped by, but I've mostly been here alone. I didn't know who else to call." He resented the break in his voice.

The two sat, knees facing. Sadie didn't reach for his hand, didn't pat his arm, for which he was grateful. Even though Mara couldn't see them—bile rose in his throat as he thought the words—he was glad there was nothing to see. He and Sadie were just friends, had always, almost always, been just friends.

"Can I ask what happened?" Sadie's blue eyes were framed in dark lashes.

"The past couple of weeks, Sade, she's been weird. Headaches, jumpy about stuff, wouldn't leave her bed. She passed out at work last Wednesday and hasn't been back since." He fell back in his seat. "She, um, had surgery last night, and had a psych evaluation done this morning." He couldn't meet her eyes, couldn't try to explain what Mara had done. "I think she's going to be here for a long time. Whatever's been going on with her, she's been really scared. I could see it." He paused, unsure how to continue. "I should have done more. I tried to love her, to tell her things were okay. I just, I didn't know it could even get this bad." There was that voice break again. He blew out a long breath.

Sadie, a deep line forming on her brow, did take his hand now. "What happened, Justin?"

He looked up, caught her eyes, searching as if maybe they held some answers. The tears came in a flood, and he let them fall. "She, she said she couldn't watch it anymore, that he—don't ask me who—couldn't have power over her anymore. I don't know what she meant. But, while I was at work yesterday she… Sadie, she took a spoon and a steak knife and dug out her eyes."

A hand flew to Sadie's mouth, the taupe-painted nails like pebbles holding in her gasp. With the other she gripped Justin's limp fingers, resting them on his knee. "What does that mean, Jus? Is she, like, going to be okay?"

"I don't know," he said, his voice trailing to a squeak. Shuddering sobs overtook him, and Sadie fell to her knees to wrap him in an awkward embrace. He leaned into her and let himself cry. Her hair smelled like coconut and mint.

After a minute or so he pulled back, retrieving a wad of tissues from the pocket of his sweatshirt and wiping his face. He thought of the bandages across Mara's eyes, the strangely serene look she'd had all day, her indiscernible whispers. Would he ever get her back?

Staring now into Sadie's crystalline eyes, he was over-come with a new wave of sorrow. "Sadie," he whispered, "I don't know what I'm going to do. I haven't told Mara yet, don't even think she'd understand; she's really out of it."

Sadie leaned in close enough he could count her freck-les.

"Sade, Mara's pregnant. The doctor said almost eight weeks."

Later, after Sadie had convinced him to let her take him home, drink a smoothie, and take a nap, he lay alone in bed, the after image of Sadie's silhouette still on his eyelids. His finger itched, then burned, beneath his wedding ring. He took it off and set it on the nightstand.

As he drifted to sleep, Justin heard distant thunder, a long drawn out grumble that resonated within the broken spaces of his heart. His last thought before blessed sleep was that a storm was coming.

# ON THE EDGE OF SANITY

Brenda Wright

"Am I going mad, or…"

I push my head deeper in my arms, rocking back and forth, repeating over and over, "Am I insane? Why am I so alone? Why do I need to do this?" Memories flash again between so many questions.

I'm inside a dark car in a vacant parking lot located who-knows-where and it's nighttime. I swear, heads are popping up and sneering at me from outside of the car. They keep me unnerved, alert and on edge. These horrible heads carry faces from my nightmares.

What is happening? I'm not normally like this. I try to breathe deeply. Will I be able to stop this torture? Please don't let me be insane, remind me there is an end, a purpose to all this. I can't help but question if maybe—maybe, I have gone too far this time.

I need to calm myself and think. I'm not so old I can't get out of this situation. The golden years have made me sentimental. My faculties may have dulled over the years, but I have an iron memory. I started playing with some memories a few days ago. What was at first just entertainment, has now left me an exhausted mess.

I remember when my elderly father hallucinated. My

siblings and I thought it was funny, but now I empathize.

While on a walk, a few days back, I had the sensation the sidewalk was lengthening right in front of me. Salt Lake blocks are long, but it didn't look overly long at first glance. As I shuffled in the twilight of the cold early autumn, panic seeped in at the same moment I realized I may never reach the end of the block in time. I craved the end of the block, the corner where streetlights are brighter, and all is safer. As the shadows deepened around me, I picked up my pace as much as old age would allow.

When I was a child, I had to sprint, sometimes two steps at a time, up the stairs from our dark basement. Something was right behind me, clawing to get me before I reached safety at the top. I would get so scared I couldn't even breathe until I hit the landing.

Remembering the monster of the basement, an evil abomination, worse than the world had ever seen, I felt it was only inches behind me once again here on the street. Struggling to get my old legs moving, my heart rate jumped faster than appropriate for my age. I was desperate for the light.

Rounding the corner, sucking in air like an asthma victim, I found a safe spot and bathed myself in the glow of the vintage streetlight.

"Silly old fool," I mouthed as my heart pounded in my throat. Then, I swear, I caught something from the corner of my eye dash into the shadows. Goosebumps erupted down my arms and legs followed by a hard shiver and hot sweat.

A mere two days later it began again. First, I remember noticing a black ooze writhing up between the cobbles of the street my friend and I were walking on. An oily stink hit me as the goo gurgled up from the gaps I attempted to tip-toe over.

"What the hell is that black stuff?" I asked Debbie while I teetered over one particularly large gap.

"What do you mean, black stuff?" she said.

"Look at the space between the stones we're walking on. Can't you see that blackness? It's a liquid, isn't it?" I pointed to an enlarging slime patch near her left shoe. The oily stink wafting up was not a typical stink for a downtown street, but a more pungent sulfur stench like those hellish bubbling hotpots in Yellowstone. I knew I was going to fall into those stink pots and be boiled alive if I didn't grip my father's pant leg as tightly as one of his wood vises.

"Oh my God that stinks," I moaned. "Careful, if you step in it, it will eat your foot away. I bet it contains an alien biological acid," I said mostly to myself.

"You must have something stuck up your nose," she said.

I ignored her impairment as we stepped onto regular cement and continued on until I was hit in the face with the smell of burnt toast. I hate the smell of burnt toast, but I wasn't going to burden Debbie with this new observation. I could tell she was already irritated as I held my nose high in the air making loud sniffing sounds. How could she not smell it herself?

Burnt toast is all my mother could make and we had to eat it no matter how burnt it was. Mother would scream, "There are starving kids in China!" and then slap the back of our heads for punctuation. "Eat it or go hungry—that's all there is. Besides charcoal will do your stomach good." I heard mother's anger all the way from childhood. I glanced around expecting to see an open window where we could peek into another torture chamber.

Needing to think of nothing for a moment, I plugged my nose and tilted my head back to gaze up into the overhead tree branches. They looked like black cobwebs clinging to the fading sky, just like father pointed out on that fateful family camping trip so many years ago.

"Why are there bats downtown?" I shrieked as Debbie was smartly tying a scarf around her neck. "Are they diving at us? Are they the blood-sucking kind? I hate bats, father couldn't get them out of our tent. And they probably carry ticks," I added for Debbie's edification. "I'm sure they carry ticks. I hate ticks. They are covered in ticks—get away from me." I flung my arms around slapping at the horrid flying monsters. Ticks climbed my legs. I slapped at them as they tickled me on their journey to get into my panties.

"Seriously, Lottie, you are irritating tonight. Please keep your disturbing imagination to yourself if you don't mind." As the last word left her mouth Debbie added an impressive stomp on the ground for emphasis. She doesn't know it's impossible to smash a tick.

Debbie is often oblivious to my world. She is such a realist. She walks through life never looking to the left or the right and therefore missing most everything evolving around her.

We entered the Eccles Theatre to discover our tickets were on the highest level, Tier Three. Not only were we to sit in the highest tier but the ultimate last row of the highest tier—the unnerving row "K." I made the mistake of looking down from up there. Sudden vertigo made the stage zoom to the bottom of the Grand Canyon in a dizzying drop. A flimsy little knee-high safety rail was all that was between me and certain death. I clung to everyone I passed in my attempt to safely slide into my seat.

In a high tense voice, I squeaked, "Tight seats, in the middle of the row, dangling high up the nosebleed section of the theatre. What else bad could happen?"

Debbie played deaf and looked away. I too dramatically turned my head, right into the face of a young man straight from the pages of *Deliverance*. The moment I caught sight of crusted teeth inside his gaping mouth, I caught a whiff of his last meal. Meat and onion aroma hung around him like a rotting shroud barely holding down the rancid body funk of his dirty t-shirt. I felt him staring at me and I dry heaved into my purse.

The boy's demeanor worsened, and the air likewise became more suffocating. It was hard to inhale a decent breath of... What do you call a warm, moist, smelly gas which hundreds of people have circulated through their lungs hundreds of times? I threw back my head and gulped like a fish thrown in the bottom of a boat. I swear the creature next to me was flicking a blackened tongue over his pointy teeth when I caught him staring at my exposed damp neck.

"I want out of this theatre now," I mouthed to Debbie. She blinked and turned away.

It took all the strength I could muster not jump up and do a running scream all the way out of the theatre. I was just sane enough to realize I couldn't stand up in the dark. I would topple over and fall forever downwards, rolling on everyone's head only to stop with an awkward plunge at my death on the stage below. But, If I stay seated much longer I knew I would spew vomit all over the people in front of me, people so close their greasy heads were leaving dandruff on my knees. Which was the least terrifying, least mortifying way to die? I couldn't decide.

"I can't breathe," I all but yelled. Debbie reached over and patted my knee—a bit too harshly.

There was no way to stop the sweat dripping off my forehead and quivering upper lip. Where the hell did all these germ-infested flies come from, and why now? I swatted at a few that were determined to dance on my moist eyes and lips.

Debbie jabbed her elbow into my upper arm with amazing strength saying, "Please settle down, you are disturbing everyone, especially me."

Scared witless, I recounted the multiple ways I could die at any moment and all she could do was worry about being "disturbed?" She looked at me again, blinking. Then, I swear, she gave me a wink.

I know a sinister wink when I see one. I asked myself how well did I know this Debbie friend anyway? As a small girl, I was locked in a tiny bedroom, all alone, by a so-called friend. I cried and pounded on the door an entire afternoon before her older sister finally let my raw remains out of the prison cell.

I stared at Debbie through squinted eyes and would not have been surprised to see her morph into a well-coiffed killer. Next thing I knew, Debbie was waking me up and explaining I missed the show and we should leave since everyone else had.

"You're lucky you didn't have to wake up a dead body," I said with scorn.

Debbie grunted, "Honestly Lottie, your imagination will be the death of you."

Walking back to our apartments from the theatre, I didn't point out the scuttling insects running out in front of us on the walkway. Nor did I mention the screams of desperate creatures caught in the cold darkness at the edges of the side-walk, a darkness so deep it easily held the tons of vermin scurrying into it.

Shaking so hard from the frights filling the night, I clung onto Debbie and sang loudly, "Jesus wants me for a sunbeam." I trusted the song would not only keep me from remembering any more but would lead us to safety. Never was I so grateful to get inside my apartment with the door closed and locked.

- - -

Routine errands yesterday kept me busy and my mind occupied for the most part, but as the day progressed I realized I needed to use a public facility. I loathe public restrooms, but waiting was not an option.

When I was a younger woman I had the occasion to use the immense restroom in a big box store. It was near closing time when I entered the bathroom from a long, dark hallway. Quietly seated in a closed stall, doing my business, I hear someone burst in, flip off all the lights and shut the door. There I was sitting in complete and utter darkness. I couldn't see my hands in front of my face. I didn't know if someone had come into the bathroom and stayed for some evil reason or if they had mistakenly left me in alone upon closing the store for the night. Being back before cell phones, I had no way of making any light. I screamed out to whoever else might also be in the restroom. I threatened loudly that I had a weapon—a purse with which I could bludgeon anyone to death.

Though I couldn't find the toilet paper, I decided I had to find the door myself. I felt myself swirling and drowning in fear and desperation. I stumbled into sinks and followed the wall around until I felt the door. No escapee from a Siberian gulag felt as free as I did.

Well, yesterday evening, I found myself facing a public restroom. I pushed the door open to a pitch-black room. Darkness and fear both slapped me in the face as I stood frozen for a few moments in the doorway. My heart began running a marathon. I took one brave cautious step into the blackness reaching for a light switch and—

BAM! The automatic lights clicked on. I screamed childishly loud and long. The *It* clown had not jumped out, but I would have said he did. My little girl scream was followed by a humiliation giggle. I finally got a hold of myself and settled down in a closed stall not realizing I had just selected a front row seat to all hell breaking loose.

The stall walls closed in on me as the overhead lights dimmed. One lone red spotlight splashed its eerie glow down over my head. Sweat popped out on every inch of my skin, even though the room was frigid. At the first glimpse of creepy crawlies coming from under the neighboring stalls into mine, I let loose another scream. The crawlies squirmed and groped to get at my legs and climb into my dropped pants. I could feel the hot stinging feet of these, these—

"Oh my God, not black widow spiders! Please, no, no mom, I can't kill them!" I yelled over and over as I stomped and slapped my way into a full-on panic attack with no one this time to hold me and calm me down.

The large hideous black widow spiders would not stop creeping towards me. Each one had dripping fangs wriggling in front of their mouths. I could see my own contorted face reflecting in the shine of their swollen black bodies. Bristly legs grew longer and thicker before my eyes. Webs clung to me smelling like vomited rotting carcasses. I seized up and no more noise nor movement came out of me. My mind switched off.

Next was the smell of Lysol and a lady poking my arm. Opening my eyes, I saw I was curled up on the counter by the sinks.

The lady was saying, "You have to get down and or I call security."

I knew everyone was looking at me as I ran out of the bathroom. Was I not dressed? Did I forget to zip up my pants? Their stares were hot as laser lights, honed-in and burning through me. Some people pointed. I heard giggling ridicule— just like the time I slipped and fell flinging my tray of food all over the floor in front of the entire school student body.

My face was hot and bright red, my eyes stung and would not focus no matter how hard I blinked. I could only make out a dark, tight tunnel stretching away in front of me. I had to make it back to my car and my sharp pencils. I dove in and locked the doors.

- - -

I've been sitting here emotionally raw, fighting memories in my car for hours. Heads are again popping up in front of the windows. Now I see that everything I have most feared in my life has been pursuing me relentlessly the last few nights. Are not these fears proof of something's unquenched lust for my sanity? I had never wished to remember nor relive a single one of those fears. Why drag them up now? Why must I overwhelm my senses with such treacherous recollections?

I sit here like a prisoner in my car as I focus and analyze every tiny detail of their devastating effects on me. This arduous task is taking a toll.

"Please, I can't take any more. You are coming at me

too fast!" I scream as I writhe in pain, shaking out my right hand. I have never been so compelled to retrace and document every sensation—every color, sound, smell, and taste associated with each of my most unsatisfied fears.

My journal is sticky with blood. My hand keeps cramping from bound, strangled muscles. Crying, shivering, and remembering, I absorb it all and let it flow through me and into my pencil.

"Am I going mad or...

         ... am I deep inside a writer's bubble?"

## LOVECRAFT'S TYPEWRITER

Daniel Cureton

"Wow, is that *Lovecraft's* typewriter?" screamed Andrew with boyish glee.

"Yep." *Plop.* The old machine let out a ding. "We just got it in today with some of his other effects," said Julie.

Andrew was beyond thrilled. An avid enthusiast for Lovecraft and horror, he collected books and memorabilia, fancying himself a quasi-expert on the subject. "Dare I touch it?" he said in a low whisper

"What?" asked the other archivist.

"Oh, ugh, nothing just talking to myself."

She turned and walked away deeper into the archive.

Andrew glanced out the window overlooking the low foothills of Brown University, *I'm living the dream,* he thought. An archivist at a university working with the collections of authors he loved and admired growing up certainly was one of his dreams.

Andrew turned to admire the typewriter. It was dusty and quiet, but glowed in the sun beaming in through the windows. He sighed audibly and returned to his work. He had piles of manuscript documents to process.

As the days went by, the typewriter sat on a nearby

table and each day Andrew noticed it became cleaner and tidier. At one point, Andrew asked a fellow archivist if anyone had been cleaning it.

"No. No one's touched it since Julie, the one who brought it in."

Andrew was perplexed.

Back in the office, he stroked his finger down the front plate of the typewriter. It was dust free.

"Wow, either this is self-cleaning or someone is giving it some elbow grease," he said to himself. Deciding to keep an eye and see if anyone was indeed cleaning it, he spoke to John, the Head Archivist, about it.

"Are we doing an exhibition of Lovecraft's papers?"

"No, not that I've heard," said John. "I mean, we've done it before, but we don't have any plans since the collection is old news."

"Well, I'm just curious who is taking care of the typewriter. It's been cleaned. And no one seems to know about it."

John shrugged. "What's your curiosity? It's just a typewriter. We'll bag and tag it into the collection and stick it on a shelf with his papers."

"It's just that it's *his* typewriter, Lovecraft's personal one. The 1905 Remington. I think that it's worth a special value–dollars–also sentimental, which we can capitalize on for a writers and enthusiasts exhibition."

"Ok…I mean, I agree. Maybe in the future we can schedule it to be set up. For now, it'll just be as is. You can keep working on your manuscript collections."

Andrew gave a nod.

Returning to his desk his thoughts caught up with him, *Well that's that, but I have a suspicion someone is up to something with the machine, even if John doesn't know.* Andrew looked at the typewriter, shining on its own (*that's peculiar, it shouldn't be so shiny not in direct light*). He walked over to it and a distinct *click* was made, as the "H" key was pushed down. Andrew took a step back, shook his head and looked again at the machine. *That must have been my imagination.*

Andrew leaned in for a closer look and didn't come upon any strange happenings.

Deciding nothing was there, he turned to walk back to his desk. Another *click* came ringing down as clear as day. Andrew swung around, hoping to catch someone typing, only to find himself alone with the typewriter, and his thoughts.

- - -

### The Brown Daily Herald

#### *Ghost and Monsters Abide within University Archives*

*"Strange happenings on the campus at Brown as staff have no answer to queries of reported shadow figures and poltergeists in the archive reading room.*

*" "No, we have only a staff of eight with a few processing assistants. It's highly doubtful one of them would be going around and play tricks on staff and patrons. This is clearly people's imaginations,' said John, Head Archivist.*

*"This paper will report more online as this story unfolds. Follow us on Twitter @the_herald to stay up to date."*

- - -

John flew around the corner. "All staff meeting."

Andrew walked to the reading room where the other staff were gathered. Some were confused, others anxious, but the general feeling was that everyone knew what the meeting was about. John walked in and immediately started.

"All right, I need whomever is responsible for the pranks to come forward." He was holding up a copy of *The Brown Daily Herald* in which the story had made the front page.

No one seemed surprised. Most, Andrew thought, were like him—more concerned over John's anger than the story.

"This ends now," John continued. "I will not have us be made the fool of the entire campus. That fool will be the one I fire!" He ended the meeting by walking out and slamming the door behind him.

Andrew pilled back to his desk and considered his options. *Should I set up a camera? What about jamming the keys so they don't work?* While deliberating, he heard the faintest—\*tap\* \*tap\*—sounds.

Instead of hurrying to the typewriter, Andrew played it cool (*Not gonna get me to run around like a headless chicken*).

Another half hour passed, the sounds on the Remington continued, but with more intensity—\*Tap\*—came the echo down the hall. Andrew ignored the sounds. \*TAP\*—the force of the stroke set him on edge.

A feeling crept down his neck, shivering down his spine like a slithering cold snake. *This is nothing. Nothing at all, just my nerves* he thought. Anxiety rising. The sudden feeling that the typewriter was aware that he was aware that it had entered his mind. Like the chill of a cold shower, a voice penetrated, "Aaaaaandrew…"

The tingling coiled down his hands as the—*TAP *TAP *TAP*—in rapid succession, rattled the mental frame on Andrew's conscious hold, and pushed him to listen to the voice.

"Aaaandrew…coooome tooo meee…" The voice sounded like a warm glow.

A feeling of lusting thirst, dark with temptation, washed over Andrew.

The tapping continued with a furious whacking, sounding as if the machine would come apart.

Andrew's heart raced in anticipation. He turned in his chair, expecting to see the person he felt in his mind, as a long-missed lover returned, when suddenly—*DING*—the bell rang, startling Andrew so much that he jumped from his seat with a yelp of fear.

He had heard enough. Rounding the corner to confront the mystery typist, Andrew found himself alone, and the machine perfectly still. Someone had inserted a piece of paper on which was typed, "Hello, Andrew."

*This is madness.* To keep an eye on it and prevent further insanity, he moved the typewriter closer to his desk, perched on another table.

*Time to take this to the director. Someone is after me.*

Andrew yanked the sheet from the platen and started towards John's desk. As he turned a corner, he ran into the director, startling the man who yelled in return, "*What's* the matter with you. Are you working or playing on that confounded machine," he said with a scrupulous look, having noticed the typewritten sheet in Andrew's hand.

"Ugh, no sir. Sorry, I just kept hearing this machine go off. I was certain I'd catch someone playing with it. Here, look, they typed a messaged to me." Andrew showed the paper to John, who glanced but failed to be impressed by the evidence.

"So? You could have just as well typed it right? Move the typewriter someplace where it's locked, like the manuscripts safe in the vault, that way it'll stay out of reach of everyone, yourself included."

"Yes sir."

John left him and Andrew let out a sigh. *Shit, this damn typewriter is trying to get the better of me. What the hell.* The typewriter was placed in the locked safe by a staff member on the other side of the archive in the rare books vault.

- - -

A few uneventful weeks passed, allowing the rumors to quell, and to let John cool his head—the staff forgot the whole mess of the hauntings as routine returned.

Andrew needed to get something from the vault in the safe. He asked one of the staff women to come along.

"I don't want any issues again, like we had last month."

"Of course," said Sarah nonchalant as they walked to the safe.

"Do you think there could be anything...*wrong* with the typewriter?"

"What do you mean?" she asked concertedly.

"Well, just that..." Andrew was uncertain about telling anyone his experience. He and Sarah had been co-workers for a few years, but they didn't know each other well.

"It was like it was taunting me," he said. "During that whole hauntings mess, it was by my desk and would go off by itself. I could never catch anyone on it."

"Oh…" She glanced out the window, her face widened in alarm.

Andrew noticed the look. "It's just that I'd hear the tapping sound and run over to find no one around, but yet the carriage had moved, paper been inserted, text typed out. It's a little spooky."

Sarah agreed and he dropped the subject, not finding a confidant in her. They arrived to the safe and Andrew entered the code: "2848-"

Andrew heard it. *Tap* *tap* *tap**tap*

Shuttering, he stopped. Sarah was far enough back to not have heard the sound. He continued the sequence "-8548."

As his fingers hit the last number the safe door flung open with an explosive *boom* and a sudden burst of wind from inside that launched Andrew and Sarah backwards into the stacks.

Boxes fell from the shelves onto the pair, papers and folders flying out. Andrew rolled on the floor, coming out of his daze and looking up.

The typewriter floated out of the safe. It gave off an eerie light. Streams of energy plasma shot out of its sides. The overhead lights flickered and went out. The vault darkened, with only the glow of the typewriter remaining.

Andrew gasped, paralyzed with the same fear that had tried to grip him those weeks ago. He looked to his left and found Sarah out cold. He was alone.

Electric current filled the air as the typewriter moved slowly toward Andrew, drawing out the breath he had recovered. The—*tap* *tap*—of the keys called to him, the ring of the carriage was the bell of welcome, and the electric arcs formed hands of ecstasy, pulling him in. Andrew sat up and stared wildly at the machine. He uttered a whimpering "No," but felt pinned to the floor by the hands caressing him as a familiar lover.

"You see Andrew, it's ok now, you can come home with me," said the machine.

Like a tap-dance of death, the keys fired with increasing speed. Papers flew out, landing in a neat stack next to Andrew. A ghostly figure appeared next to him, the shadow of a slender man who pointed down to the pages. Andrew felt compelled to move, the same slithering coil slinking its way down his arms.

"*Pick it up…*" whispered a sultry voice.

Picking up the manuscript, Andrew read "The Demon's Machine" on the masthead. All the pages were blank except for the last, which had Andrew's name typed out.

"*Picking up the pages, Andrew saw his name on the page. He looked upward, recognizing the figure of the idol he so worshiped, beckoning Andrew to join him. The choice was clear: resist with eternal pain, or let go and live forever in eternal ecstasy.*"

Andrew recognized the ghostly figure—H. P. Lovecraft—the soul of the man dead almost a century, come to life to feed.

Lovecraft's ghostly figure smiled, a deceptive demonic flash of teeth as his arms opened wide to embrace the newest guest.

*No, you're not supposed to take the souls of your fans.* He could feel the warm current flowing inside, the feelings of comfort and love in contrast with his rational brain, and the drain of energy leaving him. The life force flowed out of his body through his eyes, his mouth, and seemingly through the very flesh on his bones.

"Let me love you. Death is only the beginning of what can be…forever between us," it said in a soothing voice. The figure of Lovecraft reached down and gripped the boy's hand, letting out in the vault a sinister laugh.

The alarm in Andrew's brain exploded as he felt compelled to give his soul to the typewriter but knew it was death come to take him.

Just up the corridor came a sudden flash of light. A door swung open and there stood the backlit outline of a person.

"Not in my archive." John walked forward with a jug of motor oil in one hand and a baseball bat in the other. He was followed by an assistant carrying a potted plant.

The energy current arced forward and smashed the pot—ceramic pieces flew everywhere. John took one to the back of the head, "Owh, that hurt!" he said. A fire in his eyes ignited, but he kept his cool. The assistant screamed, but continued to hold onto the plastic which had lined the clay pot.

In the throat of the typewriter, where the ribbon reels were stretched, Andrew saw a pair of enraged eyes emerge. Hissing, the typewriter slowly moved towards John, leaving Andrew half soul-sucked with the figure of Lovecraft sneering at the pair.

"I said not today, mother fucker!" John splashed the jug of oil onto the typewriter.

It jerked to the right, only to be met with the bat swung deftly by the Head Archivist. It swayed out of the way, but caught another stream of oil as it went left. Trying to rush John, the oil landed on the keys, instantly boiling, set aflame with its own electric energy.

John stepped out of the way. "Now!"

The assistant flung loose soil onto the typewriter by the handful. The oil boiled and mixed with the dirt, slowing the machine's advance. The streams of energy began to flicker.

"Get out of my archive!" John yelled, and brought the bat down smack dab between the reels.

The furious typewriter tried to suck John's soul and spewed the dirty mix back at them, but it could only sputter and lose gravity.

John gave one final gusto blow onto the keys, smashing the metal and plastic beneath the pine. The machine let out a screech as metal parts flew out the sides and fell to the floor, lifeless. The figure of Lovecraft vanished and Andrew felt life return. The lights came back on in the vault. John stepped back, watching all the souls that had been captured slide out of the machine, off its pages, and vanish as smoke in the wind.

John moved to help Andrew, picking him up and sitting him in a chair while the assistant checked on Sarah. "Out cold sir, but she'll live," he reported.

John nodded, giving Andrew some water. Andrew,

dazed, managed to chirp out a thank you,

"How did you know?"

"Kid, you don't get to be Head Archivist without having seen your fair share of the strange and weird."

Andrew sighed, guessing that demonic typewriters counted as one of the weird. Nonetheless, he was shook. *I never thought that's how I'd meet my favorite author.*

John said, "I had a sneaking suspicion from when you first came to me about it that it was a living artifact. We get them in occasionally, but unfortunately there is no Warehouse team to deal with them, so it falls on us. I knew it was biding its time for the opportunity to strike."

"So you knew something would happen when the safe was opened the next time," Andrew said shaking his head to clear it.

"With all the ruckus on campus and your panic about the machine, I knew it would make some kind of move soon. Sitting locked up for several weeks, I'd be pissed off myself. You just happen to be the chosen target, probably due to your association with his work. Thankfully, I'm old enough to know what the bane of the mechanical era is: dust and oil. So, short of holy water, dirt and oil works best. That'll gum up just about any of those metallic wonders of the pre-microcomputer age."

"And a baseball bat," said Andrew.

"And a baseball bat." John agreed.

Andrew breathed deeply, feeling mostly alive again, and went to stand. John put his hand on Andrew's shoulder.

"We'll get this cleaned up. In the meantime, I think you can report to the Special Collections Department, they

# CRAZY FOR MORE?

IMAGINE THE MADNESS OF THESE PREVIOUS COLLECTIONS OF UTAH HORROR:

2018 Anthology

They say some only hunger for food, while others only hunger for love. But have they ever encountered a different kind of hunger: the insatiable, unstoppable appetite for fear?

Feast upon 24 never-before-published stories and poems fresh from the darkest minds in Utah's horror writing community. Sample the succulent flavors of dread and despair in these terrifying tales of ravenous zombies, piggish parasites, cannibalistic neighbors, and so much more.

When we crave the unnatural, there is no loyalty. There are no rules. There is only...THE HUNGER.

Not for the faint of heart, *The Hunger: A Collection of Utah Horror* is sure to satisfy your craving for something that will keep you up at night. Devour it...before it devours you.

2017 Anthology

Twelve Apocalyptic horsemen of the Rocky Mountains have come together in this terrifying anthology of Utah Horror. After years of dystopian fiction, these twelve writers won the challenge to portray how the apocalypse would occur.

Questionable kittens, ritualistic killing, destroying angels, ancient gods seeking punishment, lawless renegades, practitioners of the dark arts, and zombies will haunt every corner of your mind as you read these thrilling accounts of what could happen during the end of days in Utah.

Reanimated corpses of religious fanatics proclaiming salvation are the least of your worries...

## 2016 Anthology

The Great Salt Lake is a remnant of an ancient lake that was almost as long as the State of Utah. What mysteries does it hold in its briny waters? What secrets lurk in its murky shores?

…a malevolent spirit haunts a pregnant woman, luring her ever closer to the salty depths, yet what it wants is much more horrifying than death…the inversion and smog in the Salt Lake Valley carries more than just bad air…two locals find more than they bargain for when they unearth an ancient box buried in the salt-caked muck…

Whether its mystery, apparitions, ancient curses, or a modern day apocalypse, one thing holds all these tales together: The Great Salt Lake. Nestled inside the second anthology of Utah horror, are tales intended to delight a wide range of readers.

2015 Anthology

The West has always been a symbol of the wild frontier, rugged adventure, and dangerous exploration. However, if it wasn't for fear of the unknown, the West would just be another cardinal direction. *Old Scratch and Owl Hoots* delves into that fear and captures it in fourteen tales of terror set in the West ranging from the 1800s to the present day. Take a gander inside…a strange creature on Antelope Island that can never satisfy its hunger…a woman's vacation to Zion National Park that takes a dark turn when she can't stop hearing the cries of a newborn baby…an outlaw on the run from Porter Rockwell who finds more than he bargains for in the Utah wilderness…

All the stories in the anthology are written by authors with Utah connections. Some are veterans at the craft, while others are making their debut. Cozy up next to a campfire and delve into these fourteen stories and find out why it's dangerous to be out and about in the West when the sun goes down.

# ARE YOU A HORROR WRITER?

The Utah Horror Writers formed in June, 2014. If you live in Northern Utah, consider joining the Chapter. The group is for new and old writers, published and unpublished. Find out more at www.utahhorror.org and on Facebook: Utah Horror Writers.

## Call for Submissions

Each year the chapter publishes an anthology of local horror. A writer does not have to live in Utah, but the story must have a connection to Utah.

We are pleased to announce the 2020 anthology:

*They Walk Among Us*

Monsters, werewolves, vampires, and more, submissions will be accepted in four different categories:

-Flash Fiction: No greater than 1,000 words.

-Short Fiction: No greater than 5,000 words.

-Poetry: Up to 3 poems, no greater than 5 pages.

-Novelette: No greater than 15,000 words.

Multiple submissions welcome, but one per category. The call is open February 13 and closes October 31, 2019 at 11:59 pm, MST. Submit via email: utahhorror.anthology@gmail.com. Accepted authors will receive a small compensation.

Submit questions to utahhorrorwriters@gmail.com and see our website for submission guidelines.

CPSIA information can be obtained
at www.ICGtesting.com
Printed in the USA
LVHW020226040619
620065LV00002B/132